P9-BZG-318

JULIE'S EYES DRIFTED SHUT, AND SHE SLEPT.

Dreams troubled her again, nightmares of being in the center of a maze, only instead of hedges hemming her in on every side there were mirrors, mirrors stretching to infinity, and her image was reflected a thousand times over. Her every motion was repeated precisely. Yet there was one marked difference—the myriad eyes staring back at her were mocking and evil. She opened her mouth and screamed; the other mouths opened, and laughter drummed against her ears.

She awoke, a scream dying on her lips. She sat up, looking wildly toward the pier, searching for Shell. He wasn't to be seen.

There was something wrong, something missing. Then she realized what it was. *Dancer II* ! The boat was gone!

Mirrors

Also available from Worldwide Library by
PATRICIA MATTHEWS

ENCHANTED
THURSDAY AND THE LADY

Patricia Matthews

★

Mirrors

WORLDWIDE®

TORONTO · NEW YORK · LONDON · PARIS
AMSTERDAM · STOCKHOLM · HAMBURG
ATHENS · MILAN · TOKYO · SYDNEY

MIRRORS

A Worldwide Library Book/May 1988

ISBN 0-373-97070-6

This book is dedicated to my sister Nancy, with whom, I am extremely pleased to say, I have a relationship that in no way resembles that between the two siblings represented in this book.

PART ONE

Discovery

ONE

A BLUR OF WHITE caught Julie's eye, and she leaned forward in her seat for a better view out the bus window. At the side of the highway, startled by the sound and movement of the big transcontinental bus, two egrets lifted on white wings, their slender necks and streamlined bodies outlined against the flat blue of the Florida sky, like figures in an Egyptian wall painting.

Julie Malone felt tears sting her eyes at the beauty of the picture they presented. She pushed the button that moved the back of the seat forward so that she wouldn't miss anything. She was greedy for new things to see. This was a strange country, so flat and green and lush—and less than fifty yards to her left the blue-green glitter of the Atlantic Ocean. She repeated the strange-sounding place names over in her mind as she might have rolled brightly colored pebbles in her hand—Key Largo, Conch Key, Spanish Harbor, Pirates Cove, Key West.

Julie leaned her head back, suddenly pensive. Ever since she had gotten on the bus in Moorestown, she had been trying to analyze her emotions. She was still far from certain what they were. She had expected to feel sorrow and some trepidation at leaving the only home she had ever known, the people whom she cared for, Ken, the man she loved. But instead there was this tremendous excitement, this feeling of freedom. She was leaving the only world she knew, the only place in which she had an identity. She was going to a strange place where she might find out that she was someone else, someone that she might not even care to be, and yet she was filled with delight and expectancy. She shook her head at her own inconsistency.

Rummaging in her bag, she took out the letter she had received a week ago, the letter that had forged a link between her present and her unknown past. It was the letter that had placed her on this air-conditioned bus speeding down the Overseas Highway over a string of island jewels strung together by graceful bridges.

Normally she received very little mail. Consequently she had been surprised to receive the airmail letter addressed to Miss Julie Malone, Moorestown, Connecticut. The return address bore the name of the law firm of Henderson, Caldicott and Phipps of Key West, Florida. Julie had turned the letter over in her hand, filled with a curious and sudden sense of foreboding. She knew no one in Key West; she knew very few people anywhere except in Moorestown. And yet, as she had stared at the envelope, something had stirred, insect-small, in the back of her mind.

What if it was something concerning *before*?

"Before" was the term Julie always used to describe the years prior to her arrival in Moorestown. The girl who had gotten off the bus in downtown Moorestown had no name and no memories of her life farther back than a few hours before her arrival. She remembered the bus driver. A kindly, graying man with a generous smile. She remembered being on the bus and watching the trees and fences speeding past; but she remembered nothing else of any consequence.

Moorestown was a small town, and a kind town. The police department, the hospital staff and a good portion of the residents tried with every means at their disposal to learn the identity of the pretty dark-haired girl who had gotten off that bus. Her fingerprints were sent to Washington but apparently were not on file.

She was given exhaustive medical tests, but no reason was found for her loss of memory. Finally she suffered through several sessions with a psychiatrist, again with no results. The psychiatrist's final conclusion: hysterical amnesia. Such cases were extremely rare, he explained—at least those that lasted for extended periods of time. In his opinion, it had probably been brought about by some severe trauma, a shock so intense and terrible that she had retreated from the incident, pulling a merciful curtain down over it. It could last for the rest of her life, or it could lift at any given moment.

They estimated her age to be fifteen or sixteen; and when nothing could be learned of her past, and when it became apparent that *she* was not going to remember, a childless couple—the Malones—who had always wanted a daughter, took her in and gave her a home and their name.

She became Julie Malone, and she was happy. She made friends, attended the local high school and the small college, and finally took a job with the local newspaper. She was popular and well liked. At first there had been words whispered behind hands, and pointed fingers: "Girl with no past . . . girl with no name . . . probably someone's dumped bastard. . . ." But the passing years put such innuendos behind her, and she was accepted. Eventually she fell in love with Ken Dawson and the young couple became engaged.

And it was only now and then, perhaps in the deepest part of the night, or when something like the letter touched some forgotten chord in her mind, that Julie wondered about what *had* happened before. Who had she been? Who were her real parents? Where had she lived? Sometimes she was amazed at her own lack of curiosity; but she rationalized that since her present was so comfortable and secure, she would be foolish to worry about her past. Often, when she was being very honest with herself, she admitted that part of her reluctance to ponder her origins sprang from fear. What if there were something terrible behind that curtain of forgetfulness, something too horrible to confront? She didn't want to risk finding out. . . .

She sighed, bringing herself back to the present. She looked out the bus window again and saw her image reflected back at her. A pretty girl, people said, but Julie was never sure that she quite believed them. Her hair was raven black, as were her eyes. Her complexion was dusky, highlighting even white teeth and a soft, sensitive mouth.

Salespeople had often hinted that she should wear more colorful clothing, yet she always bought subdued colors—grays or browns or blacks—never quite trusting their subtly flattering words. How could a person with no past believe she was truly beautiful?

The air brakes squealed, and Julie was jarred from her reverie. This was it—the end of her journey. Whatever it was she had come to find out was here, waiting for her. She felt a strong reluctance to leave her seat; but the doors of the bus were sighing open, and the rest of the passengers were getting down their luggage and pushing toward the exit. The babble of excited voices surrounded Julie, making her feel alone and isolated from the other passengers. This is ridiculous, she scolded herself. Mr. Phipps had made all the arrangements for her—the bus, the motel, everything. There was really no problem, she was just being silly. . . .

"Miss Malone?"

She glanced up at the sound of her name, and then looked higher still. The young man towering over her had to be the tallest person Julie had ever seen. The face bent toward her looked familiar, and she decided that was because it looked like a face more suited to Moorestown than to Key West, Florida. It was long, with angular lines, divided by a regal nose, set off by a pair of large, very gray eyes and topped by shaggy red-brown brows. The mouth was wide, the expression grave.

Here, Julie thought, is a good, solid, dependable man. She began to feel better. He was regarding her quizzically now, and she realized that considerable time had passed since he had spoken.

"Yes," she said hastily. "I'm Julie Malone."

The wide lips smiled now, and the gray eyes regarded her with more warmth, making him look almost boyish. "I'm Phipps, of Henderson, Caldicott and Phipps."

"Oh, yes." Julie extended her hand. "Thank you very much for meeting me." She wondered if he had a first name.

Phipps took her hand gingerly and gave it a brief, firm shake, then released it. "I trust your trip was pleasant."

"Oh, fine. Yes, it was fine." She rummaged in her purse for a tissue with which to wipe her forehead, which was unpleasantly damp.

Phipps nodded, grinning now. "Yes, it does get quite warm here. But it's the humidity, really. You have to watch things like shoes, for example. They get mold and fungus in them if you're not careful."

She shuddered, but he didn't seem to notice.

"Now, I guess I'd better get you to your motel. You'll feel better there."

In a few moments he had collected Julie's luggage and loaded it into an ancient Jeep parked a half block up the street. He helped her in before getting in beside her. As they pulled away, Julie leaned back against the seat. The heat had sapped her curiosity and drained her strength, and it seemed to take an effort just to breathe. She had been so looking forward to seeing Key West, but now she didn't even have the energy to look at it. She wondered why a prosperous young attorney drove an open Jeep instead of a new, air-conditioned automobile, which would certainly have been a blessing.

Phipps seemed to sense her discomfort and smiled over at her. "You'll get used to it, if you stay around. It may take a little time, is all. There aren't many tourists in Key West at this time of the year, for that very reason. Only the year-round residents enjoy this climate.''

She tried to return his smile, wondering again if he had a first name. When she had more energy, she would have to ask him.

The motel, which was right on the beach, looked comfortable. Every bungalow was surrounded by palms and other tropical plants. Flowers bloomed in brilliant profusion. There was a strong breeze close to the water, and the coconut palms scraped and chattered in the wind like harsh-voiced gossips.

Julie signed her name to the register, and Phipps carried her bags to her room. The interior of the bungalow was blessedly cool. She wanted to throw herself across the comfortable-looking bed and sleep for a week, but Phipps was still there, standing tall and erect, as though on military inspection. She gazed up at him.

''I know you must be tired, Miss Malone, after your long ride. There is plenty of time to rest before you are to see Mr. Henderson in our offices this afternoon. I'll be by for you at—''

Phipps frowned down at his watch. Julie noticed that his wrist was brown and muscular.

''Will four o'clock be all right?''

He looked at her expectantly, and she nodded her agreement.

He also nodded and seemed to hesitate, about to say something more. Then he turned and left the room quickly.

Julie removed her shoes, stretched out on the bed and tried to fall asleep. Wanted to fall asleep. It was what she always did when she needed to gain time, when she wanted to postpone whatever it was she needed to face. But this time sleep would not come so easily. She sighed. Since she couldn't sleep, she might as well take a bath.

The bathroom, like everything else here, was lush and tropical. The tub was twice as large as the one at home, and it took Julie some time to figure out how the faucets operated. Instead of the handles she was accustomed to, there was a huge knob of polished chrome with a dial. At first it defied her reasoning processes, but at last she mastered the rather complicated procedure.

Long before four o'clock she was dressed and waiting, tense with expectancy. She prowled the room, stopping now and then to look out the window at the hot lemon sunlight and the lush green shrubs and flowers. The sunlight off the water was dazzling.

Her path back and forth across the room carried her close to the nightstand, where her purse lay on its side. The corner of a white envelope protruded. Julie sat down on the bed and took out the letter. She sat there for a little while, turning it over and over in her hands. She didn't have to read it; she knew the contents by heart. She had read and reread the letter until every word was imprinted neatly in her mind, somewhere just back of her forehead.

Mr. Henderson, the senior partner of the law firm, had written the letter; its contents were succinctly and clearly worded. In essence, the letter informed her that the firm of Henderson, Caldicott and Phipps had for years handled the affairs of the Devereaux family in Key West. They were almost certain that she was the last surviving child of the family. A sixteen-year-old daughter had disappeared eight years ago, and there was every reason to believe that Julie Malone was that girl. If she was agreeable, they would like her to come to Key West, where the family estate had existed for a hundred years. There they would make the final determination as to whether or not she was the young woman in question.

Mr. Henderson, seemingly capable of reading her mind long-distance, assured Julie that the letter was not a joke and closed by listing formidable references with whom she might check. After the initial shock wore off, Julie did just that. The references checked out, the firm was real, and the letter was legitimate. Only then did she tell the Malones and Ken.

The Malones were apprehensive. They had grown to love Julie very much, as if she were their very own. It hurt them to think that her life, which had been carefully planned, could change and possibly turn her away from them and from Ken. They had been so looking forward to seeing Julie and Ken married and settled happily into a house close by. They had been looking forward to grandchildren playing at their feet. They viewed the letter as a threat to that envisioned future.

And so did Ken. Everything was planned. In a few months the plans would have culminated in their wedding. He had made a down payment on a house and had given Julie an engagement ring.

Julie touched the modest diamond on her finger. Suddenly she missed Ken terribly. Missed the comfortable, solid bulk of him. His charm and gentleness, his practicality, his dry humor—all traits that had drawn her to him when he had moved to Moorestown two years ago.

What was she doing here in this strange place, with these strange people, she wondered. What if the whole business was a joke after all, or a cruel trick of some kind?

The knock she had been waiting for sounded on the door. Julie glanced at her watch. Four o'clock. When Phipps of Henderson, Caldicott and Phipps said four o'clock, he meant four o'clock.

Julie crammed the letter into her purse, took a last deep breath of the room's cool air, squared her shoulders resolutely and went to open the door.

TWO

May 28
*Today is our birthday. We are eleven years old. Daddy and
Mama gave us ruffled dresses and bicycles. I hate the dress,
but the bicycle is okay. Aunt Helen gave us gold heart lock-
ets, but the present I like best is this leather diary. I like it
best because Suellen does not have one. Aunty Pip gave me
the diary and gave Suellen a box of paints. I am not like
Suellen anyway. She is nothing but a crybaby. We look just
alike outside, but underneath I am different. I have a good
thing to use this diary for. I am going to write down all the
different things I do. I am going to write down all my
thoughts. I am going to write down all my secrets.*
   The first secret is that I wish I was not a twin.

   This time Phipps called for Julie in a large, sol-
emn-looking black car that proved, blessedly, to
have air-conditioning. She wondered why he hadn't
driven it when he'd picked her up at the bus station, but she filed the question away to ask at a later
date when she knew him better; perhaps at the
same time she asked him what his first name was.
She smiled to herself at the thought, and Phipps,
turning his head at that precise moment, smiled
back at her.

   "You'll like Mr. Henderson," he said. "He's a
fine old gentleman. A descendant of the original

Hendersons who came to the Keys in the early nineteenth century.''

''I'm sure I will,'' said Julie. ''His letter was very—'' She hesitated.

''He does write a good clear letter, doesn't he? You have no idea how difficult it is composing a good letter. I—'' He suddenly flushed a bright, attractive pink that made him look younger and more vulnerable. ''I shouldn't have said that. After all, you were an English major. You know about such things.''

Julie winced inwardly, but it must have shown on her face because he said quickly, ''I am sorry. Did I say something wrong?''

Julie attempted to ease his discomfort with a smile. ''Not really. It's just that I can't quite get used to having strangers know so much about me. I gather that your firm's investigation was very thorough.'' She added ruefully, ''It seems that I don't have many secrets left.''

''It's not that bad, Miss Malone. It's just that in a case like this we must be certain, as certain as circumstances warrant. It took years, you know. There was very little to go on. When the . . . the break came along and they found you, your life was traced back to the very day you arrived in Moorestown.''

''You said 'they.' Don't you mean 'we'?''

He shook his head slightly. ''No, I'm new to the firm, relatively speaking, and wasn't involved in your situation until just recently, not too long before you were found.''

Julie repeated the word in her mind: *found*.

Had she then been lost? The professor of her college psych course had once told Julie that she had a good sense of identity despite her loss of memory of the earlier years. Was this identity just a facade? A false front to hide someone else, a stranger whom she didn't know?

"I understand that you have no memory of your life before Moorestown?" Phipps said uncomfortably.

"That's right."

"That must make life difficult for you."

Julie shrugged, feigning indifference. "One gets used to it. I suppose a person can become accustomed to anything with time."

"Tell me, Miss Malone, why did you take the bus all the way down here? We sent you the money for plane fare."

"I had no way of being certain that this wasn't all just a fantasy, and there seemed no need to hurry." Then she sighed and said, "No, I'm hedging the truth. The truth is, I'm terrified of flying."

Phipps gave her a rather curious look but said nothing more as he pulled up before an old wooden building that looked like a residence except for the white shingle hanging over a post by the front gate. The sign proclaimed in neat, black letters: Henderson, Caldicott and Phipps, Attorneys-at-Law. The house had recently been painted, but no paint could disguise the age of the building or the beauty of its lines. It was graceful and elegant in the fashion of an earlier time. Around the house, as everywhere else in Key West, flowers and shrubs grew in a riot of color.

"The Hendersons have owned this house since 1945," Phipps remarked.

Julie could tell that this fact impressed him. Well, it impressed her, as well, she had to admit. After all, *her* family roots only went back eight years.

Although the shadows were lengthening, it didn't seem noticeably cooler outside to Julie when she got out of the air-conditioned car to enter the building. The interior of the building was cool, and as beautiful as the exterior. There seemed to be miles of polished wood; it glistened richly in the soft amber afternoon light.

Mr. Henderson's office was at the end of the hall on the lower floor. Julie suddenly wondered what the eldest member of the law firm was like. Then Phipps opened the door and she saw that Henderson was much as she had imagined him. Of medium height, he stood perfectly erect. He was slender, and although his frame appeared somewhat shrunken by age, his shoulders were still broad. His facial features were highly aristocratic. His physical appearance, coupled with the dark, conservative suit that he wore, made him look like the typical elderly attorney as depicted in movies. Julie judged him to be close to seventy.

He bowed slightly as Julie entered the room. "Miss Malone." His voice was dry and precise, but his gray eyes were friendly.

Julie smiled tentatively. "But if what your letter says is true, I don't suppose I really am, am I?"

He returned the smile. "That may be true, my dear, but even if you are—" he hesitated "—but even if you are Suellen Devereaux, you will still be

Julie Malone. After all, we are who we think we are, as well as who others think we are.''

Julie was delighted and much relieved. He was utterly charming and wise; and she had been afraid that he would be one of those stern, forbidding men, dry and as uninteresting as a law book.

''Sit down, please, my dear.'' He gestured toward a chair. ''Make yourself comfortable. Would you care for some iced tea, or perhaps lemonade?''

''No, thank you, I'm really too nervous to swallow.''

He nodded sympathetically. ''I can easily understand how you might be.'' He turned to Phipps, his voice sharpening. ''Sheldon. Do sit down. You make *me* nervous, hovering about like that.''

Julie hid a smile behind her hand. So his first name was Sheldon. Sheldon! She repeated the name under her breath, liking the sound of it; it seemed to fit him.

Sheldon flushed pink and quickly sat down in the chair opposite Julie.

''Now, my dear,'' Henderson said, ''I won't be asking you any personal questions, since we already have the answers to most that we might ask. We are all but positive that you are Suellen Devereaux, but we wanted to see you in person first, to see if the resemblance is as marked as our pictures show.''

He opened a desk drawer, took out several snapshots and gave them to Julie.

Her fingers trembled as she leafed through them. The pictures were all of a young girl, ranging in age from about two to approximately fifteen. Julie's throat tightened and the pulse in her forehead began to throb, for the face was unmistakably her own. Younger, in strange clothing with strange people in strange surroundings, but the face was her own. She choked back a cry and let the pictures fall into her lap.

Henderson moved from behind his huge polished desk and came around to her chair. "My dear Julie, I *am* sorry. I didn't realize how much of a shock those pictures might be to you."

Julie tried to stop shaking. "It's just that it looks like my face, but the pictures are of a time I can't remember. It's like...like seeing myself as a ghost, or as someone from another time, another life."

"But that's what it is, isn't it?" His hand was gentle on her shoulder. "It *was* another life, and now we are going to bring you back to it. Now, first you must meet Stella Bronson Devereaux, your grandmother."

"My grandmother?" Julie felt the words slip out of her mouth. They seemed to hang visibly in the air between them. "I have a grandmother?"

"You do indeed." The attorney nodded. "And an aunt and a great-aunt. The great-aunt is Helen Bronson, Stella's sister, and the aunt is your father's sister. Your grandmother is old now. She is dying. She has been for months. She has been clinging to life for only one reason, to see you again. It was Stella who initiated the search for you. She insisted that you were alive and could be found. You are the last of the family line."

Julie's thoughts were circling in her mind like birds that could not land. "A great-aunt and an aunt?"

"Yes, my dear."

Julie's head began to ache. "My family! and I don't even know who they are." She clapped her hands to her head in a effort to stifle the panic she felt rising in her. "I'm sorry, Mr. Henderson. It's just that I feel so confused!"

"It's a lot to take in at one time, I know. Sheldon, pour Julie a glass of brandy."

Sheldon got to his feet and strode over to a small bar in one corner of the office. He returned with a glass, giving it to the older man.

Henderson offered the glass to Julie. "Here, drink this. No refusal, now. It's excellent brandy."

Julie wasn't much of a drinker, but she obediently took the glass and sipped at the aromatic liquor. It sent warmth down her throat and into her stomach and made her feel less faint.

Henderson continued, "Now, your great-aunt Helen lives here in Key West. She never married, and has spent the last ten years of her life looking after, and being a companion to, Stella Devereaux. Your other aunt, Pippen, married a Frenchman, Antoine Delacroix, deceased now. She has been living in France but is returning to Key West to meet you.

"We are certain that you are—" he hesitated briefly "—Suellen Devereaux, but your grandmother must be certain, too. You see, there is a great deal of money involved. The Devereaux estate, which will go to Suellen on her twenty-fifth birthday, is enormous, so we have to be absolutely certain of your identity. If you feel all right now, Sheldon and I will take you to Devereaux House. It is a beautiful old place. I think you'll like it, Julie." He smiled suddenly. "You know, it's a little difficult to know what to call you. Suppose we continue with Julie for a time? It's a name you're accustomed to, and it certainly doesn't mean that we have any reservations about your being Suellen Devereaux."

Julie nodded slowly. The news about the Devereaux fortune was another shock. And now she had to face the most difficult part of all—facing this strange woman, her grandmother. A total stranger and yet blood of her blood, flesh of her flesh. This woman was her father's mother, had known her father and mother. All of a sudden Julie felt a wild, uncontrollable yearning, a need to know who she really was. For a microsecond something slipped in her mind, and it was as if a dark drapery had been pulled aside. For just that brief fraction of time she glimpsed a woman's face, a familiar face, yet one ugly with some powerful emotion. Was it anger? Terror? And then the drapery closed, closed so quickly that she couldn't retain the image, and it receded in her memory until, a moment or two later, when she tried to recall the face, she could not.

Almost in a trance, Julie picked up her purse and preceded Henderson and Sheldon out to the car.

A short time later she knew that she would never forget her first glimpse of Devereaux House. Clutching her purse in both hands, she tried not to reveal the inner turmoil she was experiencing, torn between the fear that she would suddenly remember the past and the fear that she would not, wondering if the house would look at all familiar. The building was concealed behind a high stucco wall over which rose the tops of trees. The lavish brilliance of bougainvillea wandered freely along the length of the wall.

At the entrance, Henderson honked the car horn. A few moments before the huge wooden gate opened from within seemed an eternity to Julie, who sat perched on the edge of her seat, straining for her first look at the house. Would it look at all familiar to her? Would it trigger a memory, open a window into the past?

Then the gates swung open and she could see a curving white gravel driveway and, through the trees, a large white mass that she knew must be the house.

The drive wound through the abundance of a tropical garden filled with exotic trees and plants. Although she could not identify them all, Julie had read the names in her guidebook on the bus coming down, fascinating, exotic names: royal poinciana; the orchid tree; frangipani; the woman's tongue tree; Spanish laurel; Mexican flame; and the passionflower vine. It was fantastic and beyond her previous experiences. It looked as she imagined the Garden of Eden must have looked.

The last turn of the driveway now brought the house into full view. Graceful, two-storied and circled by balconies, the house wore the patina of age wonderfully well.

The house and the garden surrounding it were both so lovely that Julie felt her breath catch in her throat; and again, just for an instant, something

stirred far back in the dark recesses of her mind
and then was once again gone.

The inside of the house matched the exterior in
beauty. The floors were of polished wood, pegged
and grooved. A graceful banister curved up a
broad staircase to the floor above. The windows
ran from floor to ceiling, reminding Julie of the
pictures she'd seen of old houses in New Orleans.
But the drapes were drawn—against the heat, she
supposed—and that made the house rather dark
and gloomy. Overall, it had a Spanish flavor about
it that Julie liked.

"It's lovely," she whispered.

Sheldon heard her and smiled. "It is, isn't it?"

When she appeared too bemused to move of her
own volition, he gently took her elbow and turned
her toward the stairs. "Come along, Julie."

He held her arm as they mounted the wide staircase, and she was grateful for his support. As they
went up the stairs, the upper reaches struck Julie as
even gloomier.

At the top of the stairs an elderly black woman
awaited them, neatly clad in a black dress and a
white apron. Her face was kind and melancholy.
She nodded at Henderson and studied Julie with
frank curiosity.

Henderson said, "How is she, Pauline?"

"She's been waiting all day," the black woman
said in a musical voice, indicating a door with a
jerk of her head.

Henderson opened the indicated door, pushed it
wide, then stepped back for Julie to precede him
into the room.

Julie, feeling a watery weakness in her legs, moved forward slowly. The main piece of furniture was a huge four-poster bed, which dominated the room like a throne. And upon the bed lay an old woman, propped up with many pillows.

Her grandmother, Stella Devereaux.

THREE

May 30

It has been a year and one day since I started writing in this secret diary. Yesterday was our birthday again, but it was dull.

Today was a good day, but it started out bad. It rained this morning, and Mama made us stay in our room and play. I had a great idea for a game but Suellen didn't want to play. She never wants to play anything good. But then the rain stopped, and Mama let us go out but she made us put on our boots.

I think Mama likes Suellen best. Well, that is all right. I think I like Daddy better than Mama anyway. Mama is all soft and mushy, like Suellen. I decided that some people are soft and blurry, like pictures that are smeary, and some people are sharp and strong. I have made a list. The blurry people are Suellen, Mama, Aunty Helen, Miss Johnson, my teacher, and Mr. Findlay, my Sunday school teacher, who lives next door. The sharp people are me, Daddy, Aunty Pip, Grandmother, Daddy's friend Mr. Thomas, who is real handsome too, and Huey. I decided that more men are sharp than women. More women are blurry, but I am different. I like being different. Daddy says there is nothing wrong about being different.

The reason today turned out good is because me and Huey sneaked through Mr. Findlay's hedge after it stopped raining. Their dog, Dingo, was asleep. He's a silly dog that barks all the time. We tied Dingo's tail to Pinky's tail.

Pinky is the cat. Pinky woke Dingo up, while we hid behind the hedge and watched. It was really funny the way old Dingo ran around barking and pulling Pinky with her claws dragging along behind. Mrs. Findlay came running out all fuzzy looking too. She was yelling and flapping her apron. She looked silly. Flapping her apron didn't do anything but scare Dingo and Pinky more. Finally Mr. Findlay came out and caught Dingo and set him loose, and the fun was over.

They never saw us or knew who it was that did it. We laughed and laughed.

The old woman was tiny, a mere wisp of a thing. She made Julie think of an apple doll, one that looked old and wizened; yet her black eyes were still fierce and shone with acute intelligence. She studied Julie for a moment, gesturing imperiously for silence as Henderson started to speak.

When Julie began to obviously feel uncomfortable, Stella Devereaux spoke in a voice not in the least enfeebled by age. "So you think you're Suellen?"

Julie bristled. She thought this old woman rude and arrogant. "I don't think anything of the sort. It wasn't my idea to come here," she said in her own defense.

Henderson spoke up. "It is our considered opinion, Mrs. Devereaux, that this is your granddaughter, Suellen."

"Come here, child." The old woman motioned with a hand as thin and translucent as waxed paper. "Come closer. My eyes are not what they once were."

Julie hesitated. It was in her mind to just turn around and march out and catch the next bus back to Moorestown. Yet her curiosity was too strong. Reluctantly she approached until her thighs struck the side of the high bed.

Those keen black eyes studied her intently. Then, as if in slow motion, one blue-veined hand came up to touch Julie's cheek, the stroking of the fingers as soft as a feather's touch. It wasn't exactly a caress, it was more of a probing gesture, as though the old woman were searching for reality.

"The eyes, the eyes are those of a Devereaux, like her father's. But the nose, the nose is not a Devereaux nose." Stella Devereaux brushed one finger across Julie's nose, then touched her own, which was noble, still large in the wrinkled face. "The blood, of course, has thinned down through the years." Then she appeared suddenly weary, seeming to sink back into the bedclothes, her head moving from side to side. Even her voice was weaker when she spoke again. "I don't know, I just don't know. She was sixteen when she left us, would she have changed that much?"

"Your memory is not what it was, Stella," Henderson said gently. "I see a strong resemblance to the girl Suellen was at sixteen."

"You're an old man, Claude," Stella Devereaux said in a scoffing voice, "and you haven't been close to a girl in twenty years."

"She looks just like Rosellen would at that age—" Henderson stopped abruptly, flushing.

Julie stared at him. "Who's Rosellen?"

He sighed and said stiffly, "Your sister, who disappeared at the same time you did."

Julie made a startled sound. "A sister? I have a sister?"

Henderson nodded somberly. "Yes, my dear. A twin. But she is dead."

Stella Devereaux raised a hand. "I have forbidden that Rosellen be discussed in this house, Claude. You are well aware of that."

"I am aware of that, of course, but in view of the circumstances, Stella . . . The girl doesn't remember any of her past, and she will have to be told of Rosellen."

"You tell her, then." The fire returned to the old woman's eyes as her gaze once more found Julie's. This time suspicion lurked in their depths. "Since being informed that you believe the young lady here to be Suellen, I have read a bit about amnesia. Most experts agree that it is usually a plot device of fiction writers and seldom exists in real life. If it does, it is only a temporary thing. But lasting eight years? I could find no such case histories."

Henderson said, "I have consulted with leading psychiatrists about this. Such cases are rare, true—extremely rare—but it is possible, Stella. If the trauma is severe enough, the mind can slam the door on the past."

"'Slam the door on the past!'" Stella Devereaux snorted. "You sound like a soap-opera doctor, Claude. Trauma indeed! What trauma?"

Henderson said stiffly, "If we knew that, we would know the answer to many questions, now wouldn't we?"

"I don't wish to talk any more today." The voice of the woman on the bed was very weak now. "Tomorrow, perhaps. Go now. Leave me alone."

Sheldon gently took Julie's arm and whispered in her ear. "We'd better go. Mrs. Devereaux tires easily."

Henderson remained behind as they left the bedroom. He said, "Wait for me downstairs. I'll be down in a few minutes."

Sheldon led Julie to the dim parlor on the ground floor. There she turned to him in bewilderment. "Not only don't I understand, but I'm a little angry. This wasn't my idea. I was asked here, and now that woman is questioning who I am. She seems to be saying that I'm some kind of a fraud. After her money, I suppose that's what she thinks. Well, I have news for her, for you and Mr. Henderson! I don't want her money. I was doing just fine before all this began."

"It isn't *her* money, Julie. The money is in a trust, to go to you on your twenty-fifth birthday. But I can understand how you feel. However, you must understand something and be patient. Stella Devereaux is eighty-years-old, and she has been very ill. She isn't always lucid. Today, unfortunately, is not one of her better days. And she tends to be naturally suspicious."

Julie sniffed. "More than that. She's paranoid if she thinks I'm after the family fortune."

"Stella does have a tendency toward paranoia," said a voice from the entryway. "On the other hand, she has some cause. There have been others before you. All impostors. Several million dollars is a powerful lure for fakers."

Looking toward the entrance, Julie saw another elderly woman who she judged was in her late sixties. But unlike the woman upstairs, this one was still robust, in good health; she wore a rather dowdy brown skirt and a tan blouse.

Sheldon said, "Julie, this is Helen Bronson, your great-aunt. Miss Bronson, may I introduce Julie Malone, the lady we are now convinced is the real Suellen Devereaux. No impostor this time. I'd stake my reputation on it."

Helen Bronson made a sound halfway between a snort and a bray of laughter. "I wouldn't risk a dime on any lawyer's reputation."

Sheldon grinned easily. "Helen is our local cynic, Julie, but then her cynicism has stood her in good stead in the past. She has fended off a number of girls claiming to be Suellen Devereaux."

The woman moved closer, peering at Julie with narrowed brown eyes.

"Well she looks like the twins. I'll grant you that. It may be that you've finally come up with the real thing! Now, if you'll excuse me, I have to tend to Stella."

As suddenly as she had appeared, Helen Bronson was gone. Staring after her, Julie said, "There are many things about all this that I don't understand, but chief among them is this . . . isn't there anything that will prove beyond a doubt that I'm this Suellen? Fingerprints? Or baby footprints? I understand that all babies born in a hospital have impressions of their feet made. And how about dental records?"

"You were never fingerprinted. All dental records have somehow been lost. And you and

Rosellen weren't born in a hospital, but right here in Devereaux House, during a hurricane. They couldn't get your mother to a hospital.''

"And that's another thing. Until today, I never knew anything about a sister. My twin, Mr. Henderson said?"

Sheldon nodded. "From what I've been told, it was impossible to tell the two of you apart. Even your own mother had problems."

Julie shook her head in frustration. "A sister, a twin. You'd think I would remember that, but I don't. What happened to her?"

"Nobody is quite sure. I wasn't in Key West then, of course, but the way I understand it, she disappeared a few days before you did. The consensus is that she drowned. Your father had a boat, and Rosellen was crazy about it. For some reason that nobody can understand she took the boat out alone, in another bad storm. She was never heard from again, nor was the boat located."

"Her body was never found?"

Sheldon shook his head. "No, but that's not unusual when a boat sinks. So much happened to the Devereaux family at that time, so much tragedy. Your parents were killed, and then you and Rosellen vanished, all within a space of ten days."

"Were my . . . my parents killed together?"

"No, Julie, not together." It was Claude Henderson, who had entered the room in time to hear her question. "Your father, Reese Devereaux, was killed first, in a plane crash. In his own plane, on a flight from here to Miami. Then, right after the funeral, your mother was killed in an automobile accident, the same night Rosellen went out in the boat. And four days later you vanished from Key West." He shook his head somberly. "It was the combined shock that put Stella to bed. She never fully recovered from it. I do believe she would have expired, but for her determination to live until you were found. She always believed you were alive somewhere."

"But why doesn't she believe the same about my sister?" Julie noticed that she was not talking as if she had accepted the fact that she had once had a sister, a twin.

Henderson hesitated. "I'm not sure why, except that Stella, for some reason I've never ascertained, didn't care much for Rosellen. You were always her favorite."

Julie said, "It all sounds too much like a soap opera!"

"Perhaps it does to you, my dear," Henderson said in a chilly voice, "but it wasn't to those of us involved, especially Stella Devereaux."

Julie said hastily, "Oh, I know, I didn't mean that the way it must have sounded. It's just that all this is too much to take in, too much to really believe."

Henderson nodded. "Yes, I can understand that. Perhaps we should go now."

As he led the way out to the car, Julie turned to Sheldon. "These hurricanes you spoke of . . . have you experienced one?"

"No. I've lived in Key West four years, and there hasn't been one since I've been here—not a bad one, anyway."

"But you're always reading about Florida hurricanes and how destructive they are. In the bus coming down the Overseas Highway, I noticed I don't know how many houses built up on stilts. I asked the driver about them and he said it was because of the hurricanes.''

Sheldon laughed lightly. ''They do hit farther north, on the mainland of Florida and on the keys in between, but Key West seems to escape the brunt of the bad ones.''

''How does that happen? Does some sort of magic protect you down here?''

''That's quite possible,'' he said with a straight face. ''Some strange things happen in Key West, you'll find.''

''Well, I certainly don't think I want to be here when a hurricane hits, magic or not. The land is so flat it looks like one big wave could wash everything out to sea.''

''I wouldn't advise that you go around talking like that in front of a Conch.''

She stared. ''What's a Conk?''

''A native of Key West. And by Conch I don't mean just someone born here, but someone whose family goes back two or three generations. They're a pretty clannish lot. I don't know how they'd view you, Julie. You were born here, your family goes back several generations, but they might consider you a northerner now.''

They had reached the car. Sheldon held the door open for Julie and Henderson to get into the back, then went around to the driver's seat. During the ride back to her motel, Julie stared out the window without seeing the passing scenery, her thoughts in turmoil. So many new things had been thrown at her, her brain felt fuzzy, confused. So much so quickly, and little of it made any sense.

As though they realized her state of mind, neither Sheldon nor Henderson broke the silence until Sheldon drove the car into the curving driveway in front of the Pier House. He got out to open her door.

As she started to slide out, Henderson touched her arm, staying her briefly. "Julie, I shall see you tomorrow afternoon. We'll go back to Devereaux House. Hopefully Stella will be better, and your other aunt, Pippen, should be there by then."

Despite the warm air let in by the open door, Julie shivered slightly. "I'm not sure that I want to go back to that house. It's a lovely place but, well, somehow it seems haunted. That may strike you as a strange thing to say, but it's how I feel."

"Don't let your imagination run away with you, my dear," he said sharply. Then he softened his tone. "Anyway, perhaps that is a good thing. Perhaps your subconscious is trying to tell you that Devereaux House is full of memories of your past."

"I suppose that's possible, yet it seems unlikely."

Henderson took her hand and patted it paternally. "All will be well, Julie. Give it time."

Julie wasn't in the mood for such bromides at the moment and had to choke back a heated retort. Without another word she got out of the car. Sheldon accompanied her to the door of the motel. "Julie, you really shouldn't be alone all evening. May I take you to dinner? They have a very good restaurant here at the Pier House."

Julie looked at him with a rush of gratitude.
Sheldon was a very perceptive young man; she
didn't want to be alone all evening. "I'd like that,
Sheldon, very much."

"Why don't you call me Shell? Everyone else
does, except my mother and Mr. Henderson."

She smiled. "All right, Shell."

"The days are long here this time of the year.
Why don't I come by at nine? Or is that too late for
you? We eat late here in the summer."

"No, that will be fine, Shell. That'll give me
time for a nap. I tried to nap this afternoon, but I
was too keyed up and restless."

He squeezed her hand. "I'll see you at nine,
then."

Julie went on into the lobby, got her key and
went to her bungalow. She was very tired now. The
combination of the long bus ride and the nervous
tension generated by the meeting at Devereaux
House had exhausted her. Removing only her
shoes, she stretched out across the bed in the
blessedly cold air from the air conditioner and fell
into a shallow sleep.

Her sleep was troubled by dreams. When she finally awoke around six, she could remember the
dreams vividly. Hurricane winds howled, tossing
bodies like matchsticks. Airplanes crashed, exploding into searing flames. And then, in the real-
ity-distortion of dreams she found herself in a
peaceful room, dancing before a full-length mirror. It was at first very pleasant, but then, suddenly, the mirrors multiplied; and she saw myriad
mirror images of herself dancing into infinity. And
then the more distant images began to glide to-

ward her. Their smiles turned dark and scowling and grew increasingly threatening the closer they came, until she was surrounded by her reflections, all reaching clawlike fingers toward her.

She awoke with a scream dying in her throat, sitting bolt upright, drenched in perspiration despite the air-conditioning. As it happened, the dresser mirror was directly opposite the foot of the bed, and she saw her frightened face reflected in it. She caught herself peering behind the single image for the others.

She turned away resolutely, slipped her shoes on and left the room. The sun was just about to drop below the horizon in the west, but it was still stiflingly hot. She walked south along the beach, which was mostly deserted now, with only a few bathers left. And then, as she walked a mile or more below the motel, the sand became a narrow strip of pebbly beach, with rocks to her left. She was alone now, not another soul in sight. She kept walking.

The sun had set, and the fast twilight of the subtropics was settling around her. She sat down on a rock, knees drawn up, and stared pensively out at the darkening sea.

She was strongly tempted to pack her bags and take the next bus going north. She was a stranger here, and everyone was trying to fit her into a mold that she didn't care for. Oddly enough, the fact that a large inheritance was at stake gave her even more reason to shy away. Julie had never yearned after wealth as such; it seemed that something deeply buried in her subconscious turned her off big money. She would be content with a nice income, enough to support and raise a family. There would be too much responsibility connected with wealth, especially a fortune coming to her so unexpectedly.

She suddenly tensed at a sound from behind her; but before she could turn she was struck a stunning blow in the back and catapulted headfirst into the sea. The water wasn't too deep here, but it was swift. She had never been a good swimmer; there hadn't been that many places to swim in Moorestown.

Flailing, she went under, but she managed to fight her way to the surface, her head exploding out of the water, fighting for air. She caught a glimpse of a fleeting figure behind where she had been sitting. Then it was gone as she struck out for the shore, swimming clumsily, fighting the strong current.

She finally came out of the water a few yards south from where she'd gone in, on a small shelf. She sprawled facedown, coughing water, gasping for breath. After several minutes she got shakily to her feet and scanned the area. It was almost dark now, and she could see no one. Had she, sitting there dozing, lost her balance and fallen into the water, dreaming that she had been pushed?

No! She shook her head in violent denial. It was too real. Someone had given her a shove. It could have been an accident, someone could have stumbled inadvertently and fallen against her. But if that was the case, why had that person fled instead of at least *trying* to rescue her?

Her head swung around as she heard a voice calling her name. "Julie? Where are you?" It was Shell.

"I'm here, Shell." She started toward him. They met on the strip of beach, a few yards from where she had been sitting.

"My God, Julie!" He stared at her in disbelief. "You're soaking wet! Did you fall into the water? It's treacherous walking along here."

"No, I didn't fall in, I was pushed in."

His eyes narrowed. "Oh, Julie. Come on now."

"It's true. I was sitting up there—" she motioned with her head "—staring out to sea. Someone came up behind me and gave me a hard push. I could easily have drowned, since I'm not the best swimmer in the world."

"But why on earth would someone do a thing like that?" he asked, perplexed.

"How do I know?" she said in exasperation. "All I know is that it happened."

He was still dubious. "You say you were sitting up there, staring out to sea. You sure you didn't dream it? The sea can be hypnotic sometimes."

"No, I didn't dream it," she snapped in annoyance. "You don't get soaked like this in a dream."

"But you could have fallen—" He broke off, his gaze raking the area. "As you can see, Julie, there's no one here."

"They're gone, whoever was here. Probably heard you calling me and ran."

"That's possible," he admitted. "I have been calling for a bit. I came to pick you up for dinner and you weren't in your room. I figured you were on the beach.''

"If I'm going to dinner, I have to change and shower.'' She started back toward the hotel, shivering now with a sudden chill. Shell caught up with her and draped his jacket around her shoulders.

FOUR

November 18

Yesterday Suellen was sick, but I think she was just pretending because she gets lots of attention from Mama that way. I wish she really had been sick and hurt a lot, because she told Mama what Huey and I were doing in the garage. Suellen must have peeked in through the window because we had the door closed. If I had caught her peeking, I would have pulled her hair good and hard and made her too scared to run tattling to Mama, but Huey and I didn't see her.

We were having such fun until Huey got scared because he heard noises outside, but it was just that silly old Dingo sniffing around. I hate that stupid dog! Mama was very cross. Her face got real red and she yelled at me that she was going to tell Daddy, but she didn't. She told me that I could get into bad trouble doing things with boys in the garage. That's all she knows. I know I cannot get into trouble like that because I haven't had my period yet. I was twelve this year. Anyway, when I get my period I know things to do so I won't get into trouble.

I got even with Dingo and I got even with Suellen too. I put some poison from the garden shed into some hamburger meat and fed it to Dingo. He is so stupid that he swallowed it whole without even looking. He'll be good and sick before long and Mrs. Findlay will carry on and flap her apron, like she always does. I wish I could see it.

Then I put on Suellen's blue dress and went over to Mrs. Turner's backyard. I didn't even try to hide. I just walked right up to her orange tree and began picking the oranges. In a minute she came running out hollering just like Mrs. Findlay. I waited until she could see me then I ran away with my skirt full of oranges. I listened in on the extension when she called Mama. I heard Mama say which one of the twins was it? And Mrs. Turner says who can tell which is which? Then Mama said, well what color dress was she wearing? And Mrs. Turner says blue.

Mama hung up and called Suellen and scolded her, and Suellen kept saying that she hadn't done it, and Mama said it must have been her because she has the only blue dress.

I wanted to giggle out loud, but they would have heard me.

When Shell Phipps came into the office the next morning, Jean Harris, the receptionist, looked up from her desk. ''Mr. Henderson wishes to see you at your convenience,'' she told the young man.

''All right, Jean. Tell him I'll be down in a few minutes.''

One thing about being made a junior partner, Shell thought, is that I don't have to jump through so many hoops.

When he'd first joined the firm, a summons from God—as he had thought of Claude Henderson in those days—would have been answered promptly. He would have been down the hall and into Henderson's office before the words were out of Jean's mouth. Now he could dally a little; now he felt it necessary to dally a little.

Not that Henderson would tolerate an undue delay, but Shell had more leeway now. Habits of years were hard to break, and Henderson still absentmindedly snapped out orders as though Shell were still a lowly law clerk. Like yesterday, when he'd ordered a brandy for Julie.

Julie. Shell leaned back in his swivel chair, thinking of Julie and last night. He knew, of course, that Henderson wanted to discuss Julie, wanted Shell's impressions of her.

He admired Henderson's honesty, his grasp of the law, his unquestioned integrity; but sometimes the older man demanded too much of others, especially those working for him.

Sheldon Phipps was a native New Englander, a natural athlete, a superb basketball player in high school. His family, while not poor, could not afford to send him to college, but he had gotten an athletic scholarship to the University of Southern California, where he had studied law. He had been the basketball team's star guard during his last two years. It hadn't been easy; most of those who attended on athletic scholarships took undemanding courses, hoping for a shot at pro ball after college. Shell had worked his tail off to get his degree and to play ball at the same time.

But he managed, graduating in the top ten of his class. He was offered a tryout with the Los Angeles Lakers but never once seriously considered it. The profession of law had always intrigued him, and he was happy enough to settle for his degree. Originally he had intended to return to Vermont and start his own practice, but the southern California weather had spoiled him; he didn't think he could suffer through those iron winters in New England.

There were no opportunities that suited him in California, but one of his law professors knew that the law firm of Henderson & Caldicott in Key West, Florida, was looking for a bright young man. Claude Henderson had once been a colleague of the professor's and was agreeable to accepting any young man his friend might recommend.

Shell accepted the position. The firm was prestigious, and there was a good chance, if he did well, of being made a junior partner in time.

The weather in Key West wasn't exactly what he had expected, especially not the summers; but he became more or less acclimatized to it, and he liked the casual life-style. In the beginning, of course, he was only a law clerk, but that was to be expected— he had to serve the usual apprenticeship.

He soon learned why he'd been employed. The two elder members of the firm dealt strictly with civil matters, giving legal advice to their wealthy clients and handling their estates, business contracts and the like. However, a change had taken place in Key West over the past years, and the children of many of their clients were being hauled into criminal court—for drug use, brawling, minor pilferage and even drug smuggling, which was becoming a lucrative pastime for the youth in the area.

Henderson and Caldicott refused to soil their hands with such matters, but they found that they stood to lose their wealthy clients if they did not stand between their rebellious offspring and the law. Thus, Shell Phipps. His apprenticeship proved of short duration—almost before he knew it he was handling criminal matters—but he didn't mind. He liked the battle of wits, despite the fact that he often despised the spoiled, arrogant youths he was required to defend. But he was made a junior partner within three years for his laudable efforts, long before he could normally have expected such an offer.

His intercom blinked. He pushed the switch. "Yes, Jean, tell Himself that I'll be right there."

Jean laughed throatily. "Someday, buster, I'm going to pass on your messages verbatim, and then you'll be in manure up to your knees."

Shell chuckled and got to his feet, his thoughts moving ahead to what he was going to tell Henderson about Julie. He chuckled again. If he kept calling her Julie, soon he wouldn't be able to call her anything else, yet she was extremely uncomfortable with Suellen.

In Henderson's office he said, "I'm sorry, sir. I had some papers to go over and got lost in them."

Henderson nodded coolly, motioning him to a seat.

"The Devereaux girl, you took her to dinner last night?"

"Yes, sir, I did."

"See here, Phipps, you're not smitten with her, are you?"

Shell gave a start, having to search his mind for the meaning of the word. Trust Claude Henderson to use such an old-fashioned term. He smiled meagerly. "I don't believe so, sir. After all, I've known her for less than twenty-four hours."

Henderson grunted. "Stranger things have happened. Aside from the fact that she stands to inherit a great deal of money, we are, in a manner of speaking, representing her, and it is a grievous error for an attorney to become emotionally involved with a client.''

''I think Julie is very attractive and a nice person,'' Shell said somewhat stiffly. ''But it doesn't go beyond that.'' Even as he spoke, he had to wonder just how accurate his disclaimer was.

Henderson studied him narrowly for a moment, then slowly nodded. From a humidor on his desk he took a long black cigar. When Castro had seized power in Cuba, most cigar makers had fled to the United States, and a number of them remained in Key West. Henderson smoked two a day, one in the morning and one in the afternoon. Of course, Shell reflected, I don't know what he does at home. Henderson had lived a bachelor's existence in a condo on the beach since the death of his wife many years before Shell had come onto the scene. Shell had never been inside the man's home, and he knew no one who had.

''How did last evening go?'' Henderson asked.

Shell shrugged. ''All right, I suppose. Julie wasn't very communicative, if that's what you mean. We ate at the Pier House Restaurant, and she went to her bungalow the moment we'd finished. I suppose it was all due to what happened earlier.''

Henderson leaned forward attentively. ''What happened earlier?''

Shell reported what Julie had related to him. ''The thing is, I'm not sure if she didn't just imagine the whole thing. I certainly saw no one when I arrived on the scene, which means nothing, of course.''

"I suppose, with all that happened yesterday, that her imagination could have been overactive,'' Henderson said thoughtfully. He exhaled a thick cloud of pungent smoke. "There was a streak of instability in her father and grandfather, you know. Perhaps even insanity. I'm not sure. Naturally, the Devereaux have never been anxious to talk about this.''

Shell made a sound of surprise. "No, I didn't know. It must be a deep, dark secret. I've certainly never heard even a whisper to that effect. And Stella Devereaux certainly shows no signs of it.''

Henderson was nodding. "That's true, but then Stella is a Devereaux only by marriage. But Reese Devereaux, Suellen's father, was . . . well, flighty. He was a brilliant man, I agree, and managed to increase the money he inherited threefold. But he was erratic at times, and he would fly up to New York several times a year to drink, gamble and womanize for days, sometimes longer.''

"That's not necessarily a sign of madness.'' Shell grinned. "If so, half the rich men I know are crazy.''

"But Reese carried it too far. More than once I had to send someone up to New York to get him out of jail. Once he was found almost dead on the Bowery, buying high-priced wine and sharing it with the winos there.'' Henderson sighed. "I can't recall how many times I'd sworn to wash my hands of him, but Stella always talked me out of it. I've been representing the Devereaux since I opened my practice here thirty years ago. That's probably why he was flying to New York, for another toot, when he was killed in the plane crash.''

"Then you think his genes may have been passed on to Julie? I find that hard to accept. She seems perfectly normal to me. The tension she's under, anyone could imagine what she did last night, if she *did* imagine it.''

"I'm not saying she is unstable, Sheldon. I'm just suggesting it as a possibility. For all we know, she could even be telling the truth.''

Shell stared. "What do you mean, sir? You mean someone really tried to kill her?''

Henderson gave a small shrug. "Anything is possible in today's climate. The dregs of society inhabit Key West these days. Drug pushers, drug smugglers and drug users. People kill just for the thrill of it. And do not forget—'' he exhaled cigar smoke ''—she will be worth considerable money when she comes into her inheritance.''

"And that isn't far off.''

"True, Julie is now twenty-four, and—''

"And her sister is dead,'' Shell finished for him.

"That is what we believe.''

"Is there any doubt of that?'' Shell asked slowly.

"Her body was never found, as you know, but her death is generally accepted. The only real doubt—in my mind, at least—concerns which one of the twins we have here, Suellen or Rosellen.''

Shell sat up, startled. "You mean you're not sure? I never really considered that aspect of it.''

"Since Rosellen died, this one must be Suellen. But how can we ever *really* be sure? After all, no one was ever able to tell them apart.'' The older man shrugged. "But then, I suppose it really doesn't matter all that much, does it?"

"You mean it doesn't matter which twin we found, so long as it's one of them?"

"I would hesitate to go that far, Sheldon, but at least we could settle for one Devereaux."

"It might matter to Julie," Shell said in a dry voice. He was thinking hard, wondering if he had been wrong in his snap judgment. What if Julie really were in danger? No, that would be too melodramatic, some relative trying to kill her for the money. "In case something happens to Julie, what happens to the money then? Does it go to the aunts or Stella?" he asked.

Henderson shook his head. "No, Stella has enough money of her own, and Reese was never on good terms with either Helen or Pippen. If both girls are deceased, without issue, the trust goes to various charities. And Stella's own money, on her death, is equally divided between Helen and Pippen and Rosellen and Suellen."

"In that case, there's really no one to benefit by Julie's death, is there?" Shell spread his hands. "So who would have a motive to kill her?"

"In that sense, I suppose you're right." Henderson brooded for a moment. "I have never been a man to indulge myself in hunches or even intuition, but somehow I have a bad feeling about this whole affair. So I would appreciate it, Sheldon, if you would sort of keep an eye on Julie, at least until we see how matters proceed." He smiled meagerly.

Julie was supposed to have a second audience with Stella Devereaux at three that afternoon. She used the word "audience" because she felt a little as though she were going to visit royalty.

She arrived at the law offices at 2:30 and found Shell waiting for her. "Mr. Henderson isn't going to Devereaux House today. He had an urgent appointment."

Julie didn't say so, but she thought it was just as well. Although she liked him, Claude Henderson intimidated her a little. As they drove away from the law offices she said, "I wish to apologize for my behavior last night. I know I was surly and very bad company."

"You had reason to be upset. I would have been, I'm sure, if someone had just tried to kill me."

She glanced over at him in surprise. "Today you believe me? Last night you said—"

"I had second thoughts, okay? I doubt very much that you would dream something like that. After all, you were soaking wet. You must be careful.

"Over the past few years a bad element has drifted in. Someone once said that it was almost as if the eastern seaboard had been tilted, dumping all the lowlife down here into the boot. Some guy stoned out of his skull could have happened by, saw you there, vulnerable, and just gave you a shove. There are some people like that, absolutely without conscience, who will kill for no motive whatsoever, just for the hell of it."

"This doesn't sound like such a nice place, your Key West," she said dryly.

"It's probably no worse than others, and better than most," he said defensively. "There's only a small fraction like that, and everything is being done to keep them under control. Unfortunately, Key West has become a mecca for dope smugglers. That seems to be the chief industry nowadays."

"Then it hasn't changed a great deal, has it?"

Shell gave her a sharp look. "I'm not sure what you mean."

"You mentioned the word Conch yesterday, so today I did a little research into its origin. It came about because the early settlers built their houses out of conch shells. And today the old-timers, the native Key Westers, call themselves Conchs. Am I right?"

"You're right on the button, Julie."

"And those early settlers had an unsavory history. Some of them were wreckers and pirates, the worst kind of bloody villains. So in that respect, Key West hadn't changed."

"I suppose you could say that. It all comes about because we're so damned isolated here, like a long finger stuck out into the ocean. We're near the shipping lanes, and we're so accessible by sea. Almost everyone has a boat, commercial or pleasure. Even I have one. So it's simply impossible to patrol the shoreline successfully. You'd need almost as many patrol boats as private boats, and that would cause a traffic jam worse than the Hollywood Freeway at rush hour."

"And the Devereaux? Were they once buccaneers?"

"Well, nobody knows for sure, of course," he said cautiously. "That's all too far back in the past,

Julie. But I'll be honest with you. The story has it that the initial Devereaux fortune was the result of piracy on the high seas. But they're not alone in that. Many old, respected families in Key West can trace their roots to pirates."

"I suppose most people would consider that a romantic background, a colorful family legacy."

"It's certainly not a stigma, if it goes far enough back into the past. It's my understanding that your great-grandfather, Jean Devereaux, was a pirate operating in the Gulf and using Key West as a base...." As they turned the corner and Devereaux House loomed in the next block, Shell slowed the car. "There's something I should tell you, Julie, and I'm not quite sure how. You'll meet Pippen Delacroix today. She flew down from Miami early this morning on her way in from France. Pippen is . . . well, she's a rather strange person. I only met her once, but she rubbed me the wrong way then."

"Strange in what way, Shell?"

He squirmed uncomfortably in the seat. "Well, it's a little hard to explain. I understand Pippen's in her mid-forties, but it would be easy to guess her at thirty. She has a caustic tongue and is liable to say almost anything at any given time."

Julie looked at him curiously. "Why do you feel you have to warn me about her?"

"Because she always fought Stella over the issue of looking for you. She always maintained that you'd never be found, so why go to all the trouble and expense of looking for you?"

"She must have some reason for thinking that. Did she ever express one?"

Shell shook his head. "Not a logical one that I ever heard. She's strange, as I said. For instance, she claims that she's often in touch with, quote, 'those on the other side.' Things like that. The thing is, I wanted to forewarn you. More than likely she'll deny on sight that you're Suellen Devereaux. She may call you a fraud, a phony, all kinds of names."

"Did you ever think that she might be right?" Julie said in a low, almost inaudible voice.

If Shell heard her, he chose to ignore it. He pulled the car up before the stucco wall and came around to help Julie out.

The same black woman answered the door. At the sight of them she leaned forward and whispered, "Mr. Phipps, Miss Pippen is here."

"I know, Pauline," Shell said with a sigh. "We're ready for her." He squeezed Julie's hand. "I hope."

As Pauline stepped back, a tall, handsome woman in a short white dress came sweeping down the staircase. She stopped short at the bottom and stared at Julie, her brilliant black eyes unsettling in their intensity.

Then she opened her arms and advanced, speaking in a throaty voice. "Why, of course it's Suellen! I don't know how anybody could have the least doubt."

She embraced Julie fervently. Past her shoulder, Julie stared at Shell; his face was blank with astonishment, his mouth open.

FIVE

March 4

I have been reading some really interesting books. Some of them I got from the library, and some of them from Huey, who sneaks them out of his father's study. I have to read them in secret though, because Mama gets all bent out of shape when she catches me reading them. I have to watch out for Suellen too. She is so naive. I tried once to get her to read one, but she practically threw a fit. So far she hasn't tattled to Mama, but I wouldn't put it past her.

Some of the books are about sex and some about black magic, which is interesting too. Aunty Pip has told me stories about communicating with the dead. Nobody believes her, but I do.

Huey and I have tried some of the things in the books of his father's. Suellen would die, just die, if she knew some of the things we do. I guess if she knew, her hair would turn as white as snow. Mama would probably drop over in a faint. I'd almost like to tell her, just to watch her face. Sometimes I think she and Suellen hate me just because I'm not like them.

Except Daddy. I know he doesn't hate me. I know I am his favorite. He is the only interesting person in this house, besides me. I think I could tell him about the things in the books, and he would just laugh. I wonder what he ever saw in Mama. She is really dull. But she is pretty, and I suppose Suellen is too, since she looks just like me. Sometimes I wish something bad would happen to Mama and Suellen, and then there would be just Daddy and me. I would keep house for him, do everything for him, and be a charming hostess to all of his friends.

I can tell that I am growing up because of the way Daddy's friends all look at me, especially Mr. Thomas. I like him to look at me because I think he is very handsome, almost as handsome as Daddy. Mr. Findlay, our Sunday school teacher, looks at me, too, even if he is one of the blurry ones. Mrs. Findlay notices him looking at me. I can tell by the way I catch her staring at me, but she has always hated me anyway, since her silly dog Dingo died.

I just hate going to Sunday school. As soon as I am old enough to do what I want, I'll never go again. Suellen doesn't seem to mind going, but she is such a fool anyway. I wonder what she would think if I told her how Mr. Findlay looks at me. I suppose she wouldn't believe it. She thinks he is a good man. I have heard her say so.

Today I found something else to read. I found it up in the attic. I was up there going through an old trunk. I guess it's really called a sea chest. Down in the bottom I found a bunch of handwritten pages so old they're about to fall apart. It's all about my great-grandfather Jean Devereaux, written in his own hand, I think. It's hard to make out, the ink is so faded. He was a pirate! I can hardly wait to read it all. But I'll have to do it in secret. I just know they wouldn't approve of me knowing what's in it.

Julie felt a strong sense of relief when Pippen Delacroix finally released her and stepped back. She had to agree with Shell's assessment—there was something strange about the woman. Not only strange, Julie thought, but frightening, as well, although she would have been unable to explain that feeling.

Pippen was speaking to Shell. "And you? I've met you somewhere. I know that."

Unsmiling, Shell said, "I'm Sheldon Phipps, Mrs. Delacroix, of Henderson, Caldicott and Phipps."

"Oh, yes!" Pippen snapped her fingers. "The attorney, the one with a name almost like mine. How could I have forgotten?" She looked at him narrowly, black eyes shrewd. "You look surprised, Phipps. Why is that?"

"Well, I . . ." Shell fumbled for words. "I suppose I'm just surprised at your accepting Julie as Suellen so easily."

Pippen gave a Gallic shrug. "Why should I deny it, when the truth stares one in the eye? She is a Devereaux. One look at her is enough to realize that."

"As I recall, you've been opposed all along to the search for her. A great waste of money, I believe you said."

"So I was wrong. I'm not infallible." She shrugged again. "Besides, I've consulted recently. Running Elk informed me that Suellen was still alive."

"Running Elk, I presume," Shell said in a dry voice, "is your spirit guide?"

"Of course."

"Why is it they're always Indians?"

"Because Indians had a great rapport with the spirits. Their god was called the Great Spirit, you may remember."

"I'm puzzled by something," Shell said. "As I recall, one of the reasons you were always so adamant about Suellen being dead was because this spirit guide of yours had told you that she was.''

''He was mistaken. The twins were so identical that no one on earth could tell them apart, not even my brother and his wife. The same thing is true on the other side.''

''So you're saying now that your spirit guide is claiming that it's Rosellen on the other side, not Suellen?''

''That's exactly right, Phipps.''

''But how did he learn of his mistake?''

''Because Rosellen's spirit told him so,'' Pippen said triumphantly.

Julie had been following this weird conversation with growing incredulity. Did Pippen, this elegantly attired, sophisticated woman, really believe all this? Julie herself had an interest in the occult, but it was an interest tempered by logic and a certain amount of healthy skepticism. Pippen's statements sounded outrageous and more than a little eccentric.

She caught Shell's gaze on her, and he winked.

''I saw that!'' Pippen said sharply. ''I know the world is full of unbelievers and I can live with that, but I don't care for being made fun of to my face.''

''I am sorry, Mrs. Delacroix,'' Shell said contritely. ''I truly am. I wasn't really making fun of you....''

''Oh, yes, you were, but I'm accustomed to it. Come along, Mother is waiting for you, Suellen.'' The woman started up the staircase, head high, not looking back.

Shell gave Julie his arm and they started up, more slowly. She whispered, "She's really serious about all that, isn't she?"

Shell nodded. "Oh, yes, quite serious. And she's right, I shouldn't have winked. I was poking fun at her in a way, and I've always tried to respect the beliefs of others, no matter how outlandish I might think those beliefs are."

"Does Stella Devereaux believe in spirit guides?"

"Not for an instant. The old girl is completely down-to-earth. Pippen may be her daughter, but you'd never know it, they're so different. I never met Reese Devereaux, but I understand that he was cut from a different mold, as well. More like his sister."

"He believed in the supernatural?"

"I don't know about that, but he liked the good life—wine, women and song—as does Pippen. Men, of course, instead of women, although I've heard rumors—" He broke off, squeezing her hand. "I hope that doesn't upset you, what I said about your father, but you're going to hear it anyway sooner or later. If not from me, from somebody else."

"Since I can't even remember knowing him, I don't suppose it matters too much. But if my...my father was such a profligate, how did he hold on to the fortune?"

"Stella keeps a tight rein on money matters, you can be sure. Reese had a talent for making money, I understand, but not for keeping it. Stella saw to it that he kept it—most of it, anyway."

"I've never been told, just how much money is involved?"

"I don't know the exact figures, that's Mr. Henderson's department, but it's several million dollars."

She made a sound of distress. "That much money frightens me."

"It does many people at first." He laughed softly. "But you'll soon get used to it. Most people do."

Julie wasn't so sure; the responsibility alone would be awesome. But she said nothing more, as they were at the door to Stella Devereaux's bedroom.

Pippen was standing at the head of the bed. The old woman was propped up against a pile of pillows. She looked a little better this afternoon. Her bright gaze found and clung to Julie's face as she and Shell stopped at the foot of the huge bed.

"Well, my girl," Stella Devereaux said in her brusque way. "To my great surprise, Pippen just told me that she's convinced that you're really Suellen. What do you say to that?"

"What can I say?" Julie retorted. "In fact, it seems that I've had very little to say about any of this from the very beginning. I feel like some sort of a bystander, or a moviegoer, watching a girl named Suellen up there on the screen, a person I've never seen before."

Stella Devereaux laughed. "You even sound like Suellen, talking fanciful like that. She had more daydreams than any girl should have."

Pippen said, almost defensively, "Rosellen, too. All young girls go through that stage."

The old woman waved her silent. "Where are you staying, girl?"

"In a motel. The Pier House."

"Move in here. There are plenty of bedrooms. No need to spend good money on a motel."

"I don't know," Julie said doubtfully. "I'm not sure that I *am* this Suellen Devereaux. Somehow it doesn't seem right to me. How can you know who I am, if I don't?"

"I'm about as sure as I'll ever be. Maybe if you move in here the familiar surroundings will help to bring your memory back."

Shell spoke for the first time. "There is something I have been thinking about. You could take her to Dr. Reardon's clinic. It's not far, and it seems to me that Julie's case would be right up his alley—"

Pippen snorted. "He's nothing but a quack, a witch doctor! Just because the press keeps doing articles on him they've made him a pop idol. These 'new techniques' of his do more harm than good!"

"Your spirit guide told you all that, I suppose?" Shell said dourly.

"That is correct, Phipps, he did," Pippen said calmly.

"Ah, you're on to her, I see, young man," Stella Devereaux said with a laugh, then turned her attention to Julie. "I'll hear no more arguments, girl. You'll move in today. I'll have Pauline prepare your old room for you."

"I think that's a good idea, Mrs. Devereaux," Shell said. "As a matter of fact, Julie, we'll go get your things right now and move you in."

Before a slightly dazed Julie was completely aware of what was happening, she was out of the house and they were driving away. Stirring, she glanced over at him. "You think it's a good idea, do you?"

"Yes, I do." He darted a quick look at her. "It's your home, why shouldn't you stay there? They've gone to a lot of trouble to find you, Julie. Now it's over."

"Is it?"

"Now what does that mean?"

"One thing nobody seems to have thought of," she said gloomily. "What if I'm *not* this Suellen Devereaux? Don't misunderstand, I'm not trying any hoax here. But what if I wake up some day soon with full memory and discover that I'm Jane Doe from Peoria, Illinois?"

He shook his head. "Never happen. The more I see of you, the more certain I am."

"I wish I was as sure." She shifted uneasily in the seat. "I'll be honest, Shell. It's that house."

"The house? What's wrong with the house?"

"It's . . . well, spooky, I guess is the only word I can use. I get a funny feeling when I'm in it."

"You know, while Devereaux House is not a castle, most people would envy anybody having a chance to live there. It's a well-built house, it cost a fortune even when it was built, and it's rich in history, Devereaux history."

"It's also steeped in tragedy," she said with a shiver. "Two people died violent deaths days apart, and two sixteen-year-old girls disappear off the face of the earth. That's enough to give you a case of the creeps right there."

THREE HOURS LATER, when Julie was settled into what was supposed to have once been her bedroom, she wasn't as uncomfortable as she had feared. The room was cheery, decorated in bright yellows; and although the furniture was old and covered with too-bright chintz, the room was attractive. The sun was slanting toward the west, flooding the room with natural light. All in all, she thought, it was very pleasant.

If she was to live here, she was determined to have her say about redecorating and refurnishing the room. Except for the bed, it was a child's room. The bed, another four-poster—were all the beds in Devereaux House four-posters?—could stay.

She caught herself up short. She was thinking as if she fully intended to live here permanently. Had she unconsciously decided that she was indeed Suellen Devereaux and that this was her rightful place in the world?

This thought brought on a wave of sorrow, sorrow for the Malones and for Ken. Which reminded her—she had yet to call them as she had promised, to let them know what had taken place down here.

She sat down at the nightstand by the bed, picked up the Princess phone and dialed the familiar number. As she listened to it ring, she heard a click and wondered for just a moment if someone had picked up an extension somewhere in the house. Then the familiar voice of Alice Malone said breathlessly, "Hello?" and Julie forgot the click.

"Hello, Mom. It's Julie."

"Julie!" The word was a glad cry. "We were getting a little frantic here."

"I'm sorry, Mom. I should have called yesterday, I know, but so many things have happened, I'm kind of overwhelmed."

"What has happened? Tell me!"

Quickly Julie told her all that happened, omitting only the near drowning on the beach.

At the end of it there was a short silence, and then the sound of a heavy sigh came over the line. "Then it looks like you really *are* this Suellen Devereaux."

"Well, everybody here seems to think so."

"I suppose I should be glad for you, with all that money involved, but I feel like we're losing a daughter."

"Oh, no, Mom!" Julie said. "You'll always feel like...you'll always be my real parents, you're all I've ever known."

"That's because your memory is gone. What if you remember everything that happened before you came to us? You'll feel differently then."

"I promise I won't."

"Julie..." Another sigh came over the line. "Julie, I just realized how selfish I'm sounding. Bob and me, we'll always be thankful for having you as long as we did. I thank the good Lord every day that you came to us. We'll never stop loving you."

"And I'll never stop loving you, you know that. Where is Daddy?"

"He's downtown somewhere, dear. Would you like him to call you when he gets back?"

"Yes, please." She gave Alice Malone the phone number at Devereaux House.

"Julie," her mother said hesitantly, "Ken has called at least twice a day since you left. He's worried, too. I think you should call him."

"I will, Mom, the minute I hang up. And I promise to call you and Daddy regularly from now on."

After she hung up, Julie sat for a few moments with her hand on the phone. She felt a strange reluctance to call Ken. She loved him, she knew she did, yet she also knew that he wasn't going to be too happy with what she had to tell him. He had been strongly opposed to her coming down here, claiming that it was all nonsense, a wild-goose chase. Why didn't she just stay home where she belonged, marry him and forget everything else? Now she was sure that he wouldn't crow with delight to learn that it was all true and that she might be staying a while.

With a sigh she dialed the number of the sporting goods store that he managed and was put right through to him. "Julie! Sweetheart, am I glad to hear your voice!" An injured note crept into his own voice. "Why haven't you called me? I've been going out of my mind here."

"I'm sorry, Ken. Things have been sort of crazy, and I wanted to get at least some of it straightened out before I talked to you."

"Get what straightened out?" he asked warily. "What's crazy?"

She gave him an abbreviated version of what she had just told Alice Malone.

"So I was wrong, maybe you are this Suellen Devereaux. But to me you'll always be Julie Malone."

"That's sweet, Ken."

"Well, Julie's the girl I know and the girl I love. But I don't understand one thing. Now that they've decided you're the missing heiress, why can't you come home where you belong?"

"It's not that simple, Ken."

"I fail to see why. You don't know anyone there. All the people you know and love are here, in Moorestown. Unless your memory has suddenly returned," he said with a rising note of suspicion.

"No such luck," she said ruefully. "I wish it had. It would make it all so much simpler."

He made a sound of impatience. "I don't understand. They can't keep you there, unless you want to stay. Sign whatever papers are necessary and get back up here where you belong. They know where you'll be if they need you for anything." He lowered his voice. "I miss you, damn it!"

"I miss you, too, darling. But I can't leave right now. For one thing, Stella Devereaux, who I suppose is my grandmother, is dying. And there are many unresolved questions—"

"Like I said, unless you *want* to stay," he broke in.

"That's not true, Ken." And yet, at the same time, she had to wonder if it wasn't at least partly true.

"I'm sorry, Julie," he was saying. "I'm being too hard on you, I know. Poor baby, all this must be confusing as hell for you, not to mention scary.''

''You're right, Ken, it is terrifying. Thank you for understanding.''

''It's just that Key West is a long way from Moorestown,'' he said with a feigned air of martyrdom. ''And I'm suffering, with no one to comfort me.''

She had to laugh. ''I'll make it up to you. Soon, darling.''

''You'd damned well better,'' he said briskly. ''If I could get away from here, I'd fly down there. Maybe I will see if I can get away—''

''No, don't do that, Ken,'' she said quickly. Too quickly, she realized. She added, ''I mean, there's no need for you to do that at the moment. Wait until I know how long I'm going to stay. Things should get resolved in a few days.''

''Well, all right. But I'm not going to wait forever for my lady to come back to me.''

''It won't be too long—'' A knock sounded on the door. ''Ken, someone's at the door. I'll call you tomorrow, I promise.''

''Okay. Remember that I love you, baby.''

''I won't forget, darling,'' she said softly, and hung up. She called out, ''Come in!''

The door opened and Pauline came in. ''I'm sorry, Miss Suellen. Didn't realize you were on the phone. But I'm leaving for the afternoon, won't be back until time to fix supper. I was wondering if there's anything I can get for you.''

''Not that I can think of, Pauline. Thank you.'' As the woman nodded and started out, Julie said hastily, ''Are you in a big hurry?''

"Nope, I reckon not." Pauline looked at her intently.

"I was wondering if we could talk for a minute?"

"Reckon so. Roscoe, that's my man, says I'd rise up out of my coffin, if there was a chance to have a good talk." She shut the door and came on into the room.

Julie gestured to the chair by the bed, and Pauline sat down, folding her hands in her lap, and looking at Julie with a lively curiosity.

"All this happened so fast, I'm dizzy," Julie said hesitantly. "How long have you worked here, at Devereaux House?"

"Ten years I've worked for Miss Stella."

Julie felt a jab of surprise. "Somehow I didn't realize that. Then you were here when I . . . when I was supposed to be here. You knew the twins, and their parents."

"Yes, Miss Suellen," Pauline said softly. "I was here then."

"You appear to accept me without any doubt."

Pauline nodded and said simply, "Yes, I know."

"But how do you know which twin I am? Everybody says it was impossible to tell them apart."

"I could always tell, 'cause Miss Rosellen was the mean one."

Julie caught her breath. "The mean one? What do you mean by that?"

"I mean Miss Rosellen had the pure devil in her. When something bad was done, always look for Miss Rosellen. I tried to tell your mama that, she wouldn't listen. I tried to tell your daddy, he just laughed. No need to tell Miss Stella. Nobody can ever tell Miss Stella anything.''

''You mean she was just full of mischief, don't you, Pauline? Kid stuff, things like that?''

Pauline shook her head vigorously. ''No, sir, I don't mean mischief, not child devilment. I mean evil, poisoning a neighbor's dog, screwing boys—excuse me—before she was hardly old enough to bleed. I suspect even worse things,'' she said darkly, ''but I don't know them for a fact.''

''What worse things, Pauline? What could be worse than what you've just told me?''

''Huey, the neighbor's boy, he died. Found hung from a rafter in his folks' attic. Nobody ever knew why.''

Julie recoiled in horror. ''You can't mean that my . . . that Rosellen did that? Surely you're not serious!''

Pauline shrugged and said cryptically, ''Nobody ever explained why a fourteen-year-old boy hung himself. And your mama, now, the night she was killed—''

''But that was an accident!''

''Maybe it was, maybe it wasn't.'' Pauline got to her feet abruptly. ''Reckon my man is right, Miss Suellen. Sometimes I talk too much.''

She departed, leaving Julie staring after her in disbelieving horror.

SIX

March 10
I finally finished reading my great-grandfather's journal. It has some of the neatest stuff in it! I've read other books about pirates, but most of them sounded like Hollywood movies, like some of the old pirate movies Errol Flynn made that I see on the late-night TV. I'm sure that these stories by Jean Devereaux are the real thing.

I wish I had lived back in those days. I've read about one or two women pirates, but I would have made a good one if I had been around then. When you wanted something, you went out and got it. When somebody got in your way, you scared them into their holes or killed them, whichever worked. My great-grandfather, I'm sure, was one of the strong, sharp people. There was nothing blurry about him.

He hid in and around the Keys between forays out to sea. He had spies in all the big shipping ports. Relays of rumors brought word when a ship was sailing with any valuable cargo, and then Jean Devereaux would sail his ship, the Shark's Fin, out to intercept them.

First, he would order the cargo vessel to heave to and turn over whatever they were carrying. If they refused, he would blow them out of the water. I don't really understand why he went to all that trouble. Why not just sneak up and attack the ship? It would have been a lot easier in the long run. Maybe he kind of wanted to toy with them, like a cat does with a mouse. Yes, that must be it!

He came upon one of his prize catches by accident. It was a ship loaded with silver and gold, sailing across the Gulf to Europe. There was a big fight, cannons roaring, swords slashing, lots of blood running across the decks. Finally the Shark's Fin won out, great-grandfather loaded all the loot on board his ship, and sank the other ship.

His own ship was badly damaged. In his journal he says there was a mutiny among his buccaneers, and he had to hang many of them from the yardarm. The mutiny made him so angry that he had three of his men bury the treasure on one of the Keys, and he shot the men after.

Great-grandfather's journal ends there. I wonder if that was how the Devereaux fortune was started? Did he use the treasure, or did his only son, my grandfather, dig up the treasure later?

I am sure the last is what happened. Oh, what a grand secret this is, to know that the Devereaux fortune was founded on pirate's gold! I'll just bet that if I told Grand-mother Stella what I know, she wouldn't be so snooty!

Julie found Helen Bronson out back of the house, trowel in hand, a garden smock covering her angular figure. She was on her knees, loosening the dirt around a group of scrawny rose-bushes, sprinkling granules of fertilizer around their roots.

Helen glanced up at the sound of Julie's footsteps. "Ah, good afternoon, child! I understand you've moved in with us to stay?"

"Well, at least for a bit," Julie said diffidently. She was gazing around the spacious, high-walled yard. In contrast to the front yard, many of the bushes were dying, weeds were rife, and the long rectangular swimming pool was empty except for a scum of water on the bottom.

Noting her glance, Helen said, "Looks almost obscene, doesn't it?" She got to her feet with an audible creak of joints and limped to a concrete bench under a nearby tree. "Sit, child, sit!" She patted the bench beside her, and Julie sat down.

"It's a shame," Helen said, "the way Stell has let this backyard go to pot. I've tried to talk her into hiring a gardener, but she won't budge. God knows it isn't as if she can't afford it, but she says why worry about having a decent backyard if there's nobody to enjoy it. Never mind that I like to putter around back here. She says I'm too old and foolish to worry about pretty flowers to look at. The only reason she keeps the front yard decent is for visitors. The same thing applies to the pool. There's nobody around to use it anymore, and Stell just let it go. Maybe now that you're here, she'll fix it up again." She looked at Julie hopefully. "Do you swim?"

Julie remembered the episode on the beach and suppressed a shudder. "Not very well, I'm afraid."

"I do like to see young people enjoying themselves." Helen heaved a sigh. "It's not good, child, to get old and have to depend on the generosity of others. Oh, not that I'm bad-mouthing your grandmother. She has her ways, but I must say that she's been more than generous. Not that I don't earn my keep, and I don't care all that much for money, anyway. Pauline cooks and cleans house, but I look after Stell. She did talk of hiring a nurse, but I won't hear of it. After all, I am family, if not a Devereaux."

"Were you here—" Julie stopped and cleared her throat. "Were you here when I was supposed to have lived here?"

"Supposed? Child, I don't think there's the slightest doubt but that you're Suellen." The older woman patted Julie's hand. "As for my being here, in Devereaux House, no, I wasn't living here then. I had a place of my own, but I visited all the time. With Stell, you and Rosellen, your folks and Pippen all living here, there was no room for me. Stell wasn't bedridden then, either. It was only after all that happened that her health failed."

"Then you weren't here the night of the hurricane?"

"Heavens, no, child. No one should have been out in that storm. What on earth possessed your mother to be out driving that night, I'll never in this world understand."

"Was there any chance that it wasn't an accident?"

Helen peered at her sharply. "I don't know what else it could have been, honey. The brakes went out, her car skidded on the wet streets and she rammed into a bridge rail, going into the water."

"But why did the brakes go out?"

"I don't know." Helen shrugged. "I never did learn to drive, never did learn to trust automobiles."

"And no one knows why she was out driving in such a terrible storm?"

Helen shrugged again and sighed. "We finally just put it down to the fact that she was terribly distraught over poor Reese's death."

"Weren't there rumors that it wasn't an accident, that her car had somehow been tampered with?"

"There are always rumors. Your mother was a prominent woman in Key West, the Devereaux are prominent people—" She broke off, looking at Julie keenly again. "Now how did you hear those old rumors? You've only been here a little more than a day." Helen's demeanor changed abruptly and she became the formidable woman Julie had seen yesterday in the dusky parlor. "I never listen to gossip, and I don't approve of other people doing so." She got stiffly to her feet. "I have to get back to my gardening if I'm to get anything done today."

She turned away without another word. Julie watched her for a few minutes, her thoughts whirling. She felt that she was becoming ensnared in an ever-growing enigma, layers of mystery wrapping around and around her like a mummy's bandages. She shivered at the macabre image and got to her feet.

She went into the shadowed house, undecided as to whether to take a walk or not. She desperately wanted to escape the house, which still gave off bad vibes, but she was a long way yet from being accustomed to the heat and the humidity, and the thought of walking under that blazing sun intimidated her.

She was standing at the foot of the stairs, trying to make up her mind, when a voice called from the gloom of the parlor, "Suellen?" Julie recognized Pippen's voice. "Would you come in here, please?"

Julie ventured reluctantly into the parlor. All the drapes were drawn, and it was almost as dark as night.

"Over here, on the sofa."

Julie finally made out the blurred outline of Pippen on the high-backed, old-fashioned sofa. Pippen wore a long, loose garment that covered her from throat to toe. She indicated the sofa beside her, and Julie sat down gingerly.

"I have been in communication with Running Elk. It's always easier here, in this house."

Julie almost got up and bolted. The last thing she wanted to do right then was to be near this woman while she "communicated" with her spirit guide, but she could think of no gracious way to escape. "You mean you're having a séance?" Julie asked.

"Not really." Pippen's laughter tinkled. "A séance usually involves several people. This is private, just between Running Elk and myself."

"Then perhaps I'd better leave." Julie made as if to rise.

"No, no, stay, dear." Pippen placed an icy, staying hand on Julie's arm. "It concerns you."

"Concerns me?" Julie said in dismay.

"Nothing to be alarmed about." Pippen smiled slowly. "Running Elk foresees nothing but good things for you in the future."

Pippen took Julie's hand tightly in both of hers and leaned her head back against the sofa, closing her eyes. Julie was hard put to understand how the woman's hands could be so cold in such heat.

"Running Elk, can you hear me?" Pippen said in a throaty murmur. "Suellen is here with me. Can you see her?"

There was a long silence before Pippen spoke again, and this time her voice was a low, masculine growl that caused Julie to jump, startled.

"Certainly I can see her, stupid woman. Just because I am one with the spirits does not mean that I cannot see you mortals."

Julie stared at the other woman closely. Was she faking? Julie supposed that she could change her voice, but it certainly *sounded* like a man.

In her own voice Pippen said, "Doesn't she look just like Rosellen? Can you understand now how you were fooled into thinking it was Suellen on the other side?"

"I was not fooled, woman," said the deep, masculine voice. "You did not supply me with sufficient information. The mistake was yours."

"Yes, of course, Running Elk," Pippen said humbly. "The mistake was mine. You must forgive me. Do you have a message for Suellen?" Again, the male voice: "She is having thoughts of leaving Devereaux House. She must not do this. She must remain among her own people."

In a spurt of daring, Julie asked, "Is Rosellen there? May I speak to her?"

Pippen stiffened, releasing her hand, her eyes flying open. She said furiously, "You must never speak to Running Elk unless I give you permission! Now he is gone."

"I just thought—"

"Never mind what you thought, Suellen." Pippen's eyes narrowed. "Are you poking fun at me?"

"No, no, not at all," Julie said hastily. "I'm sorry if I spoke out of turn."

Slightly mollified, Pippen said, "Are you a believer?"

"I don't really know. I've never given it that much thought. You're the first medium I've ever met."

"I'm not a medium," Pippen said, angry again, "I'm a channel! Mediums conduct séances for money, for the gullible. I would never humiliate Running Elk by using him for commercial purposes."

She got to her feet and stalked out of the room without another word. Julie didn't know whether to laugh or feel insulted. But she did know that she had to get out of this house, never mind the heat.

Outside, although it was late afternoon, the moist heat struck her like a blow. Doggedly she walked on, toward the beach. Devereaux House was located on the east side of town. The ocean could be seen from the upper floor, especially from the widow's walk on the east side of the house, but the house was at least a half mile from the beach.

The part of the beach that she came to first was flatter and more open than the area on the west side, and the sand was dotted with sun worshipers. Julie felt little danger.

She walked along the hard sand at the edge, deep in thought, scarcely aware of where she was or where she was going. She wondered why Pippen's advice—or that of her spirit guide—was to remain at Devereaux House. She wasn't sure that she wanted to stay there. The people were strange. Her Aunt Helen was friendly one minute, then cold and almost hostile the next. Her grandmother wandered in and out of lucidity. And Pippen . . . well, Pippen had to be considered strange under any circumstances. The only one she felt at ease with was Pauline.

But despite all that, Julie felt that the key to the baffling mystery of her past lay here. The last few years she hadn't been disturbed by her blank past, but when she had first arrived in Moorestown not knowing had been mentally agonizing; and now the pain, the desperate need to *know*, was back again. If the answer was here, she had to stick it out until everything became clear.

The sound of a car horn broke into her thoughts. She turned around, staring up toward the road, and saw Shell sitting in the Jeep he'd been driving the day he'd picked her up at the bus station. He waved to her.

She climbed up the small incline to the Jeep. Eyes hidden by dark glasses, Shell frowned at her. "After what happened to you the other night, I thought you would want to stay far away from the beach."

"With all these people nearby. I didn't think anything would happen to me." She waved a hand around. "And I can't hide away forever."

"Anyway, you should have a hat on, and sunglasses, to protect you against this sun." He rummaged in the back and found a ratty old straw hat. "Here, this will give you some protection."

She put the hat on and got into the Jeep. "Were you looking for me?"

"More or less." He put the vehicle in gear and drove off. "I got away from the office early today and I thought I'd see how you were getting along."

"You sure Mr. Henderson didn't send you around to check up on me?"

He shrugged. "Not exactly. Not today, anyway. He did tell me to look after you, more or less."

"How does it feel having to shepherd around a nutty lady who's misplaced her memory?"

"I don't mind. In fact, in your case I enjoy it. I thought maybe you'd like a little sight-seeing tour around the Key. There's a tourist attraction called the Conch Train that we could take. A guide points out all the spots of interest and tells the history of the area, but I thought maybe you'd be more at ease with me. Is there anything you'd especially like to see? For instance, there's the house where Ernest Hemingway lived all those years. It's a historic attraction now, open to the public."

"I'd rather just ride around for a little, if you don't mind. Anything to get out of that house."

He gave her a sidelong glance. "Getting to you, is it?"

"It has bad vibes, I can feel them. But it's not only that, the people are a little off the wall. Aunt Helen is okay part of the time, then she turns cold and hard. Pippen . . . well, I just got caught in one of her séances. . . . No, I shouldn't say that. It was one of her private communications with Running Elk."

"I'm surprised she let you be privy to it."

"Oh, it seems that I was the subject of the communication." Julie giggled suddenly. "I got carried away and asked Running Elk a direct question."

Shell smiled over at her. "And what did he say?"

"Oh, Pippen says he never answers any questions but hers. In fact, she got up in a huff and stormed out."

"Well, suppose we just forget about the Devereaux for the rest of the afternoon and play tourist. What would you like to see, Julie?"

"I'll leave that up to you. Pretend that I'm a tourist and you're a . . . Conch Train driver?"

"Right. Well, the city was officially founded in 1822. As you've already learned, it was a pirate and smugglers' hangout, and legend has it that when it was first officially settled huge piles of human bones were found in the mangrove clumps. It was originally called Cayo Hueso, the Spanish name for Bone Island, but down through the years it changed to Key West.

"As I told you, the original settlers and all those born in Key West are known as Conchs, which is the name of the shellfish found in great numbers in the surrounding waters. Conch chowder is a popular local dish, as is Key lime pie—"

"Shell," she interrupted, "all that is very interesting, I'm sure, but would it be all right with you if we drove north along the Overseas Highway, at least for a little while?"

"No reason why not." He gave her a curious glance. "We can drive as far as you'd like. But it's a hundred and fifty miles all the way north to the mainland."

"I'd just like to see some of the area from a car. It's difficult to see a great deal from a bus."

He shrugged. "Fine with me. We can stop off somewhere on the way and have dinner, if that's all right with you."

"That sounds great, Shell. I suppose—" she hesitated "—I suppose I should stop and call, tell them where I am. So far as they know, I just went for a walk."

Shell stopped at a service station. Julie had to ask him the telephone number of Devereaux House before she could call. She was relieved when Pauline answered the phone, and she quickly told the woman that she wouldn't be back until after dinner and that she was with Sheldon Phipps.

Getting back into the car, she said ruefully, "It seems strange, calling people I hardly know to report my whereabouts. It's something like having two families, you know."

As he drove off, Shell asked diffidently, "I haven't asked.... Are you going to stay around for a while?"

She was slow in replying. "I've almost decided to, yes. I called Connecticut and talked to my...my mother and told her that I'd probably be staying for a while. I also called my guy, Ken. Neither of them was too pleased about my staying."

Shell maneuvered the Jeep around a slow-moving truck. He said without looking at her, "You have a boyfriend?"

"Yes. We're engaged. We'd tentatively set a wedding date for October 18. I don't know now, we may have to postpone it for a while."

"Engaged? Then it must be really serious."

"Serious?" She frowned over at him, but he was staring straight ahead, his face unhappy. "Of course it's serious! I love Ken."

"Did you ever think that might change, now that you're someone else?"

"Why should that affect my love for Ken? I'm still the same person I was before."

"Well, you are and you aren't. You may gain a . . . well, a new perspective on life."

"You mean because of the money I stand to inherit?"

"That, naturally. Other things, as well."

Julie gnawed on her lower lip. "I have wondered how the money would affect me, and it frightens me, as I think I mentioned. I will confess that I hadn't thought of it in relation to Ken. One thing I can be sure of." She laughed wryly. "Nobody can ever accuse him of being a fortune hunter. I certainly had no financial worth when he asked me to marry him." She looked over at him again. "Do you have a girl, Shell?"

He shook his head. "Nothing serious. I go out; I'm no monk. But I'm not in love with anyone."

"You've never been in love?"

"No." He flashed her a grin. "Not that I've ever known about, anyway, and I understand you know it when you're in love."

"Well, of course. I certainly knew it when I fell in love with Ken."

"What would you say if I told you I thought I was falling in love with you?" he said gravely.

"Don't be silly, Shell, you hardly know me!" she said tartly, and yet she experienced a flush of warmth at his words.

"I'm not sure time has anything to do with it. I simply know that I'm attracted to you more than to any woman I've ever known."

"Of course, that could be because *you* know that I may be an heiress." The moment the words were out she regretted them. "I'm sorry, Shell." She reached out to touch his knee. "That was a nasty thing for me to say."

He covered her hand with his, and squeezed. "It's all right, I understand. I want to say one more thing, then we'll drop it for the time being. I'm just glad that you've decided to stay around Key West for a while."

They were well beyond the city limits now and driving across a long bridge.

"Shell," Julie said, "where did my mother have her accident?"

He flashed her a startled look. "You must be psychic. It's just up ahead, just before we drive off this section of bridge."

She shivered, hugging herself. "I suppose I did have some kind of a flash."

He looked at her again. "Is that why you wanted to drive up this way?"

"I guess that's the reason," she said slowly. "I didn't consciously think that, but it must have been in the back of my mind."

"Well, this is where it happened." He indicated a section of bridge railing they were passing. "She rammed her car right into the railing, broke through and went right to the bottom of the channel. It's not too deep along here, but she must have been knocked unconscious when the car struck the bridge."

"One thing I don't understand," Julie said. "Was there another car involved?"

"Not to my knowledge. Why do you ask?"

"Well, with just the brakes going out, why would she swerve and go through the railing?"

His glance jumped over to her. "The brakes? Now who told you that?"

"Why, Aunt Helen. Just today."

Shell shook his head. "It wasn't the brakes. Helen Bronson knows damn little about cars. Something went haywire with the steering mechanism. I wasn't in Key West then, but that's how it was told to me."

Julie felt a chill. "Then that must mean that someone tampered with the steering."

"That's a possibility, yes. It was considered at the time, I understand, but no concrete evidence was ever found. Anyway, it *is* possible for a car's steering to go out on its own."

Julie was thinking back to what Pauline had told her. "Do you know anything about the death of a boy by the name of Huey? I understand he lived next door to Devereaux House and that something happened to him, some kind of a mystery."

"Yes, I heard about it. The boy was fourteen at the time. Hugh Waters. It *was* a mystery and quite a tragedy. He was found hanged in the attic of the family home. No one ever knew why he hanged himself. He and your sister Rosellen were always together. She was desolated, I was told. And since he was the only child of the Waters family, they never got over it. They moved away soon after."

"Were they certain that he hung himself?" she asked hesitantly.

Shell slowed the car and gave her a sharp look. "You mean, could he have been murdered? I never heard anything to that effect, but I suppose anything is possible. But how in heaven's name did you come up with that idea?" He looked at her more closely. "You're not remembering some things, are you?"

"No, no." She shook her head quickly, then gestured vaguely. "It's just something that I heard. A rumor, probably nothing more."

SEVEN

July 21

Huey's really done it now! He's told two of the boys in his class at school what we've been doing in the garage. Worse than that, he says they want to do it with us. He must think I'm really stupid! It might be fun, at least for the one time, but I know what would happen. Those old boys would tell others, soon it would be all over school, and sooner or later Mama would hear about it.

I know what would happen then. They'd send me away to some damned girls' school. I overheard Mama talking to Grandmother about it once before. They wanted to send me away then, and would have if they'd had their way. But Daddy put his foot down. He told them that he wasn't having his Rosellen sent away to a girls' school.

But this time he might not win out. Daddy hardly ever gets cranky with me, but I know that he doesn't like gossip or scandal connected with the Devereaux name, and that's what would happen if this got out.

There's only one thing I can see to do. Damn Huey anyway! Even if I don't let the other two boys do it, Huey's going to tell others sooner or later.

I've been trying to get him up into the attic in their old house. I've been telling him that it would be fun to do it with his mother in the house downstairs, but so far he's been too scared. Now I'm just going to have to tell him that we won't be doing it any more unless he does it in the attic with me. That will bring him around, I'm sure!

There's a back way to sneak in, so no one will know we're there. The only person who'll be in the house is his mother, and she's not only dumb, but half-deaf as well.

I've been up in that old attic once before. There are high rafters going across to hold up the roof. Although Huey is bigger than me, and stronger, he's not half as smart!

I'll have no trouble at all getting him to play a game with me. We're always playing a game of chicken, and he usually chickens out first, so he's always ready to try a new game, hoping he can outlast me.

This game will involve a rope and one of the rafters. I've been practicing all week on how to make a hangman's noose!

"I think the girl's making a mistake, raking over dead coals, but if it eases her mind, Sheldon, take the time to find out what you can." Henderson laughed slightly. "After all, we have our own welfare to consider. When she inherits all that money, the firm would like to retain her as a client."

Shell had spent almost a full day digging back into the past. The police station in Key West had very little information; all the papers had been sent up to Miami. He had, however, talked to the investigating officers about the accident that had killed Melissa Devereaux and about Huey Waters's hanging. Then he'd made a trip to Miami by plane after calling Julie from the Key West airport to make a date for dinner. "When I get back, I may have some information for you."

Shell had spent four hours in the courthouse in Miami, poring over every paper he could find relating to both cases. The information he collected was meager.

The plane he caught back to Key West was delayed on takeoff, and he had to go directly to Devereaux House to pick up Julie. She came to the door wearing a soft pink dress that complemented her dark hair and eyes. His breath caught at her beauty. He realized that this was the first time he'd seen her really dressed up.

"Oh, my! We've been shopping, I see."

Julie colored and smiled, somewhat shyly. "It was Grandmother's idea. She insisted that I use her charge accounts and get some new clothes. Clothes befitting a Devereaux." She smiled demurely. "I'm still not that certain about the Devereaux part, but it seemed to make her happy, so—" She shrugged. "Besides, all the clothes I brought with me are too heavy for this heat."

"You're right, why not?"

She did a pirouette. "Do you like it?"

He stepped back a little, looking at her long, lovely legs, their sexiness accentuated by high heels. The dress, with its fitted top and flaring skirt, showed to advantage her high, full breasts and slim waist. He felt his pulse accelerate as he nodded, smiling. "I like it. In fact, I love it." He rubbed a hand over his face, with its faint stubble of beard, and looked down at his rumpled clothes. "You make me feel a little disreputable. The damned plane from Miami got off the ground late and I had to come here directly from the airport. I haven't had time to change or take a shower and shave. Maybe you'll be ashamed to be seen in public with me."

Her slow smile came. "Never that, Shell. I'd much prefer dinner with you than eating here in this gloomy place. Aunt Pippen is still ticked off at me for insulting Running Elk, and Aunt Helen is still in one of her moods.''

He faced about, holding out his arm. ''Then shall we go, my lady?''

As they started into town, Julie said eagerly, ''What's this news you found out?''

''I'm afraid you're going to be disappointed, Julie. I've spent much of the day in Miami, looking over all the reports of your mother's accident and the death of Hugh Waters.''

''Ah, that was sweet of you, Shell.'' She quickly touched his arm, then jerked her hand back. ''I didn't expect you to go to that much trouble.''

''We aim to please,'' he said lightly. ''Besides, I was curious myself. Unhappily, I found very little. On your mother's car, a locknut on the steering somehow worked loose, which meant that she had no control whatsoever over the car.''

''A locknut? I don't know much about mechanics, but isn't that a nut that isn't supposed to come loose?''

''That's the theory, yes, but there are exceptions to all theories. This particular locknut had a cotter pin holding it in place, which is supposed to mean that the nut wouldn't loosen without the pin being removed first. Unfortunately, in this case, the cotter pin sheared off, causing your mother to lose control.''

''Sheared off, or was tampered with?''

''There's always the possibility that it was tampered with, yes, but there was no evidence of that. I talked to the investigating officer here in Key West, and he said that to the best of his recollection there was no indication of tampering. And there is no mention of it in any of the records.''

''But they wouldn't have been looking for tampering, would they? They would just assume that it was an accident.''

''I suppose that would be their attitude, yes.''

''And the hanging of Hugh Waters... Surely they didn't assume *that* was an accident?''

''No, that was officially declared a suicide.''

''Suicide? A...what? A fourteen-year-old boy?''

He sighed. ''Julie, it might surprise you, but the suicide rate of kids, teens and even younger, these days is appalling.''

She was shaking her head. ''I just can't see it.''

''Why not, Julie?'' he said in exasperation. ''You weren't even here when all this happened...well, I'll amend that. You were here, but you've lost all memory of it. So why do you wonder about these two incidents?''

''I just feel...well, it's like something dreadful lurks just behind a curtain that I can't see through. It's nothing but a feeling, I know, but it's real enough to me. What if I'm right? What if this Hugh and my mother *were* murdered? Maybe that explains what happened to Rosellen. Maybe she was murdered, too.''

''You could be right, of course, but what do you expect from me, Julie? After all this time? I just don't think you should be speculating like this. It's morbid, it's not good for you.''

Julie fell silent and remained stubbornly quiet as Shell expertly maneuvered the Jeep in and out of downtown traffic. Pulling into the seafood restaurant's lot, he parked and turned to her.

"You know, something occurs to me. Maybe you're right, about one of your suppositions, at least. Maybe some memory is trying to get through. Maybe you observed a murder and that caused the trauma, short-circuiting your memory. It certainly had to be something terrible. What do you think of that for a theory?"

Abruptly, in some far corner of her mind, Julie felt something dark and forbidding threaten to engulf her. She shrank back into the corner of the car seat, shuddering, her eyes clenched shut. There was a great roaring in her ears, and she thought that she was about to lose consciousness.

Dimly she heard Shell's alarmed voice. "Julie, are you okay? What's wrong?"

She fought back the waves of blackness, opened her eyes and smiled wanly at him. "I'm all right, Shell."

"What happened? You went white as a sheet!"

"I don't...I'm not sure." She moistened dry lips. "I think it was what you said about a trauma, about my seeing something or knowing something. It was almost as if I was living some horrible experience, yet not knowing what it was. If that makes any kind of sense."

"Come on, you need a good strong drink." He touched her cheek gently. "Let's go inside."

As they started toward the restaurant, Shell said, "Tomorrow is Saturday. The office is closed, of course. I have a small boat. Everybody does in Key West." He smiled briefly. "How would you like to take a cruise with me?"

"You mean, go fishing?" she said dubiously.

"No, no." He shook his head. "I'm not much for fishing. I thought maybe we'd noodle around the Keys a little. Maybe take along a picnic lunch. I happen to know of a small island that was once inhabited. It's deserted now, but there's still the remains of a pier, and a nice cove for swimming and snorkeling. There's hardly ever anyone around. How does that strike you?"

She smiled. "Wonderful, Shell!"

THE NEXT MORNING, shortly before noon, they boarded Shell's boat. Julie stared at the letters on the side of the twenty-six-foot cabin cruiser with the hint of a smile. "*Dancer II*? What happened to *Dancer I*, if there was one?"

Shell grinned sheepishly, ducking his head. "There was, the first boat I owned down here. I ran her aground on Ramrod Key, tore the bottom right out of her. Actually, I came out ahead. With the insurance money and a little extra, I bought this baby." With swelling pride he patted the railing.

Julie couldn't help but smile at his obvious pride. She was not familiar with boats, yet she could see that this was a beautiful craft. "It's lovely," she said sincerely.

He grinned. "She. Boats are always she."

Once aboard, Julie saw that the boat was trim, with a nice cabin and a shaded cockpit. Shell started the motors and eased *Dancer II* out of the slip, moving slowly until they were out of the harbor.

The sea was calm. Shell had promised her it wouldn't be rough because he'd keep to the west side of the Keys, the Gulf side. The colors of the water were like none Julie had ever seen—deep greens and blues, so clear that she could look deep into the sea and see fish swimming beneath the surface. It seemed almost a sacrilege to Julie that the prow of the boat broke the water before them. Despite the calmness of the sea, she felt unaccountably jittery, but she could think of no reason for that nervousness.

When they reached the open sea, Shell opened the throttle and turned to smile at her. "Do you like it?"

Julie smiled back, nodding, sticking her fingers in her ears against the rumble of the motors.

"I know, it's noisy as hell," he said unabashedly. "But I'm usually alone, and I love it when I rev her up. It seems to shake the tensions out of me. I like a fast, noisy boat!"

All of a sudden, for no apparent reason she could ascertain, Julie's nervousness abated, and she felt relaxed, more at ease than at any time since she'd left Connecticut. She touched his hand on the throttle. "Put an eye patch on you, a scabbard on your hip, and you'd make a grand buccaneer, Mr. Phipps. And you do have a rifle." She indicated the rifle fastened by clips to the front of the cockpit.

He roared with laughter, throwing back his head. "You sure there isn't Irish blood in you, lass? Such blarney I've never heard! But don't misunderstand me, I love it, so keep it up. As for the rifle—" he sobered "—you can come across some touchy situations in these waters. Not often, but it can happen. I get in quite a bit of target practice with it, shooting at sharks. And some of the spots where I anchor and go ashore are infested with deadly snakes. Don't worry, there won't be any where we're going today...there!" He looked past her, pointing. "There's Smuggler's Island."

She turned, following his pointing finger. All around them were tiny islands, although most were mere smudges of greenery dotting the water; and the one to which he was pointing seemed no different from the others. It was probably about a mile distant.

"It looks like all the others to me," she said.

"It's a little larger than some. Many are little more than mangrove swamps, but this one once had a house, and a pier, like I said. The house, I understand, was flattened by a hurricane several years ago and never rebuilt. But it has a small natural cove, and it's often used by smugglers, hence the name."

"Smuggling, I gather from the things you've told me, is a big thing down here," she commented.

"Probably our biggest industry, next to fishing and tourism," he said with a grin. "Grass by the bale, cocaine and heroin, and aliens from Haiti, Cuba and Colombia. They run the Marine Patrol and the Coast Guard ragged. It's gotten so out of hand that it's no longer really controllable."

They were nearing the low, flat island now, and Shell steered the *Dancer II* into a small cove that was hidden from view by fingers of mangrove-covered land poking out on each side. Julie saw the rotting pier that Shell was steering for, the foundation of the destroyed house and a narrow, crescent-shaped strip of white sand.

As they neared the pier, she said, "That looks like an attractive beach. I'm surprised no one uses it."

"Well, for one thing you need a boat to get here, of course, and there are tales that smugglers run people off at gunpoint. Whether that's true of not, it tends to keep people away."

He nudged the boat against the pier, tossed a rope over a mooring stanchion and cut the motor. He picked up an ice cooler and the bundle of his diving equipment, then gave Julie a hand up. She had a swimsuit on under the oversize T-shirt. She hadn't been too enthusiastic about swimming after her recent experience, but Shell had convinced her to wear the suit. "Besides, I'm a good swimmer, as well as a snorkeler. Who knows, I might even teach you to like snorkeling. There's hardly a better place anywhere in the whole country for it," he had told her.

Carrying all their paraphernalia, they trudged along the narrow beach until they found a good spot to erect the umbrella. Setting everything in the shade, Shell urged, "Come on, into the water with you!"

The water was surprisingly warm, much more so, it seemed to Julie, than when she'd been pushed in the other night. But that time she had been frightened, which probably made a big difference.

The beach shelf was shallow for quite a distance out, and her fears gradually eased. Shell watched her closely for a while until it was clear that what tension she had felt was gone; then he went back to the beach for his snorkel and flippers. Wading back to her, he said, "I won't go too far away, so don't worry."

He sank beneath the water with just the snorkel pipe showing and began to slowly move out into deeper water. Julie turned her attention away and began to enjoy the sea. She swam until she was pleasantly tired, never venturing too far from shore. By that time there was no sign of Shell, yet she wasn't really worried. He struck her as a man who was more than competent at most things he undertook.

She swam back toward the spot where their umbrella was, wading the last few yards in. She opened the ice chest and found a bottle of white wine, as well as fried chicken, potato salad and vegetable sticks. She filled a plastic glass with wine and sipped at it. It was cold and delicious. Just then she saw Shell rise out of the water and start toward her.

Like Poseidon rising out of the sea, she thought, and laughed quietly at herself. But she had to admit that she liked this man. He was warm, outgoing and kind. And he was handsome, she thought; watching him coming toward her, red-brown hair slicked down like a seal's. Most tall men she knew had a rather awkward, shambling walk, but Shell walked with an athlete's flowing grace.

He kicked off his flippers and left them with the snorkel by the edge of the water and came on toward her.

As he sank down beside her in the shade of the umbrella, she said, "I'll bet you played basketball in college, didn't you?"

"Yep." He glanced at her, gray eyes twinkling. "Both high school and college. I won't ask how you guessed. I've met few men as tall as I am who didn't play basketball."

"You any good?"

"Good enough to make all-conference, good enough to have had a shot at the pros if I had wanted it." He grinned widely. "Nobody can ever accuse me of being modest, ma'am."

He reached into the cooler for the wine bottle, poured a glass and topped hers off. "I don't know about you, but I'm famished. The sea always does that to me. I eat like two horses when I'm out. Luckily, I have a great metabolism, or I'd soon resemble a horse."

"I'm hungry myself."

"Then let's eat!"

They ate cold chicken and potato salad and drank the chilled wine without much conversation. The food tasted marvelous to Julie and the combination of the wine, the sun and the sea air made her drowsy.

But ever-present in the back of her mind was her situation as the newly discovered Devereaux heir. As they relaxed after eating, she said, "I'm curious about something, Shell.... Just how did your firm track me down? I suppose through long and hard detective work?"

He glanced over at her with an embarrassed smile. "As much as I'm sure we'd all like to take credit for that, that's not how it happened. In fact, if it wasn't for an anonymous note we received, I doubt that we would ever have found you at all."

She sat up. "An anonymous note?"

He nodded. "Yep. It came in the mail one day, typewritten on an old machine, no signature, with a Miami postmark on the envelope."

"Why haven't I been told this before?"

"Well . . ." He cleared his throat in embarrassment. "I don't think Mr. Henderson wanted it widely known that an anonymous note had helped find you when all the efforts of the firm had failed."

"Just what did it say?"

He considered for a moment, eyes cast heavenward. "Let's see . . . 'If you guys are so hot to find Suellen Devereaux, look in Moorestown, Connecticut. Look for a Julie Malone.'"

"And that's all?"

"That's it."

"But how on earth did the writer of the note know where I was, *who* I was?"

"There you have me." He spread his hands. "I haven't an inkling."

"But surely that's not how you, or your firm, decided that I was Suellen Devereaux? Not on the strength of an anonymous letter!"

"Oh, no, not at all. We traced your route all the way back to Key Largo from Moorestown. The bus station here had been checked at the time of your disappearance, with no results. How you got from here to Key Largo has never been established."

"That's still hardly enough to prove anything. So you have a girl of sixteen getting on a bus in Key Largo and getting off again in Moorestown. It could be nothing but coincidence!"

"Coincidence that a girl of that age disappears at that particular time and this same girl is discovered eight years later, the mirror image of Suellen Devereaux?'' he said softly. ''A girl who has lost the memory of the first sixteen years of her life? A girl who also happens to have the same blood type as the missing girl?''

She stared at him. ''How did you discover that?''

''Your blood was typed at the hospital in Moorestown. Through proper legal channels it was easy enough to gain access to your file. Also, the file showed that you had a smallpox vaccination when you were young.'' He placed the tip of his finger on the vaccination scar on Julie's left arm. ''Suellen received a smallpox vaccination when she was ten.''

''Rosellen, was she vaccinated, too?''

He nodded. ''Of course, both of you at the same time.''

She thought for a moment, gazing out to sea. She spoke without looking at him, ''That's still not absolute proof. The blood type only proves that I *could* be Suellen Devereaux, not that I actually am.''

''Julie...'' He sighed. ''I really don't understand. Why are you fighting against this so? If our firm is satisfied, if Stella Devereaux is satisfied, why can't you accept that?''

Still looking out to sea, she said slowly, ''I have to be sure, Shell, sure in my own mind. Don't you see that?''

''I suppose I do, Julie. Yes, I understand.'' He touched her hand gently, then got to his feet. ''I'm going back in for a bit.''

She looked up at him. ''I thought you weren't supposed to go into the water with a full stomach.''

He laughed down at her. ''That's an old wives' tale. Besides—'' he patted his lean stomach ''—I'm not all that full.''

She sat with her arms wrapped around her drawn-up legs and watched him put on the flippers and the snorkel and wade out into the water until she could no longer see him. Then she lay back, arms behind her head, staring up at the brilliant blue of the cloudless sky.

The fact that the law firm had learned about her through an anonymous note made her apprehensive and uneasy. It appeared that *someone* had known all along where she was and had kept tabs on her all those years. Who could it have been? And more important, why? Another question occurred to her—why had whoever it was waited all this time to let her whereabouts be known? It was all very baffling and made her head ache.

There did seem to be one affirmative note about the whole thing. This mysterious individual apparently knew for a certainty that she was Suellen Devereaux. This should have been reassuring, but somehow it was not.

Sleepy now, she turned her head toward the pier where *Dancer II* bobbed slightly at anchor.

Julie's eyes drifted shut, and she slept. Dreams troubled her again, nightmares of being in the center of a maze, only instead of hedges hemming her in on every side there were mirrors, mirrors stretching to infinity, and her image was reflected a thousand times over. Her every motion was repeated precisely. Yet there was one marked difference—the myriad eyes staring back at her were mocking and evil. She opened her mouth and screamed; the other mouths opened, and laughter drummed against her ears.

She awoke, a scream dying on her lips. She sat up, looking wildly around, searching for Shell. He wasn't to be seen.

There was something wrong, something missing. Then she realized what it was. *Dancer II!* The boat was gone!

EIGHT

July 21

*Today is the anniversary of the day Huey died, and nobody
has ever suspected a thing. The police are stupid! They're
blurry people, most of them. I thought I saw Daddy looking at me kind of funny once or twice, but he never said a
word. He never did like Huey, anyway.*

*For our birthday Daddy promised to buy us a boat, a
power cruiser, but he and Mama fought about it for weeks.
She said we were too young yet. That's all she knows. I love
the sea and I know that I am a good sailor. Daddy told her
that just because she was afraid of the water, doesn't mean
we should be deprived of the pleasure of having our own
boat. Everybody in the Keys has a boat.*

*Suellen was upset by the fighting and told Daddy it was
all right, that we didn't need a boat, that he could get us
something else for our birthday. I just wanted to hit her! She
is such a fool!*

But it worked out okay.

*Mama finally gave in when Daddy promised that he'd
never let us sail out on the ocean alone. But we didn't get
the boat until yesterday, because the order took so long to fill.*

*Daddy took us out on the boat today, just Suellen and me.
I was crazy about it, and Daddy even let me steer for a bit,
when there were no other boats around. Mama didn't come
along.*

*Daddy told us again that Mama is afraid of the water,
and that's the reason she didn't come along. I don't think*

he's telling the whole truth. Oh, she's afraid of the water, she's afraid of just about everything! But I've been watching her and Daddy, and I don't think they get along very well. They sleep in separate rooms and I don't think they ever have sex. I've heard them fighting about it. I once heard Daddy call her a cold bitch. And I think that's why Daddy goes away somewhere from time to time. He's got another woman or women somewhere, I'd just bet on it! He always tell us he goes away on business, but I don't think so. He's afraid to have a mistress here because it might cause a scandal and Grandmother wouldn't like that.

If that's true, then it's all Mama's fault. She drives him to it. I know enough about men to know they're not happy going without sex for too long. If he was my husband, he wouldn't ever, ever have to go away!

I dream all the time about having Daddy all to myself. Suellen says she's not going out on the boat very much and Mama will never go. So maybe we'll get to go out alone, just Daddy and me.

Had Shell gone off without her?

Julie started to her feet, and then she saw him rising up out of the water, walking toward her.

She ran down to the edge of the water, pointing and shouting. "Shell! Your boat, it's gone!"

At her shout he stopped dead still, blinking at her in confusion.

Julie pointed again. "*Dancer II*, she's gone!"

Shell swiveled his head. "I'll be damned, so she is!"

He came on out of the water, discarding his snorkel and fins, then started toward the pier. Julie had to trot alongside to keep up with his long strides. "What happened, do you think? Do you think she came untied?"

He shook his head. "No way. Even if I did a sloppy job and she slipped her moorings, with the tide like it is she would have beached, not gone out to sea."

"Then what happened?"

"At the moment your guess is as good as mine."

They had reached the pier now, and Shell led the way to the stanchion where the boat had been tied off. There was nothing to see, of course; the hawser was gone, as well as *Dancer II*. With his lower lip pinched between thumb and forefinger, Shell stared out to sea, frowning.

Julie said impatiently, "Shell?"

He turned his head and focused on her. "Apparently you didn't see anything?"

"No, I dozed off. I don't know for how long. A half hour, maybe longer."

"And I was out quite a ways, out beyond the point. Even when I wasn't underwater, I couldn't see the pier.

"But what do you think happened?"

"Somebody took her away, what else?"

"But who? One of those smugglers you were talking about?"

He thought for a moment, then shook his head slowly. "Nope, they run enough risks without stealing a boat. Stealing a boat isn't like stealing a car. Not that boats aren't stolen from time to time, but it takes time to get away with it. Changes have to be made, they're too conspicuous."

"But what then?"

He scrubbed a hand across his face. "My guess would be the same person or persons who pushed you into the ocean the other evening. I suppose they were hoping we'd be left stranded out here."

Julie felt a chill as she stared at him. "You don't seem particularly worried."

"You mean, worried we'll be stranded here? No, I'm not. I'm a careful man, Julie. I never take undue chances. I told the dockmaster where we were going, told him that if we didn't show up before dark or shortly thereafter to send a Coast Guard cutter looking for us."

"You mean, you thought something like this might happen?"

He shook his head. "No, I can't take credit for that much foresight. But anything can happen out here, and it's best to always let somebody know where you are." He smiled reassuringly. "Don't worry, Julie. It might take a while, but somebody will come looking for us."

She looked at him, almost accusingly. "It seems you've finally came around to believing that my being pushed into the water was no accident?"

"I'm not sure I did until this happened," he said gravely. He took her elbow and turned her back toward the beach. "Let's get you back under the umbrella before you turn red as a lobster."

"I'm frightened, Shell," she said in a small voice. "Why should someone try to hurt me? Last week I didn't even *know* anyone in Key West!"

"You forget, people knew you before you left here, and although you may not remember them, you knew them once."

"But why should anyone wish me harm?"

"That's a good question, one that I don't have an answer for. You stand to inherit a great deal of money, but if something should happen to you, it won't benefit anyone. The money would just go to charity."

"How about Pippen or Helen?"

He shook his head. "Pippen is a wealthy woman in her own right, and Helen has always been looked after. Helen cares less for money than anyone I know. No, they're not in line to inherit. There is only one possible reason that I can think of," he said thoughtfully. "At the time of your disappearance you saw something, or learned something, that places someone in great danger. Probably the same thing that brought on your amnesia."

"But I can't remember a thing!"

"You might eventually, and someone may be afraid of that. Or this someone simply may not believe that you have lost your memory. Whatever, that's the only reason I can think why anyone would want you out of the way. Unless..." His gaze sharpened. "Unless there's someone back in Moorestown. Unless someone there might have a reason."

"At home?" she said incredulously. "Good heavens, no! Why should you even think such a thing?"

He shrugged. "Just exploring all the options, as we attorneys are fond of saying."

They had reached the umbrella now, and they sat down in its shade. Shell opened the cooler. "At least we have wine left and some food. We won't starve."

He poured wine into two glasses and gave her one. Julie sat without drinking, holding the glass in her hand, staring out to sea. Despite the moist heat, she felt a chill.

"I just can't believe there's some kind of a conspiracy against me," she said slowly. "The other night it could have been some stranger or a drug user or one of the freaks who do things for kicks. And today, well, maybe someone happened by in another boat, saw yours there, with no one watching and just towed it out to sea as a joke. *Dancer II* may be floating out there somewhere, deserted."

"Some joke," he said. "No, I can't accept that. Another boat owner would never do that, unless he was crazy."

"Then how about you? Maybe someone has a grudge against *you*."

"Anything is possible," he said with a shrug. "There are a few guys I've defended in court and didn't manage to get off. They *could* have seen a chance to get back at me and seized it. But it's highly unlikely."

The sun was nearing the horizon. It would soon be dark, and Julie didn't relish spending the night here, even with Shell by her side. What if the thieves were to sneak back under the cover of darkness...? That could even be the reason for the whole incident—to strand them here, where they would be vulnerable to an attack. If someone came, armed, in the dark, they would be virtually helpless.

Something of what she was thinking must have been mirrored on her face, for Shell reached across and rubbed his knuckles gently along her cheek.

"It'll be all right, Julie," he said gently. "You'll see." He gazed toward the setting sun. "Maybe we'll be lucky and see the green flash."

She looked at him. "The green flash? What is that?"

"On rare occasions, under the right atmospheric conditions, there's supposed to be a flash of green light on the horizon, just at the moment of sunset. Every night about this time people gather on the docks and beaches of Key West or over drinks in the bars with the proper view, looking for it. I've never seen it. Personally, I think it's a myth." He grinned lazily. "Maybe if you've had enough booze you might see it, I don't know."

He fell silent, stretching out on his back, head propped on his arms, and they both stared intently at the western horizon. The sun was soon gone, and the fast Florida twilight fell. There was no green flash. Julie drank the wine in her glass and also stretched out, moving over close to Shell.

He shifted, worming an arm under her shoulders and turning her so that her head lay on his shoulder. For just a moment she stiffened, but then she relaxed with a faint sigh. Being held like that was comforting and left her with a feeling of security. Perhaps it was a false security, but it was a feeling she welcomed right then.

They lay without speaking for some time in a companionable silence. It was fully dark now, and she watched the stars come out one by one until the entire night sky was a field of distant diamonds.

Shell moved, murmuring something inaudible, and then his head hovered over her face, blotting out the stars. His mouth descended on hers in a tender, tentative kiss. She felt no stir of resistance this time; it seemed a perfectly natural thing. His lips were soft and warm. She felt her heartbeat quicken, and almost involuntarily her hands came up to cup his face.

He muttered deeply from his throat and raised his head enough to whisper, "I want you, sweet Julie. I've wanted you since the moment I saw you get off that bus, looking lost and frightened."

It was not unexpected; her senses had awakened at the first touch of his lips, and her body yearned toward him now. Julie wasn't a virgin, yet her sexual experience was limited to a few times she'd shared with Ken, all of which had taken place after she'd known they were to be married. Without being told, her intuition had informed her that Ken was also inexperienced. None of the times with Ken had been deeply satisfying, yet the experiences had succeeded in awakening her sensuality, and she had decided that it would be better between them when they were married and free of all restraint.

But that was then, and this was right now. She recalled reading a theory somewhere that danger heightened sexual tension.

"Julie?"

She capitulated. "Yes, Shell. Oh, yes!" She arched up to his mouth, her breasts touching his chest. He moved his hand from her hip up under her T-shirt toward the soft mounds of flesh—her nipples swelling and sensitive to his every caress.

"I'll make it good for you, Julie, I will!"

And he did.

Shell was a considerate, artful lover. With Ken sex had often been hurried, almost furtive, but Shell made love with an exquisite slowness, his mouth and fingers everywhere, kissing and caressing, undressing her until finally she lay on the blanket completely nude, the sea breeze cool on her fevered skin.

And then Shell was also naked, and against her. She felt the throbbing of his erection. All reservations vanished as she felt an urgency, an aching need she had never before experienced.

"Ah, Shell!"

With guiding fingers she urged him to her, frantically waiting for him to take her. He rose above her, and a soft sigh escaped from Julie at the instant of entry. Every other consideration was swept from her mind.

His lovemaking had been so prolonged that it was over very quickly now. With a muted cry she rose and clung to him, shuddering as she climaxed; and at the same time she felt him begin to throb inside her.

After what seemed an eternity of intensely pleasurable spasms, Julie was finally still. The outside world impinged on her consciousness again, and her hearing seemed unduly acute as she heard the soft cry of a night bird, the sound of the wind in a nearby palm tree and the sighing of the waves on the beach.

Shell moved away from her, reaching for his trousers. He slipped them on without getting up and said breathlessly, "It was all I'd hoped for and more."

She moved a hand languidly out to touch his chest. Underneath her fingers she could feel the trip-hammer rhythm of his heart. She said very softly, "I know, I feel the same way."

"It's too bad the wine's all gone." He laughed shakily. "We could drink a toast to us."

"We can always pretend," she murmured.

He held a cupped hand aloft. "Here's to you, Julie Malone."

"And to you, Sheldon Phipps."

"I think I've been unconsciously looking for a woman like you for a long time and had almost despaired of ever finding one."

"I love you for saying that, but isn't it a bit premature?"

"Why do you say that?" he said, almost belligerently.

"The proximity, being alone on an island." She gestured vaguely. "And the danger, the danger may have had a lot to do with it."

"The danger, if we are in any danger, has nothing to do with anything. I felt this way before tonight."

She stood up abruptly, picking up one of the beach towels. "I'm going into the water for a bit."

As she started away, he called out, "Don't go out too far. Stay where I can see you. I'm too lazy at the moment to join you. Besides, the Coast Guard may show up at any minute."

The water was still surprisingly tepid, long after the sun was gone. Julie stayed in for only a short while before getting out, drying herself as she returned to the umbrella. Shell was sound asleep. She looked down at him with some amusement. "Some watchdog you are, buster," she whispered. She put on her clothes and stretched out on the blanket—not too close to Shell—and went to sleep at once.

She awoke sometime later to find that she had somehow managed to move close to him and now lay in the crook of his arm, her head pillowed on his shoulder. Feeling too comfortable to move, she smiled to herself and went back to sleep.

The next time she awoke she was startled awake by a blinding light and a blaring voice. "Shell Phipps, are you there?"

She shaded her eyes against the glare of the searchlight and could just make out the shape of a boat at the pier.

Then Shell was sitting up, his arm around her shoulders. "Don't be alarmed, Julie. It's just the Coast Guard to the rescue."

ON MONDAY AFTERNOON Julie went to Shell's office. She had warned him that she was coming. "I want Mr. Henderson to clarify several things for me."

Henderson studied her warily when Shell ushered her into his office and she revealed her purpose.

"I don't know what more I can tell you, my dear."

"For one thing, I'd like to see the anonymous note you received. I didn't even know about it until Shell told me."

Henderson flashed a nettled look at Shell, then shrugged. "I suppose you should have been informed about it. Fetch the file, will you, Sheldon?" While Shell was gone, Henderson said to

Julie, "It didn't seem important to show it to you. It will tell you nothing, and I suppose we were a little reluctant to reveal the fact that finding you was mere happenstance, as it were. All our efforts had come to naught, and failure always galls me. Then to have it done *for* us, so to speak..." He spread his hands in an apologetic gesture.

Shell returned with a thick file, extracted a single sheet of paper from it and gave it to Julie. A glance at it told her that Henderson was right—it could tell her nothing. Shell's memory had been letter-perfect, and the wording was exactly as he had quoted it. Julie supposed she'd been hoping for a signature, but there was none.

Her hopes dashed, she said, "I guess what I'm looking for is some positive proof of who I am. No fingerprints, no baby footprints, no dental records, just this note—" she waved the paper "—and the fact that I *look* like this Suellen Devereaux. I've been doing some reading about twins. It's true that there have been many instances of twins being separated, sometimes even at birth. But there are many look-alikes in the world. It is said that we all have a double somewhere in the world, someone who is absolutely no relation. How can you be sure that's not what I am?"

His smile was a touch supercilious. "I pride myself on knowing people, my dear Julie. And I know you are Suellen Devereaux. Call it a gut instinct, if you like."

"But you see, at the moment, anyway, I am *not* Suellen Devereaux, no matter who I was born as. I am Julie Malone, and have been for eight years."

"Julie, why do you insist so strongly that you're not who we're convinced you are?" he asked, frowning. "Sheldon tells me that you've been voicing doubts to him, as well."

"I suppose I'm of two minds about it," she replied slowly. "I would, of course, like to know who I really am. On the other hand, I'm not at all sure that I will like this Suellen Devereaux. Not if I've done something so terrible that somebody wishes to hurt me."

Henderson glanced at Shell, then back to her. "Yes, Sheldon told me about the incident Saturday. But we have absolutely no proof that it was aimed at you. It could have been a prank, somebody's idea of a sick joke. I'm sure Sheldon has told you about some of the characters infesting the area these days."

She aimed a look at Shell. "Shell didn't seem to think it was a joke."

He nodded. "I know, and I still don't believe it. Mr. Henderson doesn't seem to agree with me." He grinned. "He's not boat people, and he finds it hard to believe that boat people wouldn't perpetrate such a prank."

"Boat people!" Henderson gave a soft snort. "Boat people seem to think they're anointed by the Almighty. How about the criminals who use boats to smuggle drugs, to smuggle in illegal aliens?"

"But they're not truly boat people," Shell argued. "It's like people who truly love guns for sporting purposes, and who respect guns. On the other hand, there are those people who use guns strictly for killing other people."

Henderson snorted again. "What a perfectly dreadful analogy, Sheldon, and coming from an attorney. It's almost as bad as that asinine slogan—'Guns don't kill people, people kill people.'"

"Nevertheless, sir," Shell continued stubbornly, "boat people simply do not go around stealing boats, especially leaving someone stranded...."

Suddenly Julie ceased listening to their discussion, finding herself staring at Shell's profile; their words became a mere drone in her ears. Belatedly she was stricken by remorse.

After making love with Shell, she had felt no guilt. It was only now that she really remembered Ken and what she had done to him. She had betrayed him! What kind of a wife would she make if she fell headlong into the arms of the first attractive man who wanted her?

She could offer up all kinds of excuses—being alone in a strange place, being thrown together with Shell in an atmosphere of danger—but none of them really excused her behavior.

Was she a tramp by nature? Was that what Suellen Devereaux was? If so, Julie was even less sure that she wanted to be Suellen.

But one thing she determined in her mind. It would not happen again, and she would do her utmost to make it up to poor Ken.

NINE

July 19
We've had the boat a year now. It was just as I thought.
Mama has been out three times altogether, and she got seasick every time. The last time was five months ago, and she
swore she'd never go out again. A fat lot I care! Oh, I told
her I was sorry and everything, but of course I'm not! This
is the way I wanted it.

Suellen doesn't get seasick, but I've been working on her.
Every time we're out in the boat, I really get on her case,
and now that Mama has stopped going, Suellen doesn't go
out very often. So sometimes it's just Daddy and me, when
we take the Double Ellen out.

It was several months before we named her. I wanted to
name her Rosellen, but Mama threw a fit when she heard.
I think Daddy would have gone along but for Mama's ca-
terwauling about it. I asked Daddy why not, but he says it
wouldn't really be fair to Suellen, since the boat was a
birthday present to both of us. As if I cared about being fair
to her!

Nothing has happened yet, but it will. I just know he
wants it too, but he's fighting it. This past year I've begun
to get a real figure, and lately I've been wearing shorts and
a halter, and lying out on the foredeck, where Daddy can see
me from the wheelhouse.

I told him I wanted to get a good tan this summer, but
that's not the real reason. A couple of times, I untied the
halter and stretched out on my back. The first time I did

that the Double Ellen *swerved, almost hitting another boat. The sun's glare was directly on the windshield, so I couldn't see Daddy's face. I would have loved to!*

I've thought about taking everything off when I was sure he was watching. But I haven't dared go quite that far. Not yet.

But soon.

Once, long before he'd met Julie, another girl had told Ken Dawson that he was "square as a box." At that particular time the remark had stung a bit, yet after some reflection he'd discovered that he didn't really mind. In fact, he'd come to accept it as a compliment if it meant, as he thought it did, being old-fashioned, adhering to the old values. He had been brought up to believe that if you worked hard, remained honest and generally spurned immoral behavior, you would prosper and rise in the world.

At this particular time in his life, it seemed to him that those beliefs had come true. After graduating from business school, he had gone to work for a sporting goods firm. He had worked hard and had soon become a sales representative for the firm. And then, two years short of his thirtieth birthday, he had been rewarded with a store of his own to manage, in Moorestown, Connecticut. It wasn't a large town, yet the store serviced a wide area. He went about making friends, getting to know as many people as possible. He joined the country club and played golf and tennis. He became a member of the local rifle club and volunteered to coach a Little League baseball team.

Within a year of taking over the store he had increased sales by thirty percent. Not bad for a man not quite thirty.

Then he met Julie Malone and knew at once that he had found the woman he wanted to live with for the rest of his life. He had known very few women intimately. He had been too busy setting himself up, and he hadn't wanted to get married until he figured he was in a position to support a family. He had never patronized prostitutes, terrified of some dread disease that would render him forever unfit for marriage. When he needed sex, he would find a woman who would accommodate him. He had never once considered marriage to such a woman, of course; if their morals were so lax that they would copulate with a near-stranger, they were not suited for marriage.

When he met and fell in love with Julie—and she, wonder of wonders, fell in love with him— Ken was a very happy man. He asked her to marry him and she accepted; but it was necessary to postpone their wedding until he received his next raise and he could find a suitable house for them.

When he finally made love to Julie, he was torn by guilt afterward; but he consoled himself with the thought that the long engagement was responsible. Besides, how could it be so terrible when they were to be married eventually? Sometimes doubts shadowed his mind—Julie had consented willingly enough to his lovemaking, and that troubled him, and he could not help but wonder if she had been a virgin.

But when that damnable letter came and Julie went away to Florida, he discovered just how much he loved her, how much he missed her, and all doubts vanished.

Now his raise had come through—a substantial one, and sooner than expected—their house had been bought and was ready for occupancy, and Julie was many miles away and seemed in no hurry to come back. Suppose she *never* came back?

He decided to fly down to Key West and find out what was happening, even drag her back if it came to that. Ken smiled to himself at the thought. There was no way he could drag her back, no way, not if she wasn't ready. Although Julie was a gentle person, apparently timid on the surface, he had learned that she possessed a stubborn streak; she was a surprisingly strong woman. Still, he had worked at the Moorestown shop for two years without taking time off, and he had a vacation coming to him. If nothing else, he could consider it a nice trip; he had never been to Florida.

He made all the arrangements, and the night before he was to leave he called the number Julie had given him. She might try to discourage him from coming, but he figured that if he already had his plane reservations, she would accede to his wishes.

The phone was answered on the second ring, "Hello?"

"Julie? This is Ken."

There was a long pause, and then Julie's voice said softly, "Oh, Ken! I wasn't expecting your call. How are you, darling?"

"I'm fine. Julie—" He cleared his throat. "Julie, I'm coming down. My plane leaves early in the morning. Now don't try and talk me out of it, I'm coming down to see you!''

She laughed. ''I wouldn't think of trying to talk you out of it. I'd love to see you!''

His heartbeat accelerated. So she missed him, too! ''I have to change planes in Miami, and I'm supposed to get into Key West in the middle of the afternoon,'' he said.

''I'll meet your plane.''

''Well, okay. But I intend to rent a car. I could save you the trouble and drive out to where you're staying.''

''No, Ken, I'd rather you didn't. I want to prepare them for your visit.''

''Good, then. You won't have any trouble recognizing me,'' he said with a laugh. ''I'll be the one wearing the hat. I understand men don't wear hats in Florida.''

''Just tell me your arrival time and I'll be there.''

WHEN THE SMALL PLANE bounced down the runway at the Key West airport, Ken could see heat waves radiating off the tarmac. Although he had known it would be hot, he wasn't prepared for the humidity. As he stepped outside and walked down the steps, the damp heat struck him like a slap. He had no trouble spotting Julie at once—she was the only one waiting at the fence.

He lengthened his stride, waving, his face caught in a wide grin. She waved back. As he neared the fence, he was a little taken aback. Her clothes were different from anything he'd ever seen her wear, more colorful, and more daring. She wore a thin, short dress that whipped about her figure in the warm breeze, outlining her fine legs and breasts; and it seemed to him that she wore more makeup than he remembered. But God, she was lovely!

Coming through the gate, he set his own bag down and reached for both her hands. Holding them, he stepped back a little. "Let me look at you, sweetheart. You look good enough to eat!"

She gave him a demure look. "Do I, Ken?"

"You . . ." He gestured, spreading his hands. "I've never seen you dressed like this. It becomes you. *Florida* must become you. You've even gotten a tan."

"Aren't you going to kiss me, darling?" she murmured.

A touch startled by her boldness, he glanced around. The small terminal had already emptied except for the airport personnel. He drew her into his arms. The kiss started out to be tentative on his part, but Julie was pressing against him, her mouth soft and open on his. He could feel the firmness of her breasts against his chest. The breath left him in a rush, and he found himself returning the kiss ardently.

After a moment she broke the embrace and stepped back, flushed and looking suddenly disheveled. She brushed a strand of hair out of her eyes in a gesture that was achingly familiar. "There's probably a better place than this."

"I suppose," he said, suddenly embarrassed. "How did you come out, Julie, in a taxi?" At her nod he said, "Then I'll go rent a car."

A half hour later they drove out of the airport parking lot, with Julie sitting close to him. Ken was acutely aware of her presence. It was the first time since they'd started going together that they'd been separated for any length of time.

He followed her directions. As they drove into the center of town, Julie said, "The motel, the Pier House, is right on the beach. You'll love it, Ken."

He directed a look at her. "I thought you were staying at this Devereaux place?"

"I am, but I'll confess, I haven't told them about you yet."

"Why not?" His smile was a little strained. "Ashamed of me now that you're an heiress?"

"Oh, no, never!" She patted his thigh. "But...well, things are a little strange yet. I'm still not sure of myself." She smiled gently. "Besides, I thought we could have more time alone together at a motel than we could at the house."

Ken was silent. Her words held an implied promise that he wasn't sure he was ready for; yet, at the same time, he had to admit that the promise of intimacy started his pulse hammering. And why not, he thought happily; it's a sort of vacation, isn't it?

At the motel parking lot, she said, "You don't have to check in at the desk, I've already taken care of that."

Taking his bag from the car, Ken followed her lead as she made her way to a bungalow unit right on the beach. Unlocking and opening the door, she stood back, motioning him inside. The air-conditioning was on, and he breathed a sigh of relief. The drapes were drawn and the room was dim. Instead of turning on a light, Julie crossed the room to the nightstand beside the bed. With a start of surprise, Ken saw an ice bucket with a bottle of champagne resting in it.

"Champagne?" he said with arched eyebrows.

"I thought this was a cause for celebration," she said, and smiled brightly.

"Well, it is, of course. But you've never been much of one for drinking."

"This is Florida, Ken, not Moorestown. And besides, you're on your holiday."

As he advanced toward her, head whirling at the subtle change in her, Julie took two glasses from the ice, then picked up the bottle and felt it. "Most of the ice has melted, but it's still cold. Here." She gave him the bottle.

Ken took the bottle dubiously; he had never opened a champagne bottle in his life. Opening them had always struck him as something of an art.

Julie said, "I'll be right back." She went into the bathroom and closed the door.

Ken wrestled with the foil, then the wire, swearing under his breath. Then he began trying to twist out the cork, but it seemed to resist his best efforts. Finally, just as Julie emerged from the bathroom, the cork popped, hitting the ceiling, and champagne foamed out in a flood. Hastily he poured it into the two stemmed glasses, getting almost as much on the nightstand as in the glasses.

Julie was laughing as she reached him. "Just like the bridegroom always does in the movies."

She took the glass he handed her and clicked it against his. "Here's to us, darling, and to the future."

"I'll certainly drink to that."

They drank, Ken taking only a sip of his; he had never liked champagne. Julie finished hers and poured another.

He said, "You seem to have changed your mind. The other day when I talked to you, you didn't want me to come down here."

She gave a slight shrug of her shoulders, and his gaze was drawn involuntarily to her breasts. "Things have been pretty hectic. Half the time I don't know what I'm saying. But I'm really glad you're here. Have you missed me?"

"You know I have."

She drained her glass and set it down. In a husky voice she said, "Then kiss me. We're alone now."

Her open mouth tasted of champagne. As his arms went around her, the light material of her dress slithered under his touch with a silken sound, and Ken shivered.

She took her mouth away to whisper in his ear, "I've missed you so, darling."

The blood roared in his head, and the delicious feel of her in his arms so aroused him that he wanted her more than he had ever wanted a woman in his life. He had desired her before, but never with this blood-pounding, demanding excitement.

Afterward, Ken could never remember how it came about, but suddenly they were naked and on the bed together, hands and lips busy, writhing in blazing need. He would never forget the moment they finally came together, Julie underneath him, her body heaving in counterpoint to his.

It was a time of ecstasy beyond his wildest imaginings, and the few affairs of his past, even the few times with Julie before Key West, seemed staid and inhibited. There was nothing in the least inhibited about Julie now. She was wild, wanton and inventive, urging him on with tiny cries, and the silken vise of her thighs squeezed unrestrainedly when he shouted out his ecstasy.

For the next few seconds Ken was all sensation, with no thought at all of the outside world. When next he was fully aware, he was lying beside Julie, his heart pounding, his limbs trembling. He turned his head and looked at her beside him with wonder and a feeling of love and awe. She was on her back, her eyes closed, those firm, marvelous breasts rising and falling rapidly.

He reached out a tentative, almost timid hand and touched one breast, taken by the sudden fear that he had just dreamed what had happened, that it must be some erotic fantasy.

Then she murmured throatily and closed her hand over his, forcing it against her pulsing flesh.

"I wasn't sure it really happened, Julie," he said raggedly. "I had to touch you to make sure you were real."

Without opening her eyes she smiled dreamily. "It was real, darling, believe me. And you never need an excuse to touch me, not ever." She turned toward him, propping herself up on one elbow. "And I hope that goes for me, as well."

She touched him intimately. He gasped, sucking in his breath.

"I know, poor baby," she murmured. "You're probably worn out right now. Just lie still, I'll do everything."

"But Julie, so soon?" he protested weakly. "I don't think—"

"Don't think, just feel. It'll happen, you'll see," she said with a wicked smile.

She worked on his body with a skill that took his breath away. This was the Julie he thought he knew so well? Where had she learned all these delightfully wicked skills? His body began to leap to her stroking touch. He would have sworn that he could not be fully aroused again so soon, but it happened as she had promised. Soon she rose, hovered over him for an instant, then shimmied down, encasing him in silken heat. Ken had only performed the sex act in the conventional missionary position, but he was so consumed in passion that he acquiesced without a murmur.

When she rode him to a climax this time he was really exhausted and sank into almost instant sleep.

He awoke sometime later. It was dark and Julie was gone, yet the sheets still held the lingering odor of her perfume and the feminine smell of her. Smiling bemusedly, Ken went back to sleep.

WHEN HE AWOKE THE NEXT TIME, it was full morning. He felt marvelously refreshed and rested. In fact, he felt better than he had at any time in his life; he was starving, and remembered that he hadn't eaten any dinner last night.

Smiling at the memory of the reason for that, he bounded out of bed, took a fast shower, got dressed and went looking for a place to have breakfast. The old section of Key West began a few blocks away, so he quickly found a restaurant and ate enough breakfast for two men. Afterward he found a tobacconist's shop in a dead end street where hand-rolled cigars were made by expatriate Cuban cigar makers. Ken smoked very little, but he liked an expensive cigar when he was in an expansive mood. He paid two dollars for a long black cigar and strolled along the street smoking it. It was midmorning, the shops were opening, and tourists were crowding the streets in spite of the heat. He sat on an iron bench under a shade tree directly across from the station servicing the Conch Train—several open trams pulled by a tiny engine, a replica of a real steam engine. Smoking, he watched the tourists board the train. He even contemplated taking a trip himself, playing the tourist bit.

But every time his mind wandered, it circled right back to thoughts of Julie. He realized that last night's episode with her had wrought a subtle change in him. If someone had told him that he could experience such physical delights, he would have scoffed, and been shocked, as well. Well, he certainly wasn't scoffing; and strangest of all, he wasn't shocked. He might have been a little last night, but all that was gone. All he could think of was Julie and the future with her.

There was one tiny burr gnawing at his contentment. What had caused the change in her, and why hadn't she wanted him to come out to Devereaux House? It was obvious that she was trying to avoid that, for some reason. If they were to be married, the Devereaux would have to know about it eventually.

He got up and crossed to a curbside pay phone, dug the number out of his wallet, then started to dial it. On the last digit, he changed his mind and hung up. If he called and alerted her in advance, she might try to discourage him from coming out. But if he just showed up on her doorstep, what could she do?

He didn't even have the address of the house, just the phone number. He returned to the motel and spoke to the desk clerk. "Do you know where Devereaux House is?" he asked him.

The young desk clerk, wearing a sunny smile like a badge, said cheerfully, "Of course, sir. I doubt that there's a person in Key West who doesn't know. Devereaux House is a landmark here."

"Would you tell me how to get there, please?"

After receiving explicit directions, Ken got into the rental car and drove across town. From what little he could see of the house from the street, it looked impressive. Massive wooden gates stood open. Ken parked the car and strolled up the walk, admiring the profusion of flowers and blooming trees and shrubs.

A black woman answered his ring. "Yes, sir?"

"I'd like to see Julie Malone, please."

"Julie Malone? Who...? Oh." The woman nodded, opening the door wide. "Won't you come in? I'll fetch her. If you'll wait in the parlor, please. Right in here." She indicated an archway to her left and started up the stairs.

Ken went into the dim parlor and paced, too impatient to sit. A few minutes later his head came around at a sound in the archway.

Julie stood there, squinting in the gloom. She said uncertainly, "Yes? Pauline said someone was here to see me...."

"Ken!" She gasped, and her hand went to her mouth. "What are you doing here?"

"I know you said last night that you weren't ready yet for me to meet the Devereaux, but I thought..."

She looked confused. "You got into Key West last night? *I* told you...what are you saying?"

It was his turn to be confused. "Yes, of course I did. You met me at the airport."

"Ken..." She made a helpless gesture. "I don't know what you're talking about. I didn't meet you at the airport. I told you the other day that I wasn't ready for you to come down here."

Totally at sea now, Ken said, "But I called you the night before last and you said to come on down."

"I didn't talk to you on the phone. I didn't see you yesterday." She pushed the hair out of her eyes with a distracted gesture. "I think I'm going crazy!"

"You weren't crazy last night, unless you'd call what we did crazy. I might have felt that way at one time, but not anymore," he said, grinning. "Why, you're even wearing the same dress."

"This is the first time I've worn this dress, I just bought it two days ago." She broke off and made an obvious effort to regain control. "I think we should start over, Ken. Tell me just what happened from the moment you say you called me from Moorestown."

She motioned to the couch. Ken took the couch, but she sat in a straight chair across from him.

Julie listened to Ken with a growing sense of dismay and bewilderment. Was she going crazy?

Was she a schizophrenic, a person with a split personality? She recalled seeing the movie *The Three Faces of Eve* on late-night television some time ago, in which the heroine had three separate and distinct personalities, with none aware of the others.

As Ken drew near the end of his story, Julie tried to remember where she had been yesterday during the time Ken said she had been with him. Shortly after lunch she had put on a swimsuit and gone down to the beach and had slept most of the afternoon away. Or had she? She had started out, but at this moment the only thing she was positive about was waking up thirsty around midnight last night and going down to the kitchen for a glass of ice water. She remembered reading somewhere that overindulgence in champagne resulted in a raging thirst. And Ken had just told her gloatingly about the champagne she was supposed to have drunk last night!

As he finished and looked at her expectantly, she said slowly, "This call you made from Moorestown . . . what time was it?"

"I'm not sure of the exact time, I had no reason to check, but it was some time between eight and 8:30."

She thought for a moment. "There, you see! I wasn't even in the house. Night before last I went for a walk after dinner, and we ate at 7:30."

"But *somebody* answered the phone, Julie. She said it was you, and her voice sounded like yours."

Again, Julie thought back. It had been a depressing evening, Pippen had been out somewhere, and Pauline had left as soon as dinner was over. Julie and Helen had eaten alone, in almost total silence, and then Helen had taken Stella Devereaux's dinner up to her. Stella had been feeling a little better, and Helen had said that she was going to read to her for a bit. There was no telephone in Stella's room, and Helen refused to answer the phone. "It's often bad news," she'd said. "If it's good news, it can always wait."

There had been no one else in the house, so far as Julie knew. And then she remembered something—there had been a rain squall off the coast creating a chill breeze, and she had considered returning to the house for a sweater. Had she? She couldn't remember! Despair clouded her mind, and she wanted to get up and run from the room. What was happening to her?

Watching her, brown eyes intent, Ken said, "You don't remember? You don't think I'm lying about all this, surely?"

"I don't know, Ken, I don't know! All I know is I don't remember!"

"Your amnesia," he said thoughtfully. "Is it possible that you're blanking out things for brief periods? I know you've been under a lot of tension and stress down here. Could that be possible?"

"I don't see how it could be." She was disconsolate. "But I suppose anything is possible, if you're telling the truth."

"What possible reason could I have to lie? I wish there was some way I could prove it to you— Wait! I have it!" He snapped his fingers, smiling. "The register at the hotel, you must have signed it. You rented the room for me. Let's go check."

She hesitated for a moment, dread filling her. She wasn't sure she wanted to know. She finally said, "All right, let's go."

In the car she sat over against the far door, not looking at Ken. But inevitably her thoughts were drawn to something he'd said earlier. "Ken, you said that what we did last night might have been considered crazy. What did you mean by that? Did we—" She stumbled over the words. "Did we make love?"

"We most certainly did," he said exuberantly.

"How was it?" she said timidly.

"It was different from Moorestown. What can I tell you? It was different but great, the greatest. Being down here in Florida has changed you, sweetheart, but for the better, I'd say."

He reached out to touch her knee, and she flinched away from him. "Don't touch me!"

"Why not?" he said in a hurt voice. "Why is it so different from last night? You were all over me."

"You see, it couldn't have been me. I've never been like that." Then she remembered Saturday night on the island with Shell, and she wasn't so sure. Shell had awakened her sensuality to a greater extent than she would have thought possible.

Ken pulled the car into the motel parking lot and they went into the lobby together.

Ken said to the young man behind the desk, "The young lady here wants to check the register card to see if she signed it correctly yesterday. We have a wager going." He winked at the desk clerk. "You see, we've just gotten married, and she still has a tendency to sign her maiden name."

The man behind the desk looked at Julie with a broad smile. "Of course, I remember the young lady."

He opened the register card file, took out a card and turned it around on the desk. Julie bent over it.

There it was, Julie Malone, and unmistakably in her handwriting. A wave of dizziness swept over her, and she closed her eyes, swaying.

Ken caught her elbow. "Julie, are you okay?" he asked in alarm.

Julie shook his hand off and looked at the card again. As if further confirmation were needed, she saw the tiny circle over the *i* in Julie. When signing her name, instead of dotting the *i* in the usual way, she always drew a tiny circle.

TEN

August 24
It finally happened!

Daddy and I went out on the Double Ellen alone yes-
terday. After we were out a ways, without any other boats
around, I stretched out on the foredeck, and took my top off.
After a little while I took off the rest too. I could see Daddy
staring at me from the wheelhouse.

I lay on my back, an arm over my eyes, and waited. Af-
ter a while I heard the motor change and the boat slowed. I
sat up just enough to see that we were heading into the de-
serted cove of a small island. It was uninhabited as far as
I could see, and there wasn't another boat in sight. I lay
back down and in a few minutes I heard the anchor being
run out, and we came to a stop. I lay very still, one arm over
my eyes.

I held my arms out to him and he came to me.

The rays of the sun bounced off the clear water as it
lapped gently against the side of the Double Ellen. It was
almost noon and a pulsing heat radiated from the deck.
Sweat trickled between my breasts and my gaze shifted from
his intense focus to the horizon and the faint outline of
pristine white sails against a brilliant blue.

And then it happened. Was it only my imagination, or
was it all a dream?

Julie ran out of the motel lobby, and would have hurried right on out of the parking lot if Ken hadn't caught up to her, seizing her by the arm.

"Julie, where are you going?"

"I don't know. Let me go!" She tried to wrench her arm free, but he held her in a firm grip. Then, abruptly, her burst of panic subsided and she regained a measure of calmness. "Ken, I want to be by myself for a while. I want to think."

"I can take you back to Devereaux House—"

"No! I don't want to go back there, either, not right now."

"Julie . . . I don't understand any of this," he said gently. "That *was* your signature, wasn't it?"

"You think I understand what's happening any better than you do?" She choked back an impulse to laugh hysterically. "Yes, that was my signature. I can't deny it, but I can't explain it, either. I don't remember signing the register card, I don't remember any of the things you told me happened yesterday."

"I find that hard to accept, Julie."

"No harder than I do, I'm sure. All I can say is that I have no explanation. Ken—" She drew a deep, steadying breath. "Why don't you go home, back to Moorestown? Until I can get all this straightened out?"

He was already shaking his head, lips set stubbornly. "No, I'm staying right here. I arranged for a week off. I'm staying at least that long, if not longer. Maybe by that time you'll decide to go back with me."

"What if I'm crazy? You don't want a crazy woman!" She laughed a little wildly. "The way it looks, I could easily be mad."

"I can't accept that, either."

Suddenly she was annoyed by his stubbornness. "Stay, then! You may regret it for the rest of your life. But right now I want to be by myself."

She headed away with plunging steps, leaving him staring after her in dismay.

A few blocks up Front Street she came to the Conch Train station. The train was half-filled with sightseers, and on an impulse she bought a ticket and boarded, finding a seat on the last car, by herself. Sunk in thought, she heard very little of the operator's spiel as he narrated the history of Key West, giving a brief talk about the points of interest they passed—the Turtle Kraals, the Ernest Hemingway home, the Audubon House.

Was she crazy? If she wasn't, she soon would be, she thought wryly. There had to be some explanation for her behavior yesterday. She was accustomed—or as accustomed as she ever would be—to having lost the first sixteen years of her life, but nothing like *this* had ever happened. Almost a full day lost?

She felt overwhelmed, and it took all her self-control to keep from breaking into tears. She sat up suddenly, looking around to get her bearings, for the first time since she'd boarded the Conch Train. Over the past several days, by dint of walking, she had become fairly familiar with Key West; and she realized that she was only a few blocks away from Shell's office.

She called up to the driver, "Could you let me off here, please?"

He turned, looking back. "Sure, lady, no problem."

He pulled the train over to the curb, and Julie hopped off. She walked with a determined stride toward the offices of Henderson, Caldicott and Phipps.

It was just short of noon when she walked into the reception room. The shapely brunette behind the desk recognized her. "Miss Devereaux! How are you today?"

"Is Shell . . . Is Mr. Phipps in?"

"Yes, but I think he has a luncheon appointment." She touched the intercom. "Mr. Phipps, Miss Devereaux is here to see you."

Julie could hear his voice over the intercom. "I'll be right out."

In a moment he came striding down the corridor, his broad smile a warm welcome. "Julie! I'm delighted to see you." Then he frowned slightly. "Is something the matter?"

"I need to talk to you, Shell."

"Sure." He took her hand and started to lead her away. "I'm not to be disturbed, Jean."

"You have a luncheon engagement with Mr. Michaels at 12:30."

"Oh, hell!" He paused, thinking. "Call him, will you? See if we can't make it for tomorrow. It's not that urgent, anyway."

In his office Shell shut the door and led Julie to the short couch by one wall and sat down beside her. Holding her hand, he said, "Let's have it, Julie."

"First, Ken is in Key West. He flew in yesterday."

"The boyfriend from back home? Why did he come down, just to see you? Or try to take you back to Moorestown?" His grip tightened. "I hope you're not going?"

"No, not right now . . . ."

"Good!" He smiled.

"But that's not the reason I'm here." She paused and took a deep breath. "Shell, Ken says that he called me the evening before last, that I told him to come down and that I was with him last night." She could see that he was hurt by her revelation.

"You said, 'Ken says.' What do you mean?"

"I mean that I don't remember any of what he says happened. As far as I know, I was on the beach yesterday until late afternoon and spent the evening at home, at Devereaux House."

Shell blinked and passed a hand over his eyes. "I'm sorry, Julie, that's a little hard to take in. You don't remember anything at all? Could Ken be lying to you?"

"That was my first thought, but why in the world should he lie? And then I saw the register card at the motel. I signed it, Shell, there can be no doubt about that. . . ."

"Motel? You went with him to a motel?"

She looked away from his intent gaze. She didn't want to hurt him, but he was the only one she could talk to. "That's what he said. But I don't remember it."

"Incredible," he muttered. He got up abruptly and crossed to the window to stare out. After several minutes of thought he turned around again.

With the light behind him, she couldn't see his face. "I can't think of an explanation, either. I suppose it's possible you could have blanked out those hours for some reason, but it seems highly unlikely."

"That was what Ken thought, too."

"Isn't there anyone at Devereaux House who saw you during the time you were supposed to be with him?"

She hesitated. "Not really. I mean, I couldn't swear to it. Everything has happened so fast. My whole life has changed around. I've been doing a lot of walking, both to get out of that house and to think. Sometimes it seems I walk for hours, and later I can't always remember where I've been."

"But even so, if you were at Devereaux House, certainly someone must have noticed you."

She shook her head. "I don't know. I have vague memories of being there, but nothing clear. And frankly, I don't want to ask them, I don't want them to know. You're the only person I've talked to about it, Shell."

He came to the couch, sat down and took her hands in his again. "I'm pleased you felt that you could confide in me, Julie, but I must confess that I'm just as baffled by all this as you are."

"The other day you mentioned a psychiatrist," she said slowly.

He nodded. "Yes, Dr. Paul Reardon. Despite what Pippen says, he has a good reputation. Many people swear that he has helped them with various problems. Do you want to see him?"

"I don't know. I've always associated psychiatrists with crazy people, but the way I'm feeling right now, I may be crazy, or going crazy."

"You're not crazy, Julie," he said emphatically. "Just because you have amnesia doesn't mean that you're crazy, and besides, there's no stigma attached to going to a psychiatrist."

"I had a number of sessions with one back in Moorestown when I first showed up there, and he wasn't much help."

"I think it's a good idea. As the saying goes, it couldn't hurt," he said with a faint grin. "I know Dr. Reardon, we've used him a couple of times in court cases. He's a nice guy, understanding and kind. Shall I make an appointment for you?"

She was slow in answering, then said in a rush, "If you would, please. I have to do something!"

AT FIRST SIGHT Julie wasn't sure that she agreed with Shell's assessment of the psychiatrist, Dr. Paul Reardon. He was tall, rumpled and shaggy, walked with a stoop, wore half glasses perched halfway down a huge nose *and* had a dour countenance. His office was untidy, with books and papers piled on his desk, on the floor and on the furniture.

And he had no couch. How could he be a competent psychiatrist without a couch, Julie wondered? The one she'd gone to in Moorestown had had a comfortable couch with an elevated head that he'd covered with a clean cloth after each patient.

Then he smiled, and the smile changed his face completely. His brown eyes *were* kind, and understanding.

"Come in, my dear," he said in a deep, flowing voice. He indicated the one empty chair, an easy chair in front of his desk. "Please make yourself comfortable."

At least, Julie thought, I won't have to worry about his fee. On Monday morning her grandmother had opened a twenty-thousand-dollar checking account for her.

Dr. Reardon went around behind his desk, leaned back in his swivel chair, removed his glasses and pinched the bridge of his nose where the glasses had rested. "Shell told me the bare facts of your problem. It sounds unusual and intriguing. Otherwise I probably would not have accepted you as a patient, since I already have a heavy caseload. If it's all right with you, for the time being at least I'll call you Julie, instead of Suellen."

"It's all right with me." Her smile was twisted. "I'm so confused as to who I am, it doesn't much matter anyway."

He smiled reassuringly. "Well, I can't promise to alleviate your confusion, but hopefully we can cut through some of it. Now . . ." He caressed the bridge of his nose again. "I understand from Shell that you suffer from a rare form of amnesia, that you suddenly appeared eight years ago in a town in Connecticut with no memory of anything prior to that time. Suppose we begin there. Don't be concerned about time." He waved a hand. "This won't be a regular one-hour session. I've cleared the whole afternoon for you."

"I want you to know that I'm grateful for that, Doctor." She paused for a few moments, arranging her thoughts. Then she began, telling him everything she could remember. Dr. Reardon interrupted her frequently with probing questions, and she dug things out of her memory of those eight years that she had forgotten.

Some of the questions were very personal, and at one point she said, "Doctor, I fail to see what the minute details of my life in Moorestown have anything to do with this. Especially my relationship with Ken! That's private."

His smile was warm as he said gently, "We never know in the beginning what may turn out to be important. Just think of it as reconstructing a complete picture. By the time we're through I hope to know you better than you know yourself."

Two slow hours had passed before she finally got around to her arrival in Key West and the events that had followed.

When she had finished telling him of the supposed call from Ken and the events that allegedly had occurred the day he arrived, the psychiatrist pursed his lips, rubbed his nose furiously, then returned the glasses to their perch. He looked at her owlishly and said thoughtfully, "Do you believe him?"

"At first I didn't. But what reason would he have to lie to me?"

"Well...he badly wants you to return home with him, from what you tell me. Could he have made up an elaborate story in an attempt to frighten you into returning with him?"

"I never thought of it in quite that light. But then there's my signature on the register card, Doctor. I signed it, it's my signature!"

He was silent for a long moment, his eyes closed. Without opening them he said, "There are two possibilities that occur to me. First, since you already suffer from amnesia, it is possible that you blanked out those hours, as well. You told me that you don't remember that day clearly. I am forced to admit that it's farfetched, but then there are many things we don't know about the human mind. It can do some very strange things."

"And the other possibility?" She took a deep breath. "Could I be a multiple personality like the woman in *The Three Faces of Eve*."

"Movies!" he said with a touch of scorn.

"But it did happen, it was based on a real case."

He nodded. "That much is true, and of course it's possible. But also extremely difficult to diagnose. My dear Julie, I can see why you're so upset if you're thinking that, but let's not go that far afield this early on."

"Then if not that, what is the other possibility that you mentioned?"

"There are many curious things about the relationship of twins, especially identical twins, which apparently you and your sister were. After I made your appointment with Shell, I did some reading on the history of twins.

"There have been instances of twins separated at birth, living for years without seeing each other or even knowing of one another's existence and being brought up in entirely different environments. And yet, amazingly enough, they still grow up very much alike. They experience the same illnesses, even die within hours of one another.

"Many instances of documented ESP communications between identical twins have been observed, often with the twins a whole continent apart. To make my point clearer, twins growing up apart still develop an astounding rapport with each other. Due to their different environments, or other factors, they may develop different personalities, yet that strange psychic rapport remains."

Julie was baffled. "I fail to see what that has to do with me, Doctor. My sister is dead . . ."

He was nodding. "Yes, I know."

" . . . and even if she wasn't, how would all this explain what happened between Ken and myself?"

He studied her silently for a moment, then spoke carefully. "Now please don't be offended, but from what you've told me, there are hints that your sister Rosellen had a different personality. As I recall, you quoted the Devereaux housekeeper as saying, Rosellen was the mean one. Is that substantially correct?"

"Yes, that's what Pauline told me, and I didn't tell you all she said—" She hesitated, uncertain whether to proceed. "She said some other things that I didn't want to repeat. She apparently didn't like my sister at all, and she may have been saying them out of spite."

"Tell me, Julie. Nothing you say here, to me, will be repeated."

"Well, she said that a boy next door, a friend of Rosellen's, was found hanging from a rafter. And Pauline even hinted that my . . . that the accident in which my mother died wasn't an accident."

Dr. Reardon leaned forward intently. "And that your sister may have been somehow responsible?"

"She didn't come right out and say that, and she refused to say anything else, but her meaning was clear enough," Julie said, somewhat reluctantly.

The psychiatrist removed his glasses and rubbed his nose. He murmured, "That is interesting, very."

"I still don't see what you're getting at, Doctor."

"It's a little difficult to put into words, but what you've just told me adds a little more credence to the theory. This was told to you *before* the events with your friend Ken?"

"Yes."

"Then it's feasible that you were acting out something that you thought your sister might have done, then blanked it out of your mind. Even though she is no longer alive, a sort of psychic transference could have taken place."

"Then that must mean that if she was bad, so am I?" Julie said in dismay.

"It strikes me that you have an extremely active imagination, young lady," he said, obviously amused.

"So I've been told."

"Well, it doesn't mean that at all. You've been under a severe strain, and something in your subconscious evidently impelled you to act out a fantasy, act the way you've been led to believe your twin sister would act. And then, since it's out of character for you, you blanked it out." He sat back with a satisfied smile, as though he was pleased at reaching a solution to a vexing problem.

"And that's it, that's your answer for what happened?"

"No, not at all," he replied, suddenly grave. "And if I gave that impression, I'm sorry. It takes time and effort to peel back the layers we all erect around our psyches and get to the real root of a problem. We must have many more sessions. I'll have my secretary arrange a series of appointments for you—at your convenience, of course." He reached for the interoffice phone.

"No, Doctor." Julie held up her hand. "I'm not sure I wish to go through all that again. I did once, in Moorestown, for weeks, and nothing came of it." She stood up abruptly. "I must think about it before I decide. Thank you for your time."

As she started out, he said urgently, "Julie, I think it's extremely important that we continue with this. It could be dangerous for you. What if you do have a multiple-personality disorder? I'm not saying that you do, but I need sufficient time to discover the truth, one way or another."

"I'll think about it, Doctor. If I decide to come back, I'll call for an appointment."

Julie left the office more confused than when she had arrived. Her mind felt as though it had been scrambled in a mixer. She recalled something Ken had told her once—Ken, who had a healthy disrespect for the psychiatric profession. "The only thing a shrink does, baby, is screw up your head."

KEN WAS LYING ON HIS BED in the motel room, staring unseeingly at the flickering television screen, when a bold knock sounded on the door.

He sat up, listening. The knock sounded again. He crossed to the door. "Who is it?"

"It's Julie, darling."

He opened the door and stared at her. She wore a tight red dress and stiletto heels, her hair was brushed until it shone, and her face was heavily made up. Her bright smile grew a little strained as he continued to stare at her without speaking.

"Well, aren't you glad to see me?"

"I'm not sure," he said slowly. "Which Julie are you?"

"Which...?" She frowned briefly, but then her face cleared. "Oh."

She stepped close, pressing against him. She kissed him with an open mouth. "That Julie! Now, are you going to invite me in?"

Wordlessly he stepped back, and she brushed past him. Ken closed and locked the door behind her.

ELEVEN

September 21
It finally happened again!

It took me almost a full month to make it happen. Daddy wanted to, I could tell, every time we were out on the Double Ellen, but he kept away. He wouldn't even come close to me, not even when I was full naked on the foredeck, but I could always feel his eyes on me.

He even flew to New York, or somewhere, for a whole week, and I knew why. He went to find a woman, but I am sure that after what had happened between us, he would never be satisfied with anyone else.

Two weeks after he came back, yesterday, we went out on the boat. I heard him talking to both Mama and Su-ellen, trying to talk them into coming along. Suellen said she had something more important to do, and Mama said she wasn't feeling well.

I believe that Mama is beginning to suspect something. I can tell by the way she looks at me every once in a while. Sometimes I even wish she would find out! It would be real interesting to see what would happen then. I may even see to it that she does find out!

Julie was already in the booth, toying with a glass of white wine, when Shell walked into the restaurant to keep their luncheon engagement.

''Hi.'' He stooped to kiss her cheek, then slid into the booth across from her. ''Where were you last evening? I called the house and Pippen said you were out somewhere.''

"I was walking again.'' She motioned vaguely. "I had a lot of thinking to do.''

A waitress came to take their order. Shell ordered a beer, and they both chose shrimp salad. Shell looked at her curiously. "Thinking about what? The session with Dr. Reardon yesterday?''

"That, and other things.''

"How did the session go?''

"I'm not really sure.'' She looked at him, wondering whether she should tell him all that had transpired. "It lasted long enough, almost three hours.''

He nodded. "He told me he'd made arrangements for all the time you needed. You seeing him again?''

"I haven't made up my mind yet.'' She gave a rueful shrug. "He may not care to see me. I was somewhat hostile.''

"I understand that's par for the course in the beginning,'' he said with a smile. "What happened exactly? You don't have to tell me if you don't care to. But I am interested, I'm interested in everything about you.''

Shell accepted his beer from the waitress and took a swig.

Haltingly Julie related the essence of what had gone on in Dr. Reardon's office, ending with the psychiatrist's theory about the blank spots in her memory two days earlier. Before she was finished their salads arrived and they began eating, Julie just picking at hers.

"I'm no judge of something like this," Shell said carefully. "I know that Dr. Reardon is fond of saying that very little is yet known about the workings of the human psyche and the brain. And I'm more ignorant than most. But it *is* an explanation, and I'm sure more will emerge after a few more visits."

"I've just about decided, as I talked to you, that I'm not going back."

He stared at her appraisingly. "Why not?"

"I'm not a nut case, Shell!"

"Nobody thinks you are. I know I don't, and I'm sure Dr. Reardon doesn't, either. But your amnesia is a problem that could respond to his help."

"It didn't before, immediately after it happened. So why should it work now, after eight years?"

"I'm sure I don't know," he said with a shrug. "But I can't see that it'll do any harm."

"Just *going* to him makes me doubt my own sanity!" Despite herself, her voice was climbing dangerously.

"Julie..." He looked around worriedly and reached across the table for her hand. "Don't get so excited, people will hear you."

She snatched her hand away and retreated into silence.

After a moment she heard him sigh, and then he said in a low voice, "Julie, look at me."

She looked up into his eyes. They were grave, and his face was set and determined. "Julie, I didn't want to tell you this, and wouldn't except for the turn things have taken. I think you should be made aware of what I'm about to tell you. But first I want you to understand something. What I'm about to tell you has no bearing on what I feel for you."

"Tell me what?" she said with a sinking feeling, intuitively knowing that it was bad news.

"Apparently there's a—" He stopped, swallowed, pushed his unfinished salad away and drained the rest of his beer.

She leaned forward tensely. "There's a what, Shell?"

"There's a streak of instability on the Devereaux side of the family," he said in a rush.

"Instability? What does that mean?"

"Your father...according to Mr. Henderson, was unstable. He often flew up to New York, had flings with women. He gambled and drank heavily. Except for Stella's steadying influence he would likely have squandered all the Devereaux fortune."

"According to Mr. Henderson? Why has nobody mentioned this to me before? I don't believe you!" she said wildly. "I think you're just trying to frighten me into going back to Dr. Reardon! How does the fact that a man drinks too much, gambles and chases women make him crazy?"

"I didn't say he was crazy, Julie," he said gently. "I said he was unstable. Mr. Henderson told me that he had to bail him out of jail several times in New York, and once he was found drunk in a gutter with some winos. He almost died that time."

"Mr. Henderson!" She slapped her hand down onto the table. "What does he know? Look at

Grandmother. As old as she is, she's still sharp. She may have vague periods, but that's nothing unusual at her age.''

"Mr. Henderson has been the Devereaux family attorney for close to thirty years, he knows them all very well. And it's true what you say about Stella, but then often things like that skip a generation. Your great-grandfather was a pirate, you know...."

"So were the great-grandfathers of others here. You told me so yourself!"

"But the stories have it that he did some pretty terrible things. And look at Pippen. She's not what you'd call your normal person."

"Many people believe in the supernatural, and even some scientists are coming around to believing in psychic phenomena."

"I can understand why you're fighting this so hard." He tried to catch her hand, but she evaded his grasp. "All right, look at your sister, Rosellen. I won't go so far as to say that she killed Hugh Waters and your mother, but she was a strange child. Pauline told you that, and I've heard stories about her from other people."

"Then you *do* think I'm crazy!" she said with a gasp. "You think my sister and I inherited a streak of insanity from my father!"

"That's not what I think at all. I was afraid you would misunderstand."

"Oh, I understand quite well. You think I'm crazy!"

"Julie, don't be stupid—" He stopped short, as though realizing that his choice of words was unfortunate. He began again in a more reasonable tone. "What I'm trying to do is encourage you to continue seeing Dr. Reardon. Look, you've admitted that you're confused about many things. God knows, eight years of complete memory loss would confuse anyone."

"I wasn't confused until I came down here and met you and all the others. I was finally adjusted to it, like a person adjusts to a deformity, as much as that is ever possible. Thank you very much for the lunch, Mr. Phipps," she said coldly. "I'll be going now." She started to rise.

Swiftly he reached across to clamp his hand around her wrist. "For God's sake, Julie!" he said in a fierce whisper. "I'm only trying to help you, I'm on your side!"

"As the saying goes," she said, a little wildly, "with friends like you, who needs enemies?"

She succeeded in wrenching her arm out of his grip and marched out of the restaurant, walking almost blindly, stumbling once against the corner of a table and bruising her hip.

Outside, she stood blinking in the bright sun, feeling disoriented. For a moment she didn't even know where she was, and then she finally realized that she was only a few blocks from the Pier House. She paused for a moment. Then, realizing what she had to do, she started walking toward the motel.

When she reached Ken's door, she took a deep breath and knocked loudly. There was no sound from inside, and she knocked again. Still no response. Where could he be? In exasperation she pounded with both fists.

Finally she stood back, taking a calming breath. In her agitation she had forgotten the time. He couldn't be expected to be in his room all the time; it was the lunch hour, he was probably eating somewhere.

In her blind rush to his bungalow she hadn't taken notice of anything else. Now she saw a heavyset woman standing by a cleaning cart in front of the next unit down, staring at her curiously. She appeared to be Spanish.

Julie said, "Do you speak English?"

"Little beet," the woman said.

"The man in this bungalow, Señor Dawson. Do you happen to know where he went?"

"Swim." The woman pointed toward the beach.

"Thank you very much."

Julie made her way down to the beach. In the heat of the day, there weren't many people there. Then she saw an umbrella with a man lying under it. She started toward him and saw that it was indeed Ken. He was propped up, reading a newspaper.

She paused for a moment, studying him. He was a handsome man, probably better-looking than Shell but not nearly so tall or so well built. He was slender, with a rather large head, a mop of curly brown hair and brown eyes. The word for Ken, she just realized, was intense; he was intense about everything he did—too intense, she thought.

She resumed walking, and at the sound of her footsteps he glanced up, recognized her and put down the paper. He didn't speak, and he had a wary, waiting look on his face.

"Ken, I've been looking for you."

"Well, you've found me," he said in a neutral voice. "How are you this morning, Julie?"

She set herself. "I want you to go home, Ken. Today. I don't want you here any longer."

Expecting an explosion, she was startled by his calm demeanor. He got to his feet, brushing sand off his swim trunks. "That's what you want, is it?"

"Yes! Things are happening to me here, and you will only be hurt."

"I'm a grown man, Julie. I can take care of myself. And don't order me about like that!"

"Ken, please! I don't want you here."

"Well, *I* want to be here. I still have five days of my week left, and I'm staying. Julie . . ." He took her hands and drew her close. "What about last night?" He was watching her closely.

"Last night? What about last night?"

"Never mind, I have my answer." He shrugged and let go of her hands. He turned and scooped up the blanket he had been lying on, and the newspaper. "I'm ready for a shower, Julie. I don't suppose you'd care to join me?" He looked at her with a wicked gleam in his eyes, then shrugged again. "No, I imagine not. When you want me I'll be around, baby."

He walked off, and Julie stared after him, completely baffled. This was a different Ken from the man she thought she knew so well, and she didn't understand any of it.

All of a sudden she was swept by a feeling of dizziness, and she swayed, almost falling. The combination of the hot noonday sun and her mental upset was taking its toll. With difficulty she made her way back to the motel lobby entrance, intending to call a taxi. Luckily, one was just discharging a passenger, and she caught it back to Devereaux House.

For once the dimness and the almost eerie quiet were welcome. She was sure that Pauline had already left for the afternoon, and Helen usually took a nap right after lunch. Julie had seen very little of Pippen the past few days except at dinner time. She went upstairs, removed her sticky clothing and took a cool shower. Feeling better afterward, she changed into fresh clothing and marched down the hall to her grandmother's room. She knocked determinedly on the door. After a moment she heard a stirring inside, and a faint voice called out for her to come in.

She opened the door and went in. With all the drapes drawn and no lights on, the room was very dark. She made her way to the bed. "Grandmother, I must talk to you."

The old woman on the bed raised her head. "Who is it? Is that you, Melissa?"

Melissa? Julie's heart sank. Was the old woman having one of her bad spells? Helen had warned her that Stella Devereaux often lived in the past.

Taking two steps, she swept back one of the drapes, letting bright light in. Her grandmother cried out weakly, shielding her eyes with one arm. "The light, it hurts."

Steeling herself, Julie said firmly, "I'm sorry, Grandmother, but I have to talk to you. It can't wait."

Stella peered up at her, some intelligence seeping back into her eyes. "Oh, it's you, girl. What is it you want?"

"Grandmother, I've been told that there's a streak of insanity running through the Devereaux family."

Stella raised her head, her eyes suddenly fierce. "Who's been filling your head with such nonsense?"

"It doesn't matter who." Julie waved a hand. "Is it true?"

"Of course it's not true!"

"I understand that my great-grandfather was a pirate and a smuggler."

"That much is true, but that doesn't mean he was crazy."

"Didn't he murder people?"

"Murder? He probably killed a few people in his time, but that doesn't mean..." She gestured. "Help me to sit up, girl. Prop some pillows behind my head."

Julie gathered together three thick pillows and helped her grandmother to sit up while she put them behind her back.

Stella folded her hands primly in her lap and looked at Julie with a stern expression. "Those were bloody times, the times when Jean Devereaux sailed the Gulf. In the course of his piracy he may have killed people, yes, but I'm sure it was unavoidable. This country has a violent past, child, and a great number of the ancestors of people living today would be considered murderers in modern times. Although, come to think of it, with some of the things happening today, I don't know if it was any bloodier back then.''

''My father,'' Julie said relentlessly. ''I was told that he was unstable, not too sane.''

''That's a dastardly falsehood! Your father was wild, I'll admit. He was a man of strong appetites, appetites that you, Melissa, apparently couldn't satisfy. If a man like Reese can't find his pleasures at home, he'll go elsewhere.''

Dismayed, Julie said gently, ''Grandmother, I'm Julie, not Melissa.''

''Of course you are, girl! You think I don't know that?'' The old woman glared. ''Next thing you'll be accusing *me* of being crazy.''

Julie smiled tightly. ''No, Grandmother, you're far from crazy. But how about Rosellen?''

Stella's face went cold, and her voice grated. ''What about Rosellen?''

''I've heard some strange things about her, about some of the bad things she did.''

''Rosellen was...Rosellen was...the bad seed, the bad seed.'' All of a sudden her face went slack, her eyes going out of focus. She said petulantly, ''Tired now, Helen. Go 'way, leave me alone.'' She turned her face aside, covering her eyes with one thin arm.

Julie hesitated, feeling frustrated. Was the old woman faking so she wouldn't have to answer any more questions? Or had she slipped over the edge again? With a sigh she said, ''All right, Grandmother.''

She pulled the curtain back and made her way out of the room, closing the door softly after her.

The brief conversation had only confused her more. Standing before the door, she looked down toward the far end of the hall and saw the pull-down steps she had noticed before but had never investigated. She assumed that the steps gave access to the attic. She listened intently for a moment; the house was quiet. She started purposefully down the hall.

She reached up for the bottom rung and pulled. The steps started down but made an awful racket. She froze, listening for a few moments. When she heard nothing, she pulled the steps all the way down. Apparently they were rarely used.

This surmise was confirmed when she poked her head up into the attic. Dirty windows at each end let in sufficient light for her to see that the attic was packed with all kinds of junk: trunks; boxes; broken furniture; piles of old clothing; and, here and there, like headless bodies, women's dress forms draped with clothing dating decades into the past. Dust lay thick over everything.

And yet, when she finally stood upright in the attic, she saw a set of recent footprints in the dust, making a trail toward the back. They were small, and had to be a woman's.

Curious, Julie followed the footprints. She found herself tiptoeing, holding her breath. She had the strange feeling that the person who had made the footprints had preceded her by only a few minutes. Yet nothing stirred except dust motes disturbed by her passage. Could someone be hiding up here? It didn't seem likely. The roof sloped steeply down on both sides, and the only place she could stand fully erect was the narrow space down the center. Everywhere she looked, all available space, except for the lane down the center, was occupied. There hardly seemed to be space for anyone to hide.

"Is there anyone up here?" she said softly.

There was no answer, no sound, and Julie scoffed at herself. Why on earth should anyone be hiding up here?

She followed the footprints, which led to the far end of the attic and to a trunk so old that the leather straps were rotting and disintegrating. Julie saw where someone had been kneeling, and she knelt in the same place.

She held her breath as she slowly raised the lid, not knowing what to expect. Her first look inside was disappointing. All she could see were dresses piled to the top. They were folded neatly and looked as if they had been undisturbed for years. But when she touched them no dust flew, so she knew that they *had* been disturbed, and not too long ago.

More curious than ever, she began to take the dresses out one at a time, stacking them on the floor on each side of her. And then, halfway down she came upon a leather-bound book with a button clasp. It looked years younger than the clothes.

She picked it up, turned her back to the light from the nearest window and leaned against the trunk. She unbuttoned the book and saw that it was a journal of some kind, half the pages covered with handwriting.

She flipped to the first page, and began to read: "Today is our birthday. We are eleven years old. . . ."

TWELVE

October 2
Daddy is dead!

When I heard, I locked myself in my room and cried for the first time in years. Aunty Pip and Grandmother tried to get me to come out for supper, but I wouldn't. Finally I stopped crying and got really angry, madder than I've ever been. I wanted to kill somebody, most of all Mama. It's all her fault!

There was no longer any reason for Daddy to go away somewhere, not when we could be together on the Double Ellen. Mama drove him to it. They had a terrible fight last night. I tried to listen but I couldn't hear enough. I think it was about me.

I think Mama now knows what we've been doing. She has been looking at me in a strange way for the past few days. I know it's me she's wondering about, because I wore one of Suellen's dresses a few days ago just to see, and Mama was fine with me then.

She drove Daddy away and I could kill her for that!

It's true, Mama did drive him to it.

When I came out of my room this morning, she way-laided me downstairs and said to me that she was shamed by what I'd done, and asked me how I could do such a thing, how I could live with myself. I pretended that I didn't know what she was talking about. But I did. She did find out.

Because then she said, "You know why your father's dead? Because he couldn't stand the shame of people finding out. He deliberately flew his plane into the sea."

I screamed at her then, calling her a liar, and ran at her, beating her with my fists.

She was lying, I just know she was! Daddy would never deliberately do a thing like that. If he did, she drove him to it.

I have decided now. She has to die. I know how to do it too, and no one will ever know. A little while ago there was a telephone call from Marathon Key. The Coast Guard there says that a piece of a plane's fuselage floated ashore, and Mama is driving up there to see if she can identify it as a part of Daddy's plane.

The radio has been broadcasting hurricane warnings, and Grandmother and Aunty Pip have tried to keep her from going, but she said she's going anyway.

She's in her room now, getting ready. It will only take me a few minutes to slip down to the garage.

As I look out the window of my room, I can see that it is already dark and windy outside, with rain blowing across the ground.

It will be a perfect night for it.

Julie was numb with shock when she finished reading the last entry in Rosellen's journal. As she'd read, the attic had grown dim, and she'd had to squint to make out the lettering. Her eyes burned, the back of her neck ached, and she was cramped from sitting in one position for so long.

But her physical discomfort was minor compared to the mental anguish she felt. She found it difficult to believe that anyone could be so evil— and her own sister, her twin!

She closed her eyes, rubbing them tiredly, and leaned back against the trunk, her thoughts a maelstrom. Suddenly it seemed as if an awful abyss widened before her, and she could see images flickering in the depths, familiar images, and she sensed that the curtain obscuring her memory for eight years was about to drop away. . . .

And then the feeling was gone. The past had slipped away once more.

She looked down at the journal in her lap and a thought came to her. Perhaps this journal, this outpouring of evil, was just a child's fantasy, something Rosellen had made up.

No, it had the ring of truth, and it confirmed things that she had already learned. And besides, it all sounded familiar—somehow she *knew* everything was true. She had the sickening feeling that she had witnessed much of what was in the journal.

And then an even ghastlier possibility occurred to her. Suppose *she* was Rosellen, not Suellen? She squinted at the handwriting. It wasn't quite the same as her handwriting now, but the journal had been written eight years ago. And then she noticed the clincher—the *i*s all had a circle over them instead of a dot.

If she was Rosellen, it would explain many things. Her thoughts jumped back to something that had always bothered her—the fact that her hymen hadn't been intact when she'd first made love with Ken. If she was Rosellen and the journal was correct, she certainly hadn't been a virgin then.

But could she possibly have had sexual relations with her own father? Her whole being recoiled from the thought, her very soul revolted. And could she have done the other things? Been responsible for the death of Huey and her mother? Her hand flew to her mouth, stifling a scream; she bit down hard on the flesh of her hand until the blood came. Dear God in heaven, could it possibly be true?

She felt unclean and scrubbed her hands up and down her bare arms as though trying to rub away a layer of filth. She jumped up, dropped the journal back into the trunk and slammed the lid. Tears burning her eyes, she started toward the steps and then stopped as she noticed again the footprints in the dust. Had she made those tracks?

The footprints had been made by someone in her stocking feet. Julie slipped off her shoes and fitted her feet into the prints—a perfect match. Had she, in one of her recent blank spells, come up here and placed the journal in the trunk? And since she and Rosellen were identical twins, wouldn't their feet be exactly the same size?

Julie put her shoes back on and left the attic, pulling the steps back down into place, then trudged down the hall to her room. The house was still very quiet, and it almost seemed that she was the only person in it.

She removed her outer clothing and stretched out on the bed, staring up at the ceiling. It was completely dark now, and she didn't turn on a light. She willed her mind blank, yet thoughts kept chasing one another around in her brain. Finally she drifted into sleep.

The mirror dream began. This time she was in the attic, surrounded by mirrors; but instead of her own reflection, the journal was mirrored a thousandfold. The pages turned lazily, as though caught in a gentle breeze, and then stopped, as one page became enlarged and the damning words leaped out at her—"It finally happened!" Now human figures formed on the page, and Julie saw herself naked and writhing on her back, a man between her legs. The form of the man was as nebulous as smoke, and she could see only his back. . . .

A sound intruded on her dream, and she struggled awake. A light knock sounded on the door, and Pauline's voice said softly, "Miss Suellen?"

"What is it?"

"Supper will be on the table in about twenty minutes. Will you be joining us?"

Julie's first inclination was to say no, but she suddenly yearned for company, and she wasn't up to facing either Shell or Ken at the moment. "Will any of the others be there tonight?"

"Both your aunts will be eating here tonight."

"All right, Pauline, I'll be down, and thanks."

She removed the rest of her clothes and took a quick shower, then donned fresh clothing. The horror of what she had learned, of what she *feared* she had learned, still lurked in her mind, but she had to cope with it or risk losing her sanity.

THE FIRST THING that struck Julie at the dinner table was Pippen's attitude. She was relaxed, chatty; evidently her pique over Julie's insult to Running Elk had run its course. Helen Bronson sat silently for the most part, concentrating on her food, and scarcely seemed to be aware of Julie and Pippen talking back and forth across the table.

"I haven't seen much of you the past few days, dear," Pippen said brightly.

"I could say the same for you, Aunt Pippen," Julie pointed out.

"Yes, that's true. I had to drive up to Marathon Key a couple of times on some business. It took up more time than I thought. What have you been up to?"

"Not a great deal. On Sunday I went out on Shell's boat, and we were marooned on Smuggler's Island, until the Coast Guard rescued us." She watched Pippen carefully but detected no reaction other than mild concern.

"Good heavens! How did that happen?"

"He took me to the island on a picnic. I went to sleep, and Shell was snorkeling. When I woke up the boat was gone."

"Shell? That's the young man I met the day I came back, the lawyer?"

"That's the one."

"Are you getting . . . well, romantically involved with him?"

"I wouldn't call it that," Julie said, somewhat defensively. "I've been out with him a couple of times, that's all." She hesitated. "The young man I knew back in Moorestown, Ken Dawson, is in Key West. We're engaged to be married."

"Are you now?" Pippen smiled mockingly. "My, our little Suellen's a busy girl, isn't she? If he's here, why haven't we met him?"

Julie felt herself flushing. She said, "I don't think the time is right."

Pippen began to frown. "I hope you're not seriously thinking of getting married. I don't think that's a good idea at this time."

"Why not?" Julie said challengingly.

"Running Elk told me that this is no time for you to get married. You must wait. After all, you stand to inherit a good deal of money on your next birthday. You have to be sure the man you marry isn't just after your money."

"That worry wouldn't stop me, but you don't need to be concerned. I'm not going to get married until I get my head together."

Pippen looked at her narrowly. "Now just what do you mean by that?"

"Until I find out who I really am, until I remember what happened in that part of my life up until I was sixteen."

"I wish you'd stop that," Pippen said irritably. "There's no doubt you're Suellen. Running Elk assures me that's who you are."

"Running Elk may know, but I'm not so sure."

Pippen looked down at her plate. "As for your memory, how do you stand with that?"

"Sometimes I almost have it, everything seems about ready to come clear to me, then it slips away."

"Well, I wouldn't push it. All in good time, dear." Pippen took a bite of food. "This lawyer's boat, has he found out what happened to it?"

Julie made a startled sound. She had forgotten about Shell's boat, and she hadn't talked to him since she'd stalked out of the restaurant in a rage. She said, "He hasn't told me if he has. Aunt Pippen—" she looked directly into the woman's eyes

"—do you know exactly what happened to my . . . to Rosellen?"

Pippen's eyes went blank, and she glanced away. "There's no absolute proof, if that's what you mean, but Rosellen took the boat, the *Double Ellen*, out that night, and neither she nor the boat was seen or heard from again."

"But why would she take the boat out alone? I understand there was a bad storm that night, a hurricane."

"There was," Pippen said curtly. "Foolish girl. No boats were supposed to be out, and I understand that no others were. We were already in the middle of the hurricane. From what little information was finally gathered, Rosellen went out in the eye—in the center of the hurricane. When the eye moves in it's quiet for a period of time, no wind at all, but when the eye moves on, then the storm hits again, usually worse than at first. That's when Rosellen took the *Double Ellen* out, in the eye."

"But surely she knew all that?"

"Of course she did." Pippen shrugged. "The girl was very knowledgeable about boats and the sea."

"Then why did she do it?"

"One can only hazard a guess. She was distraught, that we know. Her father had recently been killed, and her mother had just died in an automobile accident. We don't know for sure if she knew about her mother's death, but we can only assume that she did. A phone call came about the accident, and we assume that Rosellen listened in on the extension. I answered the phone and was so upset by the news that I wouldn't have noticed.

"It was about an hour after the phone call that I discovered her missing. The news had been a great shock to Stella, and I was busy consoling her. When I finally had time to go look for Rosellen, she wasn't in the house. Naturally, it never occurred to me that she would be so foolish as to go out in the boat, or I would have tried to stop her."

"How about me? Where was I? Was that when I disappeared?"

"Yes, although we didn't know it at the time." Pippen looked at her closely. "Shortly after the phone call I heard you and Rosellen quarreling in her room. I heard loud voices and came out of Stella's room just as you slammed out of Rosellen's room. You refused to tell me what had happened and ran on out of the house. Stella called me back into her room. I thought you'd just gone out of the house to cool off. When I finally got a chance to go looking for Rosellen she was gone, too."

Julie closed her eyes tightly. Something had opened and closed in her mind, and she caught an almost subliminal flash of loud, vicious voices raised in a bitter quarrel. But what about? And who was quarreling? The door in her mind had opened and shut with the speed of a camera shutter, and the brief glimpse she'd had was not enough to tell her anything. Was she never going to remember, she thought in despair.

As if from a distance she heard Pippen's voice. "Is something wrong, Suellen?"

She opened her eyes and stared across the table at Pippen's concerned features. Julie shook her head. "No, nothing. Not really."

"You went white as a sheet."

"For just a second I thought I remembered a quarrel, but . . ."

Pippen looked at her keenly. "And that's all?"

"That's all. I don't even remember what it was all about. Aunt Pippen . . ." She looked down at the table, aimlessly moving her fork around on the tablecloth. Without thinking, she pressed down hard on the tines. "Did Rosellen put a circle over her *i*s, instead of a dot?"

Pippen got a startled look. "Why, yes, come to think of it, she did."

Involuntarily Julie pressed down hard, and the fork tines bent out of shape. Quickly she pushed the fork under the edge of her plate, out of sight.

Pippen was going on in a musing voice, "But then so did you. It was absolutely amazing how many things you did alike." She chuckled. "When one got sick, the other got sick. When one developed a certain habit, the other soon picked it up. That's what happened with the circle instead of the dot, you started it and Rosellen picked it up. You know, from what I've read of the study of twins, identical handwriting is rare. Often a difference in handwriting is one way to tell the difference between identicals. But not so with you two." Her gaze sharpened. "Why did you ask, anyway?"

"Oh . . ." Julie gestured vaguely. "I'd like to learn as much as I can about Rosellen."

"Well, study yourself and you'll see her," Pippen said with a laugh.

Helen spoke for the first time. "That's not true, Pippen, and you know it. They may have been as alike in looks and habits as two peas in a pod, but in temperament they were totally different."

"That's what you and Stella always said, but I could never see it," Pippen snapped. "Oh, Rosellen may have been a little...well, a little more volatile, more mischievous, while Suellen was more restrained."

"Volatile, my foot! That's not the way I saw it," Helen said dourly. She got to her feet. "But then nobody ever listened to me, anyway. I have to take Stella her supper."

As Helen left the room, Julie said, "What did she mean?"

"Oh, don't pay any attention to her. Helen's an old maid and set in her ways. People always have favorites, and you happened to be the one she picked. I don't care what she says, she could never tell the two of you apart, either, not until Reese and I put our foot down and made your mother stop with the clothes."

"With the clothes?"

"Yes, Melissa wanted to do what so many mothers of identical twins do, always have you wear identical clothes, down to the color of your panties. Doctors will tell you that's not good for twins. Everybody needs *some* individuality. It took Reese and I a long time to get Melissa to allow you to dress differently, but we finally won out. After that you never wore the same dresses on the same day. Thank God, people could finally tell you apart, at least when you were together."

"But about Rosellen . . . no sign of her was ever found, not even wreckage from the boat?"

Pippen shook her head. "No, nothing. But that's not unusual, not for a hurricane. In a bad sea a boat can break up completely. It's happened innumerable times before."

"Didn't she have a radio on the boat? Couldn't she have sent out an SOS, or whatever it is they do under those circumstances?"

"Certainly, the *Double Ellen* had a radio. Either she was hit too suddenly and without warning or Rosellen was too stubborn to radio for help. If she had a fault it was her stubbornness, her pride. Even in rough weather she probably thought she could make it through all right."

Julie said slowly, "It certainly appears to be a remarkable coincidence that we would both disappear on the same day, within hours of each other."

"Unless there's a connection."

Julie gave a start. "How could that be?"

Pippen shrugged. "If you don't know, I certainly don't. But there is one difference."

"And what is that?"

"You're alive and Rosellen isn't."

IN HER ROOM AFTER DINNER Julie sat for some time with her hand on the telephone. Finally she made a decision, picked up the receiver and dialed Shell's home phone.

It rang a half-dozen times before it was picked up on the other end and Shell said breathlessly, "Hello?"

"Shell, it's Julie. I was beginning to think you weren't home."

"I was in the shower. Late getting home." He sounded wary. "I thought of calling you a couple of times, but then I thought I'd give you time to simmer down."

"I'm sorry I blew up like that. I had no right."

"You probably had every right. I was out of line."

"No, you just told me the truth." She added hastily, "But that doesn't mean I'm going back to Dr. Reardon. Shell, have you had any word of *Dancer II*?"

"Not a peep. It's beginning to look like I was wrong. She may have been stolen after all. Otherwise she would have surfaced before this. Either that..." His voice turned glum. "Or she's sunk without a trace."

"Oh, I hope not, Shell," she said in distress.

"Well, so do I. Julie, is everything okay with you?"

She hesitated for a moment.

"Julie?"

"No, nothing's wrong. Not any more than before," she said with a trace of bitterness. "I just wanted to hear your voice and let you know that I was no longer angry with you."

"You don't know how relieved that makes me feel, Julie," he said softly. "Look, I haven't had anything to eat yet. I was about to throw a frozen dinner into the oven, but I'd much rather take you out."

"I've already eaten, Shell."

"Well, how about this then. I'll have my TV dinner, then you join me at Tony's Bar for a drink?"

Her first impulse was to refuse. From the intimate note in his voice she concluded that he would want her to go back to his apartment, and she wasn't sure she was up to that. Then she thought of the journal. She had to discuss it with someone, and who better than Shell? She said, "I think I'd like that."

"Fine! What time should I pick you up?"

Again she hesitated, remembering Pippen's remark when she'd told her aunt about going out with Shell. She said, "I'd rather you didn't do that. It's now almost eight. Why don't I meet you at Tony's at 9:30?"

"But why don't you want me to...? Never mind, I'll see you at Tony's then, 9:30. I'm looking forward to it."

After she'd hung up Julie sat for a bit, thinking over her decision. Would it be a mistake to show the journal to him? If he reached the conclusion that she was Rosellen, he might never want to see her again. She decided it was a risk she had to take. Shell, she realized, was becoming very important in her life, and it would accomplish little to hide things from him.

A few minutes after talking to Shell, Julie heard a car start up in the driveway, and she knew it was Pippen driving away in her rented car. She usually went out shortly after dinner. Neither Stella nor Helen owned a car, and the two-car garage alongside the house had been converted into a tool shed. Julie had asked Pauline about that, and the black woman had told her: "Miss Stella hasn't allowed us to own an automobile since your mama died in that car accident. I have to do all the grocery shopping by cab."

Julie changed into fresh clothing and cracked the door slightly. She listened intently; all she could hear was the murmur of Helen's voice reading to Stella in the old woman's bedroom.

Julie moved quietly along the hall and pulled down the attic steps as slowly as possible, hoping they wouldn't squeak this time. They made almost no noise at all. Had someone oiled them? She went up the steps into the attic, which was quite dark, with only a little illumination coming up from the hall light.

Reaching for the light switch, she flipped it on. A small bulb in the center of the attic came on, giving off a faint, yellow glow.

She lifted the lid of the trunk and went down on her knees beside it, groping with one hand under the old clothes. She couldn't find the journal. Frantically she tossed all the clothes out, emptying the trunk.

The journal was gone!

Mind reeling, she got slowly to her feet, then froze as the floor creaked behind her and a mocking voice said, "Is this what you're looking for?"

She whirled around, and for a moment she thought she was looking into a mirror. Everything about the figure standing halfway between her and the attic entrance was identical—the features, the hairdo and every item of clothing. There was one difference—the journal was held in the other woman's hand.

Now the woman raised the journal; her smile was cruel and taunting. "I said, is this what you're looking for, sister dear?"

"Rosellen!" Julie gasped out.

"Oh, no. How can that be? Rosellen is dead, everybody knows that." Rosellen laughed; it was a light, girlish sound that was at odds with the cold expression on her face.

And with that the curtain of eight years that had been hiding Julie from the past fell away, and she remembered everything.

"What's the matter, sister dear?" Rosellen said, moving closer. "You've turned pale as a ghost! I assure you that I'm real enough, that I'm not a spirit that Aunty Pip conjured up."

"I . . . I remember. . . ." Julie said faintly.

Rosellen laughed again. "Oh, do you? I've heard about your loss of memory, although I've never believed it. It was all too convenient."

"Oh, dear God!" Hand at her mouth, Julie stared at her sister in mounting horror. "It's all true, what you wrote in the journal. What you did with . . . with Daddy, and I saw you under Mama's car, tinkering with it. I didn't think anything of it at the time. But when the call came, telling of the accident and Mama's death, I knew! You had tampered with the steering mechanism. *You* killed Mama!"

"She deserved to die," Rosellen said calmly. "She was responsible for Daddy going into the ocean. If she hadn't gone on so about me and him. If she hadn't made him feel so guilty."

"You . . . you enticed him into—" Julie broke off, unable to finish.

"*Enticed* him?" Rosellen laughed. "I only let him do what he wanted to do all along. You never did learn much about the birds and the bees, did you, sister?"

"But with your *own* father," Julie whispered, her face twisted in disgust.

"It was great, sister," Rosellen said with a shrug. "But then you never would have, would you? And of course Daddy would never have dreamed of doing it with you."

"And it was you with Ken, wasn't it? Not me."

"Your guy's not all that bad, once you get him acquainted with what it's all about."

"You put that journal where I'd find it, didn't you? Why?"

Rosellen shrugged again. "I thought it was time you knew what was going on. As I said, I never did believe that lost-memory bit, but I thought that if it was true, reading my journal would help you remember."

"But why, *why*, did you want me to remember?"

"Because I want you to suffer before you die," Rosellen said sweetly.

"Die?" Julie said in confusion. "I don't understand."

"We're trading places, sister dear, and since Rosellen is dead, it seems appropriate that you be!"

Julie recoiled. "You must be insane!"

"Why? Because I'm telling you all this? Do you think you can just run out into the street yelling, 'Rosellen is alive!' Nobody will believe you. I understand that people are beginning to believe that you're playing with less than a full deck now. Try to tell them that I've come back from the dead and you'll qualify for the funny farm. The only way anyone will believe you is to see the two of us together, and that will never happen, believe me.''

Julie shook her head. Things were coming at her too rapidly. She couldn't believe that she was having this impossible conversation. "But why, why, do you want to kill me?"

"The money, sister dear, the Devereaux money," Rosellen said casually. "In eight months you're twenty-five, *we're* twenty-five, and the money comes to Suellen Devereaux. And I'll be Suellen. It's as simple as that.''

Fear clogged Julie's throat, and she backed up a few steps, her hands coming up defensively.

Rosellen laughed harshly. "Oh, don't worry, I'm not going to do it now, not here in the house. I have all of eight months, and I want you to live part or all of those months in terror, always waiting for it to happen." She smiled sweetly. "I know what you're thinking, you're thinking of going to the police, aren't you? Do you think they would believe you? A ghost is out to kill you?''

"There's no need for this," Julie whispered. "I don't want the money, you can have it all.''

"Now you must think I *am* crazy.''

"If you come back, showed yourself alive, you'd be entitled to half.''

"I don't want half, I want it all. And when I come back, it will be as Suellen. I want you *dead*, dear sister. I've hated you ever since I can remember. I've always had to share everything, everything except Daddy. I want you to suffer. Mama didn't. I made a mistake there, but I won't with you.''

"You *are* crazy!"

"We'll see who's crazy after you spend weeks or months being frightened of every shadow." Rosellen stepped aside, motioning with a mocking gesture. "Go now, sister. Run before you're forever cemented to that spot!"

Julie edged past her, her gaze never leaving her sister's smiling face, until she reached the attic steps and started down them, almost falling in her haste.

PART TWO

Flight

THIRTEEN

SITTING ALONE in the main cabin of the *Adventuress*, Rosellen raised her glass of champagne in a toast to the game to come.

Her plans were going well; so well, in fact, that it was almost too easy. It was too bad that her sister didn't offer more of a challenge. It was going to be a very one-sided contest.

But then, Suellen had always been a mouse and she, Rosellen, was a cat. It was well-known that cats liked to play with a mouse before the kill. Let's see how you like to play the cat and mouse game, sister dear, Rosellen thought.

The image pleased her and she laughed aloud, reaching for the half-empty bottle of champagne. Yes, things were definitely going her way; but then they always had. She was one of those people whom fortune favoured. It wasn't all good luck, though; her own cleverness was also a factor.

Looking out the window of the comfortable cabin cruiser, Rosellen could see the smooth blue water of the harbor where the boat was docked. She liked living aboard the cruiser and didn't mind the inconvenience that came with living on the water.

The *Adventuress* was really the *Double Ellen* in disguise, just as Bettina Powers was really Rosellen Devereaux in disguise; it was a parallel that amused her.

The metamorphosis in both instances had been amazingly easy. Just a week before his death her father had purchased supplies to repaint the *Double Ellen*, and the paint had been on board when Rosellen had fled Key West for the deserted cove where she and her father had first made love.

She had reached the cove just as the eye of the storm passed, only minutes before the full force of the hurricane returned.

The cove was well protected, and the *Double Ellen* rode out the storm unscathed as Rosellen drank champagne and wept for her dead father. She drank until she was deathly ill and then vomited until her stomach was sore.

The next morning was clear and calm, and she put her grief behind her with the storm and began painting the boat, painting out the name first. It took her ten days to finish the task.

She had anchored the boat under the concealment of the trees that overhung the water; and although several times she saw planes overhead—planes she was certain were searching for her—she was not discovered. She half expected a Coast Guard cutter to nose into the cove looking for her, but during her stay there she never once saw another boat.

At the end of the ten days, her food supply was gone and she knew that she had to leave the cove.

She was fortunate in one respect—she wasn't without resources. She and Suellen had always been given generous allowances, and their father had also given Rosellen additional sums of money from time to time.

After he and Rosellen became intimate, he also began to give her jewelry; small pieces, but of considerable value. Since Rosellen knew that if she wore the pieces the rest of the family would begin to wonder where she got them, she hid them away. She thought of them as her secret treasure trove.

In addition she managed to take several large and very expensive pieces of her mother's jewelry. Her mother was very careless with such things and often left them lying on her dresser. Since her carelessness was well-known, no one ever suspected theft.

Consequently, on the night she left Key West, Rosellen did so with more than three thousand dollars in cash and jewelry worth at least ten thousand more. The latter she intended to sell discreetly, confident of her ability to handle such a transaction and not get cheated.

So, on the eleventh day of her disappearance, she took the newly painted *Adventuress* into the harbor at Key Largo.

Under cover of darkness she located a drugstore, where she purchased a large bottle of Egyptian henna, and by morning her hair was a deep red. The next day she bought clothing, choosing styles that would make her look older and more sophisticated.

She also visited an ophthalmologist, using the name Bettina Powers and telling him that she was an actress and needed blue lenses for a film role. The lenses made the transformation complete.

Even after her new look was established, Rosellen was careful. She remained secluded on the *Ad-*

venturess for over a month, leaving only for necessities, meanwhile planning her future moves.

The first thing she had to do was get false identification papers for herself, mainly a birth certificate under the new name showing her age to be twenty-one. First she got a social security card under the new name. The card presented no problem, but the birth certificate was a different matter. She needed money, so she went scouting around the underside of Miami, where it was said that almost anything could be bought or sold. By dint of shrewd bargaining, she finally sold the jewelry for close to ten thousand dollars.

It cost her two thousand dollars to have a birth certificate forged under the name of Bettina Powers, plus a false bill of sale for the *Adventuress*. But at least she could now go about registering the boat legally under her new name.

The next thing she had to do was going to be more difficult, she knew. Although Rosellen considered herself fully capable of operating the boat on her own, she realized that she needed a man for what she had in mind.

After several forays into various bars along the east coast of Florida wearing her "adult" clothes— spike heels, a short skirt and a blouse with a low neckline—she found the man she was looking for in a waterfront bar in Fort Lauderdale.

It was early afternoon, and she was perched on the bar with a glass of champagne. The bar had only a few patrons; she was the only woman present.

As he served her, the bartender leaned close to growl, "No working this bar, girlie. No hookers in here. Do you read me?"

"Oh, I read you, loud and clear." She looked around with a sniff. "I don't see anyone here worth my time anyway. Can I just have a glass or two of champagne and some peace and quiet?"

"Just so long as that's it."

Rosellen hid her smile in the glass of champagne. She wasn't too displeased at being mistaken for a hooker. It wasn't exactly the image she'd meant to convey, but it would do.

She glanced around again. In a far corner at the back of the bar, a man sat alone in a booth, hunched over a drink. He had on rough clothing, and from his appearance Rosellen was sure that he was a seaman of some sort. He was big, with bulky shoulders and thick, dark hair curling out from under a cap. His face was dark, scowling.

After a moment she made up her mind. She ordered another glass of champagne and walked back to the booth. He didn't look up until she slid into the booth opposite him.

Then he looked up with angry black eyes. "Buzz off, sister," he said in a deep voice. "I'm not in the mood. Besides, I don't have any money, even if I was horny."

She said with a bright smile, "I just noticed that your glass is empty. I thought I might buy you a drink."

"Why?" he said challengingly.

Close up, she saw that he wasn't too bad-looking, and the big hands wrapped around his glass looked capable. He leaned toward her. "I asked you a question. Why come on to me?"

"I'm alone and so are you." She shrugged, dipping her shoulders forward slightly so that he could get a good look at her cleavage. "You looked lonely and I just thought you'd like some company. Just some conversation, that's all I'm after. And since you say you're broke, I'll buy the drinks."

"I've never been known to turn down a free drink, but I would still like to know—"

He was interrupted by the bartender looming over the table. "Is she hustling you, Gus?"

For the first time, a glint of humor struck the man's eyes as he looked over at Rosellen. "I don't know. Are you?"

Rosellen looked up at the bartender. "All I'm doing is buying the man a drink, bartender. So why don't you just bring us another glass of champagne and whatever he's drinking?"

The bartender's gaze locked with hers for a moment. Then he shrugged and returned to the bar.

"So you're Gus?"

"That's right, Gus Tatum. And you're...?"

"Bettina Powers."

From approaching other men such as this one over the past few days, Rosellen had developed a feel for it. "Gus, I'd guess you're a sailor, right?"

"Yeah." Gus retreated into sullenness again. "Or was. I'm thinking maybe I should take up another line of work."

"Why? I gather from what you said that you're broke. Lose your job?"

"Lost my boat is more like it. The boat I was skippering. It was confiscated last night, and it looks like I won't even be able to collect my back salary.''

"Confiscated? For what, smuggling?"

"Hell, no! If that was the case I'd be in the slammer, now wouldn't I?'' He glowered at her. "The guy who owned it owed the banks a bundle. They took it away from him—'' He broke off, staring at her narrow-eyed. "How come you mentioned smuggling?''

Rosellen shrugged. "Half the boats on the Keys are into smuggling.''

He looked outraged. "That doesn't mean that I'm involved in smuggling.''

The bartender came with fresh drinks, and Rosellen paid him, pointedly not tipping him.

She raised her glass. Gus already had his big hand wrapped around his. She said, "Here's to smuggling.''

Gus gave her a quizzical look, then tasted his drink.

"I own a boat,'' Rosellen said casually. "A big fast mother, faster than most.''

His eyes narrowed. "*You* own a boat? You're putting me on.''

"I own her free and clear, no banks will confiscate her. And I need a skipper. I can skipper her myself, but for what I have in mind I need a man.''

He eyed her speculatively, and Rosellen was pleased to note that he was showing an interest in her as a woman for the first time. The fresh drink must have tickled his libido.

"How old are you?''

"My age has nothing to do with anything.''

"That all depends. In some ways you look old enough, and then again I get the flash that you can't walk into a voting booth yet."

"For what I want I don't need to vote." She looked at him boldly. "I'm old enough, Gus."

"I'll bet you are, I'll just bet you are, by God." He chuckled hoarsely and downed the rest of his drink in one gulp.

Rosellen turned around to catch the bartender's eye and motioned for another round.

"You're free with the booze, I'll say that for you," Gus said.

"I like to see a man get what he wants."

"Do you now? The question is, what do *you* want?"

"I told you, I'd like you to skipper my boat."

"And what will we be doing? Shrimping? Taking out those rich northern dudes to catch the big one?"

"Smuggling. We'll be smuggling whatever's the most profitable."

Gus stared at her, then threw back his head and roared with laughter. "You don't waltz around the tree, do you, girlie? By God, you've got gall! I think I like you. I think we can do business."

IT WAS THE BEGINNING of eight exciting, lucrative years. At least once a month during those eight years the *Adventuress* had run in a load of coke or grass, and now and again a load of illegals. Rosellen didn't like ferrying the aliens—they fouled up her boat, defecating or urinating whenever or wherever the urge struck them. She only resorted to alien smuggling when she could hike the tariff to double the going price.

Never once during those years was she caught. A few times they were stopped by patrol boats as searchlights pinned the boat in a blaze of light like an insect. But it was never anything more than a routine patrol, the patrol boat having encountered them by chance, and Rosellen always came up on deck, squeaky-clean, dressed demurely and looking as innocent as an angel. They were never searched, not even when several million dollars worth of cocaine was in the hold below. These encounters scared Gus speechless, but the danger always gave Rosellen a rush.

In the beginning Gus surprised her. She had figured that he would come on to her, but he had fooled her. He kept his distance, which not only puzzled her but piqued her a little. She had been sure in the bar that he was sexually attracted to her.

Finally, after several months, she said bluntly, "I want to ask you something, Gus. You've never made a move on me, not once."

He looked at her, his eyes unreadable. "That's right, and I ain't about to."

"But I don't understand. In the bar, you—"

He interrupted her with a nod. "Yeah, you made me horny that day. But after watching you for a bit, I realized something."

"And what is that?"

"You can't be much over seventeen, kid. Oh, most of the time you act older, but little things give you away. I like the way you handle yourself, and I think we can make some bucks together. But I'm not a cradle-robber, so if you expect me to bounce you, forget it. I'll stick to the tramps, that's more my style anyway. Now if that sticks in your craw, tell me and I'll walk.''

"No, no. We'll work well together. I was just curious.''

Rosellen maintained a low profile. She kept pretty much to the boat in whatever port they were in, and for a while contented herself with the excitement and danger of the smuggling. That never palled, but in time it wasn't quite enough. More than a year had passed since she'd left Key West. In the beginning she had bought all the newspapers, but the story of the disappearance of the Devereaux twins had soon died when nothing new had developed. Clearly she was thought dead at sea; as for Suellen, she had simply disappeared without a trace.

At last she felt secure enough to venture out, at first only in the larger cities—mostly in Miami— where she courted anonymity. By now she didn't really have to dress and apply thick makeup to look older, yet she continued to dye her hair and wear the contacts; there was always the possibility, however remote, that she might be recognized. She met men in singles bars, where she could saunter in and choose a man without being thought the worse for it.

All in all, she was content with her life. With her looks and figure she had no trouble getting all the casual sex she wanted, which was the way she wanted it. She didn't miss permanent attachments. It was rare that she ever slept with the same man twice.

She had all the money she needed, and the thrill and excitement of smuggling had never lessened, for the possibility of being caught was always there, every time the *Adventuress* nosed among the Keys with a load of dope or illegals. . . .

Rosellen was jolted back to the present by a slight movement of the boat, followed by the sound of footsteps on the deck. She sat up, listening intently. She was expecting a visitor, but the footsteps were wrong—far too light.

A knock sounded on the locked cabin door, and a woman's voice said, "Rosellen, let me in."

Rosellen set her empty champagne glass down and crossed to the cabin door to unbolt it. Pippen Delacroix rushed in, disheveled, eyes blazing with excitement.

"Pippen," Rosellen said crossly, "how many times have I told you not to come without letting me know in advance?"

Pippen waved a hand impatiently. "I tried to call, but your line is out of order."

Rosellen sighed. "Not again! Well, I assume something important brought you up here. What is it, Pippen?"

"Oh!" Pippen collected herself. "Suellen has flown the nest again. Just after you were at Devereaux House, she packed up and left."

Rosellen shrugged. "I can't say I'm too surprised."

Pippen stared. "I must say you're taking it calmly enough. She was packed and out before I knew it. By the time I learned of it, she was long gone. I have no idea where. Pauline saw her leave, but she claims that Suellen didn't tell her where she was going. But then, Pauline might be lying. I never did trust that woman, and she took a fancy to Suellen.''

''We'll find her,'' Rosellen said calmly.

''How? You probably never would have found her the first time if I hadn't noticed her leaving the house and followed her, then saw her hitch a ride with that truck driver. It took me years and a lot of money to track him down and learn that he dropped her off in Key Largo, and that she'd taken a bus from there to Connecticut.''

''And I'm sure that's where she's gone this time. Where else could she go? Little sister doesn't have the guts to hide among strangers. She probably thinks she's safe there, but she'll soon find out how wrong she is.''

''There's one other thing. It's different this time. That senile old woman opened a bank account for Suellen several days ago, twenty thousand dollars! I checked at the bank this afternoon. Suellen drew it all out before she left Key West.''

''Well! It appears that little sister has more spunk than I gave her credit for. But the money won't do her any good. I'll catch her sooner or later.''

''I still don't see why you didn't finish it while she was here.'' Pippen sighed in exasperation. ''Stealing a boat and leaving Phipps and Suellen stranded. A fat lot of good that did! And when you pushed her into the water, you should have hit her over the head first so she couldn't swim.''

''I wasn't ready for her to die. I want to have some fun with her first.''

''Fun! You know, the longer this thing stretches out, the riskier it becomes.''

"She has it coming to her. I want her to know that she's going to die, I want her to know and suffer. She's been free these eight years, while I've had to live in hiding."

"You've hardly suffered, my dear Rosellen," Pippen said dryly. "And besides, much as I'd like to see her dead and you in her place, it isn't Suellen's fault that you've had to hide."

"Yes, it is," Rosellen said obstinately. "She's just like Mama."

"Rosellen..." Pippen sighed again. "For God's sake, end it, don't let it drag out."

"I'll do it my way, Pippen. You have no say in it." Rosellen's voice was cold and unyielding.

"You've changed, Rosellen. Eight years have changed you. You've developed a sadistic streak."

Rosellen laughed suddenly. "I'm no different now than I was eight years ago, Aunty Pip. You just didn't know me very well back then."

"I'll never understand why you waited six years to come to me, letting me think that you were dead all that time!"

Rosellen shrugged. "I thought it best that no one knew where I was, or that I was alive. And I had everything going for me. Sure, it bugged me that I'd never be able to claim the Devereaux money when I became twenty-five, but I didn't see any way that I could. If I came back, how could I explain where I'd been for six years?"

"Not to speak of all the trouble you'd have been in," Pippen said dryly.

Rosellen nodded. "That, too. Then I read that column in the Miami paper that the law firm of Henderson, Caldicott and Phipps was intensifying the search for the missing Suellen Devereaux, the vanished heiress who would come into millions on her twenty-fifth birthday, and I thought, why should Suellen get all that money? That's when I decided to get in touch with you, see if you had any idea where she was. It was a long chance, I knew, but I figured there was a possibility that you *might* know. After all—'' she grinned sardonically ''—there was always Running Elk.''

Pippen ignored the gibe. ''And it's a good thing you did. And you did take a chance.'' She got a sly look. ''I could have tattled on you.''

''I knew you would never do that. If I couldn't trust you, Aunty Pip, who could I trust?''

Pippen fell serious. ''And you were right. You always were my favorite, Rosellen.'' She stepped forward and embraced the younger girl.

Rosellen suffered the embrace for a few moments, then stepped back. ''Of course, one reason you're helping me could be because I promised you a cut of the inheritance.''

Pippen shrugged. ''One can always use more money. There is never enough, and it's nice to have a cushion for my old age.''

''You'll get your share, Pippen.'' Rosellen smiled cruelly. ''When Suellen has her twenty-fifth, when I come back and take her place.''

''Meanwhile, what are you going to do about Suellen?''

''I'll take care of her, you can be sure. Let her run free awhile, thinking she's safe . . . then, zap!'' She made a chopping motion with one hand.

"Well, I just hope you know what you're doing." Pippen sighed. "It was a hot, sticky drive up here. I think I'll take a quick shower."

"No!" Rosellen said sharply. "I'm expecting someone, Pippen," she said curtly. "You'll have to leave. I told you to always warn me when you're coming up."

"Expecting someone?" Pippen said in a complaining voice. "Who?"

"If you must know, a man."

"What man?" Pippen exclaimed.

"Now that, Aunty Pip, is none of your damned business."

"Don't get so high-handed with me." There was a shrill note in Pippen's voice now. "You owe me a lot. I don't think it's too much to ask—"

"It *is* too much to ask," Rosellen interrupted in a cold voice. "Now, leave."

"You're hard and cruel."

Rosellen laughed. "It's a hard, cruel world, Aunty Pip. To survive, you have to be cruel in return."

"I don't see how you can treat me this way after all I've done for you."

"What have you done for me lately? You helped me find Suellen, granted, but am I supposed to be grateful for the rest of my life for that? Besides, you're getting paid, well paid. Now I want you to leave, Pippen, before my guest arrives."

Pippen opened and closed her mouth, then turned huffily and marched out.

Rosellen turned away to the champagne bottle, poured another glass and sat down. She wondered if Pippen would linger somewhere on the dock to get a peek at her visitor. Rosellen shrugged. Let her get a look, for all the good it will do her.

Ten minutes later the boat rocked and she again heard footsteps on the deck. Heavier this time.

At the knock on the door, Rosellen got to her feet, arranged a seductive smile on her face and opened the cabin door. "Come in, big guy. I thought you'd never get here."

FOURTEEN

IT WAS EDGING INTO AUTUMN when Julie returned to Moorestown. A few leaves were beginning to turn, and the night air was brisk. A marked contrast to Key West.

There were other contrasts, as well. An air of peace hung over the town. No brightly clad tourists were visible, and the conservatively dressed men and women on the streets went about their business in a brisk, no-nonsense manner.

As Julie went along the tree-lined street toward the Malone residence, she felt peace steal over her soul. She felt safe here, protected from all harm. She was Julie Malone. Suellen Devereaux did not exist, had never existed.

The feeling of safety was an illusion, of course. If Rosellen intended to kill her—and little doubt existed in Julie's mind as to that—she would eventually come after her here. What had she said? "I have all of eight months, and I want you to live part or all of those months in terror, always waiting for it to happen."

Even if Rosellen didn't guess where she'd gone, it would be easy enough to run her to earth. Julie had made no effort to hide her tracks; she had caught the commuter flight from Key West to Miami and then the first flight north, leaving her just an easy train ride to Moorestown. Strangely, this time she had felt no dread of flying.

On the trip north her mind had often focused on Shell. What had he thought when she hadn't kept the date with him? And what had he thought when he'd discovered that she had fled Key West again? Of course, with the strange way she had been acting, it was quite likely that he had simply washed his hands of her, deciding that he was better off without a weirdo cluttering up his life.

She experienced a moment of regret. She liked Shell, she liked him very much, but how did she know that he wasn't in cahoots with Rosellen? She didn't dare trust him, she didn't dare trust anyone!

Not even Ken. Would *he* worry that she had disappeared? More important, would he suspect that she had fled back to Moorestown and come after her? Julie had the feeling that Rosellen would keep her affair with Ken going. She might even let him in on her dark secret. There was scarcely any doubt in Julie's mind which of them he would choose if he ever got the pair of them sorted out.

But whatever happened between Rosellen and Ken, one or the other would soon be coming after her. Unconsciously her step quickened. No, Moorestown wasn't a refuge; it could even end up a trap. She would have to be on her way somewhere else, and soon. But first she needed a day or two to draw a deep breath and think it all through. She had fled Key West in a blind panic, yet she knew that it had been the right thing to do.

The story of Rosellen's perfidy, her disappearance and her return was all too incredible for anyone to believe unless she could produce Rosellen in person, and how could she do that?

There was one fortunate factor—the twenty thousand dollars Grandmother Devereaux had placed in the bank account for her. Julie hugged her purse tightly under her arm. She had experienced a few moments of guilt about that; she had felt almost like a thief, sneaking that money out of the bank. Yet why should she? She was a Devereaux, there was no longer any doubt of that in her mind. So the money was rightfully hers. And she would certainly have need of it if she expected to hide from Rosellen; but the thought of running, of hiding, depressed her. When would it ever stop? Her only hope was to invent a new identity for herself and cut all ties to anyone she knew, including Ken and the Malones. Maybe in time Rosellen would be exposed for what she was and be made to pay for her crimes. Yet Julie realized that this was unlikely; her sister was too clever, fiendishly clever. When the time came she would simply show up as Suellen Devereaux, and who could expose her, or even suspect her?

Julie turned a corner and there it was, the big two-story house with the huge elms in front and the sweep of lawn enclosed by a brick fence. The lawn was turning brown, and the elms were losing a few leaves. The elms, more than a hundred years old, had escaped the elm disease that had swept through the east a few years ago.

Julie paused at the gate, setting down the one bag she had carried with her. She felt a strange reluctance to enter the house; at the same time she wanted to run inside and close the door against the terrors pursuing her. She had always felt so safe and loved in this house. But how could she ever feel that way again? To allow herself to hide there as if in a sanctuary would be a grave mistake.

She drew a deep breath, picked up her bag and pushed open the gate. At the front door she hesitated again. She had a key to the house, but since she hadn't called to warn of her sudden return, it might not be wise to let herself in. Her unexpected arrival would be shock enough.

She rang the doorbell, knowing she would have to wait a minute or so. It was near the dinner hour, and Alice Malone would be in the kitchen preparing dinner. She loved to cook, as her ample figure showed, and was quite famous at church socials and county fairs for her pies and cakes, jams and jellies.

Then the door swung open and Mrs. Malone stood there, an apron around her waist, wiping her hands on a towel. Her face was flushed from kitchen heat. The woman's gray eyes flared wide, and she gasped, "Julie! Goodness me, what a surprise!"

Then Julie was in her arms. Voice muffled, she said, "Oh, Mom! It's good to be home!" She knew that she would always think of this woman as her mother.

"I'm so glad you're home, dear, but..." She held Julie away from her. "Is anything wrong?" Alice Malone asked.

Julie had wondered all the way up here what she was going to tell her adopted parents; but now that the moment was at hand, she knew that she could tell them little of the truth. The less they knew, the better off they would be. She realized belatedly that she could be putting them in danger by just being here. She said, "Not really. It's just so...so strange down there. I guess I was homesick."

"Well, I'm just glad to see you. Come on in, don't stand there. Wait!" She moved to peer outside. "Did Ken come back with you?"

"No, Mom. He's still in Key West. That's one reason I came back. Ken and I . . . well, we had a quarrel."

"A quarrel? Oh, my, I'm sorry to hear that."

"He's staying down there for a while. He said he had some vacation coming."

"That boy works hard enough, he probably needs it." Mrs. Malone smiled complaisantly. "It's just a lovers' spat, I'm sure. It'll all blow over."

"I doubt it, Mom. Ken's...well, he's changed."

Alice Malone looked distressed. "Oh, I would never have thought..." Her glance sharpened. "Is it because of the money you stand to inherit?"

Julie seized on the excuse eagerly. "I think that may be it."

"It has been decided then that you're actually this Suellen Devereaux?"

"I don't think there's any doubt about that." Julie sighed. "But it's . . . it's complicated."

"We'll talk about it later." The woman shut the door. "I'm in the middle of fixing dinner. I must have had some idea that you were coming home. I'm frying chicken, just the way you like it."

"Is Dad home?"

"He'll be back directly. He walked downtown for some pipe tobacco."

"I'd like a bath and a change before dinner. It's been a long, tiring trip."

"Of course, dear. You go right on up to your room." Mrs. Malone smiled. "I haven't touched it while you've been gone, except to clean and dust. By the time you're finished, dinner should be ready."

Julie went up the stairs to her old room. It was on the east side of the house, getting the full benefit of the sun in the morning. The room was indeed just as she had left it—an old-fashioned fourposter with a colorful quilt that Alice Malone had made with her own hands, and comfortable furnishings. Closing the door behind her gave Julie such a sense of security that she almost wept. Perhaps it was a false security, but it was welcome at the moment. She wandered around the room, touching things. There were many pictures on the walls—Julie in various stages of growing up from age sixteen: her graduation picture from high school, a picture of her in the short skirt of her cheerleader's uniform for the high school football games, and many others.

There had been times in the past when she had felt the room lacked something. She would be visiting the rooms of girlfriends, rooms filled with dolls that were no longer played with—at least not acknowledged—and there were none in her own room.

It was strange, she thought. Her old room in Devereaux House had remained unchanged during her long absence, and she had lived there for sixteen years of her life, yet this room seemed more like home to her.

She even had her own bathroom off the bedroom. She removed her clothes now, went into the bathroom and ran hot water into the porcelain tub resting on its four claw legs.

After a long and leisurely bath she felt much better, and more relaxed. In the closet in her bedroom she found her clothes as she had left them. She put on a pair of slacks and a sweater and went downstairs. Marvelous smells met her from the kitchen, and she realized that she was starving. Except for a luncheon snack on the plane, she hadn't eaten all day.

As she reached the bottom of the stairs, Bob Malone came out of the living room, a glass in his hand.

"Julie, I couldn't believe it when Alice told me you were back," he said in his slow, deep voice. "Welcome home!"

He held out his free hand and she snuggled into it, burrowing against his jacket. He smelled of pipe tobacco and a strong shaving lotion.

He held her away from him. "Let me look at you." His blue eyes searched her face intently.

Bob Malone was a tall, loose-jointed man with thick gray hair and a face lined and weathered with age. He had been in construction all his life until retiring a few years ago, and had owned a small construction firm that had had an unmatched reputation for reliability. He was a deliberate man who refused to be hurried, and he was the most unshakable person Julie had ever known.

"What happened, Julie?" he asked. "Why did you come back so quickly and without letting us know?"

There it was again, the question she didn't want to answer.

Apparently reading indecision on her face, he said, "Come on into the living room, Julie, and let me pour you a drink. We can have a few words in private. I think there's time before dinner."

Julie's thoughts were a tumble of contradictions as she followed her father into the living room. He picked up his pipe from the stand by his easy chair, relighted it, then went over to the small corner bar to pour her a drink. She watched him, this good, kind man, his movements economical and deliberate.

"White wine all right?" he asked.

"That will be fine, Dad."

It would be a great relief to tell him what had happened. She never for an instant doubted that he would believe her, no matter how fantastic her story. Bob Malone hated liars with a passion. He had ingrained this philosophy in Julie, and she had never once lied to him, no matter what the provocation. Could she lie now, or evade the truth, without his realizing it?

But if she told him everything, he would want to take some immediate action. He would want the police informed, and she wouldn't put it past him to insist on going to Key West to confront everyone involved. If he did that, Rosellen wouldn't hesitate to kill him. No, it was better that he didn't know all that had happened.

Julie felt a wave of sorrow. Soon, tomorrow or the day after, she was going to have to leave, leave without telling the Malones the reason or her destination, and they would be sorely hurt. They didn't deserve that, but what choice did she have?

Bob Malone came across the room with a glass of wine for her. He gestured to the couch across from his easy chair. "Sit, Julie."

Julie sat down, uneasy under his probing gaze. She said quickly, "Before you say anything more, I can't tell you very much."

His gaze didn't leave her face. "Can't? Or won't?"

"Won't, if you wish to put it that way," she said with a sigh. She tasted her drink. "To begin with, it's a crazy story."

"And you're afraid I wouldn't believe you? You should know better than that. I don't think you've ever lied to me, and I'm sure you wouldn't now."

"No, Dad, that's not it. I'm sure you'd believe me. But I don't want you and Mom involved."

He exhaled a cloud of aromatic smoke. "We want to be involved in anything that involves you."

She shook her head violently. "No, not this time."

"We've always thought of you as our own daughter," he said slowly, sounding a little hurt. "And we always thought you felt the same way. But I suppose now that you've discovered who you really are, maybe your real parents—"

"No, that's not it, either!" She leaned forward. "I will always think of you and Mom as my real parents. Besides, I found out that my real parents are dead, only my grandmother is still living. Dad, please respect my wishes in this. It has nothing to do with how I feel about you."

"Julie, are you in some kind of trouble? Or maybe in danger?"

She steeled herself not to look away. "No, nothing like that."

It was a moment before he spoke again, his gaze holding hers, and she was beginning to wonder if she had lied convincingly enough. Finally he nodded slowly. "Of course, we'll respect your wishes, Julie. You must have your reasons."

"I do, really I do. There's something else, Dad. In a day or so, I'll be leaving again."

"Back to Key West?"

"No. Not right away, at any rate."

"Where, then?"

"I'm sorry, I can't tell you that. It's better that you don't know."

He stared at her blankly. "Better that we don't know? How can that be?"

"Please, Dad. Don't ask any more questions. I can't answer them."

His face tightened. "You *are* in some kind of trouble, I can feel it. And you're acting very strangely, not like you at all."

"Strangely?" Her laughter had the scratching sound of near-hysteria. "You don't know how apt that is!"

"Bob? Julie?" Alice Malone stood in the doorway, beaming. "Dinner is on the table."

Bob Malone got to her feet. "Yes, dear, we'll be right in."

As Mrs. Malone went back into the hall, Julie hurried across to catch her father's arm. "Dad? Don't tell Mom any of what I told you. Please?"

He grimaced. ''I don't know anything I *can* tell her, you didn't tell me anything. But what is she going to think when you just up and leave without a word?''

''I know, and I'm sorry about that,'' Julie said wretchedly. ''It'll hurt her, it'll hurt both of you. But that's the way it has to be.''

THREE DAYS LATER, Julie still hadn't left Moorestown. When she'd awakened the first morning back home, it had been raining, and the rain had continued all that day and evening—as good an excuse as any to postpone her departure.

For most of the morning she had sat in the living room, a magazine in her lap, alternately reading and staring out at the driving rain. Alice Malone, a soap-opera addict, came in before lunch. ''Dear, is it all right if I turn on the TV?'' she asked tentatively. ''My favorite show is about to come on. But if you'd rather I didn't . . . ?''

''No, no, of course I don't mind, Mom. You go right ahead.''

She sat beside her mother on the couch, watching the melodramatic doings on the screen. She found the parallel between the myriad troubles of the TV characters and her own wryly amusing. Who would have thought a week ago, even days ago, that she would be caught up in events as unbelievable as a soap-opera plot?

After a bit she got up and wandered upstairs to her own room, and once again she found herself sitting on the bed staring out at the gray day. She felt lethargic, without energy or direction. She had decisions to make, but every time she tried to think in a straight line, her thoughts veered off on a tangent.

The trouble, she thought, was that she was totally out of her depth, as she suspected any civilized person would be. The survival instinct was in everyone, she knew, but in people like her, people whose lives had never been endangered, it atrophied from disuse. Someone like herself did not stand a chance against a truly ruthless person like Rosellen!

But perhaps her fears were groundless. Maybe Rosellen wouldn't pursue her. The threat to hound her might just have been meant to frighten her away from Key West and Devereaux House, and in that her sister had certainly succeeded. To come after her, Rosellen would be running some risk herself.

And so her thoughts ran, caught in a maze, blundering into one dead end after another.

Her third day at home dawned sunny and cool. At the breakfast table she said abruptly, "I think I'll take a walk uptown, maybe go to the park."

Bob Malone, absorbed in the morning paper, looked across the table at her in sudden alarm.

Julie shook her head slightly. "I won't be gone long. I'll be back, I promise."

"But of course you'll be back, dear," her mother said. "What a strange remark to make! But what if Ken calls while you're out? What should I tell him?"

"I don't think he'll be calling, Mom," Julie said tightly. "But if I'm wrong and he does, don't tell him anything. Please! Don't even tell him I'm here."

"Well, now, dear, I don't know. I don't much like to lie." Alice Malone glanced at her husband.

He said, "Don't worry about it, Julie. If Ken does happen to call, I'll handle it."

As she went upstairs for a sweater, Julie felt another wave of guilt. Now she had Bob Malone lying for her, a man who was adamantly opposed to falsehoods. She could only hope that Ken didn't call.

The downtown section of Moorestown wasn't very large—a three-block area of business establishments—and the Malone residence was only a few blocks away from Main Street. On the way Julie passed the two-story brick high school she had attended. She was assaulted by a wave of nostalgia as she walked past. Like most children, she hadn't been able to wait until she graduated and got out into the world of adults. Now she thought how nice it would be to still be in school, with nothing to worry about but homework, grades and dates! With a wry grimace she walked on. The real world had turned into a nightmare, but thinking back with longing to happier days would serve little purpose.

She met a few people she knew as she entered the business district. She nodded and spoke cordially enough to those who wished to chat for a bit.

She approached the Moorestown Sport Shoppe. She hesitated for a moment, then hurried on.

Then a voice called after her, "Julie?"

Her heart fluttering with dismay, she paused, turning back. The young man hurrying toward her was Ronald Harris, Ken's assistant in the store.

He skidded to a stop before her. "I thought I was seeing things when I looked out and saw you. But it is you, isn't it?"

"Yes, Ronald, it's me. How are you?"

"I thought Ken said you were down in Florida, in Key West?"

"I was, but as you can see, I'm back."

"Did Ken come back with you?"

She tensed. "I'm afraid not."

"I'm puzzled. He said he'd only be gone a week at the most, but I got a telegram two days ago saying he'd be away indefinitely. I called the motel where he was staying, but they told me he'd checked out. Do you know where he went?"

"I'm sorry, Ronald, I can't help you."

"But you must know why he's staying down there!"

"Ken and I had a fight. I'm afraid he didn't bother to confide in me."

"But what am I going to do?" Ronald's voice rose. "If he doesn't come back soon, the front office will find out and he'll be out of a job! I can't cover for him indefinitely."

"Apparently he found something better to do than run a sporting goods store," she said in a low voice.

He frowned. "What did you say?"

"It's not important." She gestured. "I'm sorry I can't help you, Ronald. I have to run now. Goodbye."

Without a backward glance, she hurried away. She continued to walk fast until she was out of the business district and approaching the park along the river that ran through the south edge of town—

Moore's Park, named after the founder of the town.

The park was oblong, running for about a half mile along the shallow, slow-moving river. There were a pedestrian path and a bicycle path, with benches and picnic tables, a cleared area for a baseball diamond and several swings for children to play on. The trees were shedding, and leaves lay scattered across the green grass. It was cool along the path, and the park was deserted. Julie pulled her sweater close around her and walked slowly, her head down against the chill wind.

She had often ridden her bicycle along here on weekends and afternoons after school, and she had met Ken here, almost two years ago. As a promotional gimmick he had outfitted a Little League baseball team with uniforms that had Moorestown Sports Shoppe emblazoned on the back, and he had also volunteered to coach the team. He had been supervising batting practice one spring afternoon and Julie, sitting off to one side on the grass, had been watching them. She noticed that he eyed her several times, and she also noticed that he was very good-looking.

Then one of the boys hit a foul ball in her direction that came at her low and fast. Slow to react, she just managed to turn her back and hunch her shoulders as the ball thudded into her right arm.

It stung for a moment, and she was rubbing her arm when Ken came loping over. "I'm sorry, miss. Are you hurt?"

She looked up into his eyes and smiled through the sting of tears. "Not really. I probably should have caught it, but I never was very good at catching a ball.''

And that was how it began. It seemed a long time ago now. . . .

So engrossed had she been in her thoughts that she hadn't heard the rising growl of a motor behind her. Whirling, she stood frozen—a large, heavy motorcycle was roaring down the path.

Her first thought was that it was illegal for a motorcycle to be on the path.

Hunched over the handlebars, the rider wore a helmet and goggles and a black leather jacket. No features were recognizable, and it was impossible to tell if the rider was a man or a woman.

Belatedly Julie realized that the machine was aimed right at her. This recognition broke her stasis, and she threw herself to one side. The wind created by the speeding cycle whipped at her sweater as she hit the ground. Gravel spraying up from under the spinning wheels stung her face. She hit the path and rolled over once onto the dead grass.

Then the motorcycle was gone, its roar diminishing. Julie's hands burned from contact with the gravel, and the breath had been knocked out of her. She lay prone for a moment, dazed.

Then a thought exploded in her mind. The rider had deliberately tried to run her down, there was no doubt of it.

She sat up in a panic, looking west along the winding path, expecting the cycle to come charging back, but the sound was fading into the distance. Only the sounds of birds annoyed by the unaccustomed noise disturbed the silence of the park.

She got slowly to her feet. Except for the gravel burns where her hands had skidded on the path, she appeared unharmed. She dusted herself off, and with a last glance back along the path in the direction the motorcycle had gone, she turned back toward the center of town, walking quickly.

After a few steps a voice behind her shouted her name, "Julie!"

She stopped, turning, and saw a man hurrying along the path toward her—a very tall man wearing a black leather jacket. Was he the motorcycle rider? Had he hidden his machine and come after her on foot?

The voice called her name again, and Julie recognized the man—Shell Phipps! She half turned to flee and then forced herself to stop and wait for him. She was almost to the street now. Cars were moving along the road, and people were on the sidewalk. If it had been Shell on the motorcycle, he wouldn't dare harm her with possible witnesses so near.

He caught up to her, breathing hard. "Julie! Damn it, I'm glad to see you!" He took her hand and gazed down into her eyes. "Even if you did stand me up and take off without a word."

She let her hand lie unresponsive in his. "How did you know where to find me?"

"Well, I figured that Moorestown was the logical place to look for you."

"I mean just now."

He looked blank for a moment. "Oh! I stopped by your house, and your mother told me you said something about the park.... Hey! What happened to your hand?'' He held it up, and Julie saw that it was blood-speckled from her fall.

She snatched her hand back. "I fell, stumbled and fell on the path back there.''

He took her arm, and they started walking on the sidewalk. "Julie, why did you just take off like that?''

For an instant she was on the verge of telling him about Rosellen, but she caught herself in time. "Because somebody was trying to kill me and nobody would believe me!''

"*I* believed you,'' he said reproachfully. "I'll admit that I didn't at first, but I came around to it.''

"You certainly didn't act like it.'' She stopped, facing him. "Shell, why did you come up here?''

"I should think that would be obvious. I came to see you.'' He spread his hands. "I was angry at first, your leaving like that, but it didn't last.''

"Nobody sent you?''

"Sent me?'' His brows furrowed. "Oh, you mean Henderson? No, I told him I was coming, of course, and he gave me leave to go. But he made it clear that it was on my own. He said that the firm had discharged its responsibilities in finding you.''

"You say you believe someone was trying to kill me in Key West. Would you believe someone just tried here?''

He stared at her. "Here? Are you sure?''

"That's how I got these.'' She held up her bloody palms. "I didn't just fall, a motorcycle tried to run me down back there on the path. I threw myself out of the way just in time.''

"A motorcycle? On the bicycle path?" He looked back into the park. "You sure it wasn't just an accident?"

"I'm sure it wasn't an accident. Besides, motorcycles are forbidden in the park."

"Maybe the rider didn't know that."

"There's a sign." She pointed to a sign posted at the beginning of the path: Motor Driven Vehicles Forbidden.

"How long was this before I came along?"

"Only a few minutes." She looked him directly in the eye. "And the motorcycle roared off down the path in the direction you came."

"That's funny, I didn't see or hear a thing. Of course, I didn't come the whole length of the path, I cut in from the side.... Wait a minute!" He gave a start. "Surely you don't thing that I—?"

"I don't know what to think!"

She turned and started along the sidewalk, hurrying.

"Julie!" He caught up to her and took her arm. "Julie, I wouldn't harm you for the world."

"I don't know that!" She tore her arm out of his grasp. "After all the things that have happened to me, I don't trust anybody. I'm going home now, don't follow me."

"But when can I see you, Julie?" he said in dismay. "I came all the way up here."

"Then go back, go back to Key West!" she said wildly. "I don't want to see you. I'm leaving Moorestown anyway."

"But where will you go?"

"I'm not telling you, I'm not telling anyone," she said in a choked voice. "So go back to Key West, Shell. Please!"

She hurried away, almost running, her eyes burning with tears. She glanced back once and saw him standing where she'd left him, staring after her.

"BETTINA?"

"Yes, Pippen?"

"I see you got your phone fixed."

Rosellen sighed. "Is that the reason you called, Aunty Pip?"

"Well . . . partly. I was wondering if you'd had any word of Suellen?"

"My dear sister ran right back to Moorestown, as I told you she would." Rosellen gave a chilling laugh. "She almost had a fatal accident two days ago. A motorcycle almost ran her down. Can you imagine something like that happening in a quaint, peaceful Connecticut village?"

"Another close call?" Pippen's windy sigh came over the line. "How long are you going to keep this up, Rosellen?"

"As long as I choose to!"

"Well, at least we know where she is."

"Oh, she's no longer in Moorestown. She took off the next morning."

"Damn! We've lost her again."

"On the contrary," Rosellen said calmly. "She took a bus to Texas, to Fort Worth. Out where the pickups roam and the wind blows free. Only dear sister is not free. I can jerk her chain any time I want to."

FIFTEEN

ONCE AGAIN Julie was on a bus, but she was heading west this time. Since recovering her memory she had lost her fear of flying, but she somehow felt that it was less likely she'd be followed if she took the bus instead of a plane.

Carrying only a small bag and her purse with the twenty thousand dollars in it, she had taken an early train from Moorestown to New York and then taken a cab to the bus station. As far as she could ascertain, no one followed her onto the train; and when she left it at Grand Central she was positive that she was lost in the crush of early-morning commuters. Certainly she saw no one paying her undue attention.

Of course, she was forced to admit to herself, she was new at this game of fugitive and pursuer; but when she was finally settled on the big cross-country bus, her destination Dallas-Fort Worth, she was fairly sure that no one had followed her on board. As the huge vehicle lumbered out of the terminal and into the heavy New York traffic, she leaned back and tried to relax.

As she had warned Bob Malone in advance, she had left without a word to her parents. She had left a brief note on the dresser in her room telling them goodbye, apologizing for her abrupt departure and promising to be in touch.

As for Shell, he had called last night and she had refused to talk to him. Bob Malone had taken a message, the name and telephone number of the motel where Shell was staying. As he had relayed the message, her father had given her a questioning look. Julie had turned away without a word.

Maybe she was wrong about Shell Phipps, maybe he had nothing to do with trying to run her down, but she was taking no chances. If her situation was ever resolved and she learned that he wasn't allied with Rosellen, she would apologize.

For a time she had believed herself in love with him. But then, she had thought she was in love with Ken. Now she wasn't sure about either man.

In any event, she had more important things to do than worry about the two men in her life. She had to survive; and for that she needed a new identity and a place to hide. Also, she had to find a job. Twenty thousand dollars was a great deal of money, but it wouldn't last forever.

Rosellen had assumed a different identity and remained hidden for eight years. Was she any less clever than her sister? Of course, there was one large difference—no one had been looking for Rosellen. She had been thought dead.

Eight years! It seemed like forever! And in her case it might be forever. The very thought filled her with despair. Somehow she would have to find it within herself to turn and fight her tormentor. Even a cornered animal turned and fought in the end, no matter how hopeless the battle.

But first she had to prepare herself, not only physically but mentally, as well. She had to put herself in a state of mind in which she *could* fight back. Three days ago she would never have considered such an action, but anger had been growing in her. Strangely enough, she was even more angered by the attack in Moorestown than by the two attempts in Key West. Moorestown was, as the saying went, her own turf!

No, she decided as the bus rolled on into the night, I'm not going to roll over and play dead. If I can't fight back somewhere along the line I'll have to run forever, and I can't live that way.

THE FIRST THING Julie decided as she got off the bus in Fort Worth was that she'd buy a weapon. She, who had never held a gun in her hand, much less fired one.

When she'd left Moorestown she hadn't had the vaguest idea where she was going. Now she suddenly realized that there was a subconscious reason she had decided to head west. It was probably the influence of television dramas, but she associated Texas and other southwestern states with great stretches of space, freedom to move around and the inherent right of a person to stand up to one's enemies—with a gun, if need be—and be praised for it. She also had the vague notion that it would be easier to purchase a weapon in Texas.

This, at least, she found to be true. Leaving the bus station, she walked into the first gun shop she came to and stared in dismay at the bewildering display of weapons.

A middle-aged man she assumed was the proprietor beamed at her from behind the counter. "Howdy there. Can I help you, little lady?"

She approached him hesitantly. "I'm looking for a handgun, but I know nothing about them."

"Glad to be of help. That's my business." He appraised her shrewdly. "For yourself, or a gift for someone?"

"Oh, for myself," she said. "I've just taken a job where I have to travel a lot, by car, and I'll be traveling alone," she improvised.

"I understand." The proprietor nodded solemnly. "Pays to carry a piece nowadays, especially a lady alone. Now, something you can carry in your purse?"

"Well, yes. I suppose that's where I'll be carrying it."

"I think we can find you something." He drywashed his hands. "Let me show you what I have in that line."

He spread a piece of felt on the countertop, unlocked the cases and placed several guns side-byside.

"Oh..." Julie made a helpless gesture. "I don't know one from the other."

"Well, here's a nice .38. Pick it up. Go ahead."

Reluctantly Julie picked up the gun indicated. It was heavy, it was ugly, and it looked alien in her hand. Almost involuntarily she gasped and dropped it.

The gun shop owner nodded, smiling slightly. "That one's a mite heavy, I'll admit. Here." He picked up another one. "Try this one. A .25 automatic. It's smaller, lighter, can fit into your purse without any trouble. It's easy to fire. It doesn't have the kick of a .45 or a .38, but it ain't too accurate over a distance. Still, she'll do the job at close range.''

Gingerly she picked up the .25. It was certainly lighter, and it was flat and compact. It also felt more comfortable in her hand. She turned, raised it and then lowered it again. ''It's not loaded, is it?''

''Never, little lady. No loaded guns in my shop. The pieces and the bullets go out of here separately. Don't want nothing going off accidentally.''

Julie raised it at arm's length as she vaguely recalled seeing a female detective do on a TV show and aimed it out the plate-glass window, looking down the sights. At that precise moment a man came walking along the sidewalk, right into her sights. She lowered the gun hurriedly.

Turning back to the proprietor, she caught him covering his mouth with his hand, and she was sure that he was hiding a smile.

''You recommend this one then?'' she said tightly.

''That one should do her,'' he said, solemn again.

''Then I'll take it. And bullets, of course. Three boxes, or however they come, and I'd appreciate it if you would show me how to load it.''

Julie filled out the appropriate forms and then, with the automatic and the boxes of bullets in her purse, she returned to the bus station, retrieved her suitcase from the locker and went down the street to a car rental agency. She wished she had a fake driver's license; but since she didn't she rented a car under her real name, putting down her destination as Houston. But instead of heading toward Houston, she drove due west out of Fort Worth on Interstate 20, past Mineral Wells and on toward El Paso.

I'm getting very good at lying, she thought ruefully, but then I'm going to have to be good if I'm to succeed at this.

After she passed through Odessa late that afternoon the countryside became more deserted. Flatland stretched for miles in every direction, with only an occasional ranch house marring the horizon. She started looking for a turnoff and soon spotted a gravel road leading to the right.

She swung onto it and drove until she was out of sight and sound of the highway, then pulled to the shoulder of the road and got out of the car. There were a number of empty beer cans littering the ditch. She gathered up a dozen and lined them up on a rock. Stepping back about twenty feet, she took out the little automatic and awkwardly slid in the clip the way she had been shown.

Raising the gun with both hands, she aimed at a beer can and squeezed the trigger. Despite what the gun shop owner had told her, the gun had a surprising kick, and she found it difficult to hold it steady. She peered at the can. It was untouched.

Grimly she kept at it until she had fired one box of shells. She had learned not to flinch as the gun went off, and she had improved at least to the extent that she could hit the can she aimed at one out of three or four times.

Still, the big question remained—could she kill someone, even to save her life? Well, she wouldn't know the answer to that question until the time came.

She got into the car, turned it around and drove back to the main highway. There she drove west again into the setting sun.

ON BOARD the *Adventuress*, Rosellen answered the ringing phone. "Yes?"

"I lost her."

Her hand tightened around the receiver. "You what?"

"She rented a car. Since she seemed to stick to buses, she caught me by surprise. I still would have been able to stay on her tail, but I had some bad luck. My damned car stalled. It had been running hot the last hundred miles before I got to Fort Worth, but I didn't dare stop to have it looked at or I would have lost her earlier."

"Where are you now?"

"Still in Fort Worth. My car is being repaired now. A hose had sprung a leak. I'm just lucky that I didn't burn out the motor. I did manage to worm some information out of the girl who rented her the car. According to her, Suellen put down that she was driving to Houston and would leave the car there."

"Unless she's stupider than I think, she isn't going to Houston. She's likely headed in the opposite direction."

"That's about the way I figure it."

"Well, she'll have to drop the rental off somewhere, so eventually they'll find it. Stick around Fort Worth until *you* find out."

"By that time the trail will be cold."

"At least that will give you a starting point. She's not smart enough to just vanish off the face of the earth. I turned this job over to you, big guy, because I thought you were smarter than she is."

"I *am* smarter. This time she lucked out on me. By the way, she bought a gun in Fort Worth."

"Did she now?" Rosellen's smile was slow, cruel. "Did she indeed! Little sister has more spunk than I gave her credit for. This game may get exciting after all!"

IT WAS QUITE LATE when Julie drove into El Paso, and she was exhausted. She turned into the first motel with a vacancy sign and got a room for the night. She took a hot shower and got into bed, but even as tired as she was it took a while to fall asleep.

Behind her tightly closed lids the endless highway unrolled before her eyes; the lights of passing cars flared like strobe lights, then were gone, leaving her following the cone of her own headlights. She shook her head violently and opened her eyes to stare up at the ceiling.

She thought of where she was. El Paso, right on the border, with Mexico just a few minutes away. Should she try to disappear into Mexico?

No! She shook her head again. It would be much too complicated. She didn't know the language or the customs. Even if she could successfully hide there, what would she do when her money ran out? It would be many times more difficult to find a job in Mexico.

Still, thinking of Mexico gave her an idea, one she would act upon in the morning.

IN THE MORNING she packed her small bag, stopped at the first coffee shop and ate a leisurely breakfast. Then she drove the rental car through the city toward the border entrance. There were several parking lots provided near the point of entry for people who left their cars and walked across the bridge into Mexico for shopping.

Julie parked the car in one of the lots, then wrote a brief note explaining where the car was parked. She put the note, the parking ticket, the rental agreement and enough money to cover the rental and parking costs into an envelope. She got out, locked the car, put the keys into the agency's heavy manila envelope and sealed the envelope. Carrying her suitcase, she walked out of the lot, dropping the envelope into the first mailbox she came to. She calculated that the envelope would not be delivered for a couple of days, and by that time she would be long gone. Hopefully anyone following her would think she'd slipped over into Mexico.

She caught a cruising cab and was driven to the bus station. The first bus into New Mexico left in an hour. She bought a one-way ticket to Albuquerque, and an hour later she was once again on her way west.

THE NEXT DAY, IN ALBUQUERQUE, Julie found a rooming house and paid a month's rent in advance. Then she found the social security office, where she filled out an application for a social security card using the name Janet Marlowe. She was told that she could expect the card in about six weeks.

Six weeks seemed such a long time, since she didn't dare do anything under her own name. She couldn't get a new driver's license until she had the card.

She knew that it was possible to buy all the forged documents she needed to establish a new identity, but she hadn't the faintest notion of how to go about it. She was positive that she had eluded any pursuers; on the other hand, she was convinced that Rosellen wouldn't give up easily.

So she would just have to keep a low profile and not call attention to herself in any way. She had told the lady who owned the rooming house that she was grieving over the sudden death of her parents and that she had come to New Mexico from New York to find a new life for herself. The landlady seemed to accept her story without question, and Julie was sure that the woman wouldn't bother her so long as the rent was paid on time.

Julie decided to spend the time getting to know Albuquerque and perhaps take the bus to Santa Fe and Taos. She had heard that Taos was beautiful, and an artist's retreat.

"THE RENTAL CAR was left in a parking lot in El Paso, Rosellen. Just a few minutes walk from the border. Do you suppose she hopped over into Mexico?"

Rosellen thought for a moment, then said slowly, "I doubt it very much, it doesn't feel right to me. It wouldn't hurt to check it out, but I'm convinced she wants us to *think* that's where she's gone."

"You think she's that smart?"

"She got away from you in Fort Worth, didn't she?" Rosellen said sharply. "Where are you now?"

"Still in Fort Worth. I just found out about the car a while ago. But my car is fixed now, and I'll head for El Paso as soon as I finish this conversation."

"All right. When you get there check out the border crossing. If there's nothing there, start with the trains, airlines and buses. I'm sure she won't stay around El Paso, not after dumping the rental car there. Try the bus lines first." She smiled coldly. "My dear sister seems to have a thing for buses."

IT WAS NOVEMBER NOW, and it was cold in the higher reaches of New Mexico, where Julie was spending a few days. Although she understood that Taos had grown considerably over the past few years, with the addition of new, modern buildings, it still retained most of its old charm. The air was crystal-clear and invigorating. The old adobe town had been built around a square, and Julie thought that it had to be one of the most charming and colorful squares in the world.

As she strolled around, she heard a musical mixture of tongues and saw a dazzling display of color, both in the clothing the people wore and the breathtaking display of artwork. Taos had long been a mecca for artists.

Since it was a sunny day, many artists had their work in the open around the square. Bold paintings bursting with color; metal and clay statuary, both modern and old in design; intricate gold and silver work of every imaginable kind, including beautifully wrought jewelry; and Indian blankets and handmade clothing. In addition to the out-door displays, the square was lined with shops specializing in local crafts.

Julie wandered, absorbed in the marvelous things on display, forgetting her troubles for most of the afternoon.

She had often wished that she could be an artist. She had always had a great appreciation for art, but she had quickly learned that she had absolutely no talent.

Thinking of the money she had now, she itched to buy something. There were many things she would have loved to have, yet she knew it wouldn't be wise. Aside from the fact that she might need every dollar she possessed, she couldn't afford to load herself down with things; she might have to travel fast and light at any time.

Sometime later, she began to notice a number of men eyeing her closely. None of the faces struck her as familiar, but then, Rosellen might have hired strangers to follow her.

Then, as she stopped to admire a painting of a beautiful Indian maid, a good-looking, casually-dressed young man with his shirt open to his navel and a silver chain dangling around his neck sidled up to her.

"I've been watching you, and you seem to be alone," he said throatily. "You're a beautiful lady, did you know that? Could I buy you a drink?"

Julie drew back in alarm, tensing to flee, then made herself relax. "I'm sorry, but I'm expecting someone."

"You are?" He looked around exaggeratedly. "He's a little late, wouldn't you say? You've been wandering around alone for quite some time now."

"No, I just came early. I wanted to do some shopping," she said quickly. "I have to go now."

Ducking her head, she hurried in the direction of the bus station. It would soon be time for the bus back to Albuquerque, anyway.

After a few steps she slowed, looking back. The man had already turned away, walking in the other direction. Julie had to laugh to herself. My paranoia is showing, she thought; he was only trying to make a move on me. I should be flattered instead of spooked.

A MONTH LATER she received her social security card in the mail. The same afternoon she went down to the license bureau, received a temporary driver's license and was told that her permanent New Mexico license would be mailed to her in about a month. This was a disappointment. She was beginning to feel nervous about remaining in Albuquerque and felt it was time to be moving on.

It certainly took a long time to establish a new identity, she thought in annoyance.

When she returned to the rooming house, the landlady intercepted her on the way to her room. "There was a guy here looking for you today."

Julie felt a chill. "Who was he?"

The landlady shrugged plump shoulders. "How should I know?"

"You mean he didn't even give his name? You talked to a perfect stranger about me?"

"Oh, he gave me a card saying that he was an insurance investigator, but I know a liar when I see one. No more an insurance investigator than I am." The woman shook her head. "Besides, who says I told him anything? He was looking for a Julie Malone." Her faded gray eyes were shrewd. "But you're Janet Marlowe, ain't that right? Leastways, that's what you told me."

Julie tried to hide her relief. "Yes, of course," she said hastily.

"'Course I didn't believe you, not for a minute. Like I said, I can always spot a liar. But it ain't no skin off me. I never did like the law and never give them the time of day if I can help it, so I told him that no Julie Malone lived here."

"He was a police officer?"

The woman shrugged again. "Of one kind or another, would be my guess. Maybe a private cop. But I'm going to have to ask you to move on, girlie. I don't want no trouble to disturb my place, and running from the law like you are..."

"But I'm not running from the—" Julie bit the words off.

"But you're running from somebody, ain't you? If you're this Julie Malone and this guy comes back and finds you here, there's bound to be trouble. I can smell it coming."

"Don't worry, I'll be gone first thing in the morning."

JULIE DIDN'T WAIT until morning. She packed her bag and slipped out of the house shortly after dark. As far as she could tell, she left unobserved. She had noticed a motel on the highway about a mile from the rooming house. She walked all the way there and got a room for the night.

In bed, staring sightlessly up at the ceiling, she pondered. How could Rosellen's cohorts have discovered that she was in Albuquerque? She realized that she was totally inexperienced at hiding, but she thought she had covered her tracks fairly well. Clearly she had not. She wished now that she had used another name at the rooming house. If the landlady hadn't lied to her, she had not told the man looking for her that Janet Marlowe was Julie Malone. Apparently she had not, or the man would most certainly have been waiting for her. Julie had needed a mailing address for her social security card and her driver's license, so she had used her new name at the rooming house. Now she realized that she should have had them sent general delivery.

Julie was first in line at the license office the next morning. She told them to forward her permanent license to Phoenix, Arizona. She told the clerk that an aunt was dying and she had to leave for Phoenix at once.

Two hours later she was on another bus going west. As the bus left the outskirts of Albuquerque behind, a sudden thought occurred to Julie. Why hadn't she asked the landlady for a description of the man searching for her? If it was a man of un-usual height, it had to be Shell Phipps. She shook her head in disgust at herself.

SIXTEEN

WHEN SHE GOT OFF the bus in Phoenix, Julie was rumpled, tired and disgruntled; and as she lugged her bag out of the station and saw the stream of people on the street, she felt a flare of rebellion. Was she going to have to run and hide forever? Damn Rosellen! Julie knew that this was just the reaction that her sister expected and wanted; Rosellen was undoubtedly enjoying herself immensely, thinking of Julie in just this kind of situation!

She stood back against a building for a few minutes, out of the press of the pedestrians. There was a coin-operated newspaper dispenser right beside her. Through the dirty glass she could read a blaring headline: Winter comes to the east. Record cold.

Here the sun shone brightly and the temperature hovered near eighty. At least, she thought, if she had to play hide-and-seek, she had picked a good place for it. The warmth was certainly preferable to a raging blizzard.

Moving to the curb, she flagged down a taxi and asked the driver to take her to a medium-priced hotel, where she registered under yet another name.

Once in the room, which was neat and clean if not luxurious, she drew a steaming bath and sank into it gratefully. Julie let the hot water soak away her fatigue as she thought of what she would do next.

She would have to stay in Phoenix until her New Mexico license arrived, for she had to have that as proof of her identity as Janet Marlowe, an identity she meant to finally establish as soon as the license arrived. It didn't matter that her pursuer obviously knew her new alias.

Leaning her head back against the tub, she closed her eyes. Such a short time ago, life had been so uncomplicated. What had she done by opening the Pandora's box of her past?

"I'M SORRY, Rosellen, but she's gotten away from me again."

Rosellen tightened her hand around the receiver. "What happened this time?"

"Well, as I told you, I've tracked her as far as Albuquerque. She took a bus here from El Paso. But this is a fair-sized city, and after getting off the bus she just plain dropped out of sight. I've worn out a pair of shoes canvassing hotels, motels and rooming houses for over a month. So far, no Julie Malone, no Suellen Devereaux."

Rosellen snorted. "You think she'd be using one of those names? She may be a little dense, but she's not stupid."

"Then it strikes me as pretty damned hopeless."

"Nothing is hopeless. If she is establishing a new identity, she'll need at least two things, a driver's license and a social security card, under whatever name she's using."

"I don't have the clout to dig up that kind of information. I don't know a soul in New Mexico."

"You can get to know someone, can't you? Use that charm of yours, get acquainted with one of those female clerks in the license bureau."

"That's going to take time and money."

"We still have plenty of time, still four months until *our* twenty-fifth birthday. And I'm supplying the money." She smiled coldly. "Just think of it as an investment that will pay off soon. You *are* sure that Suellen got off in Albuquerque, not someplace else?"

"Oh, she got off here, there's no doubt of that. I had to work my way through damned near every bus driver in the company, but one finally recognized her picture."

"Then when you find out what name she's using, start working on bus drivers again. I'd say check with those going west first. For some strange reason, dear sister seems to be headed west."

JULIE MADE GOOD USE of the time while she waited for her driver's license. She bought a mousy brown wig and started wearing large glasses with tinted lenses and black plastic frames. She also bought new clothing, staying away from her favorite colors, veering toward rather dowdy styles. By the time she received the New Mexico driver's license and checked out of the latest of a series of motels and hotels—she had been moving every five or six days as she gradually changed her appearance—she concluded that she had disguised herself about as much as she could.

Finally she studied a map of Arizona, trying to decide on her next destination. She decided upon Sedona and Oak Creek Canyon. According to the guidebook, the weather was nice most of the year and the scenery was marvelous. It was also a small town, unlike the larger cities where she had been stopping, and so would break her pattern. If someone was still following her, this might throw them off the trail.

Arriving in Sedona, she was forced to agree that it was indeed lovely. The trees along the creek running through the town were a riot of colors, and in that respect reminded her of home. To the north towered the pine-studded slope leading up to the plateau that eventually ended at the Grand Canyon. Also to the north and the west bulked huge buttes of many colors. She had read somewhere that many Westerns had been filmed in the area, and she could easily see why.

She got a room in a motel near downtown Sedona and settled in. She spent the first week sightseeing, taking the bus to Jerome, which had once been a booming mining town and then a ghost town for a long period of time. It was now bustling again, having become a haven for artists and writers. Jerome perched right on the side of the bluff that formed the south side of the valley.

On other days she wandered along Oak Creek and around the village. Sedona had once been small, but it was growing, and many fine homes had been built. Yet it was still far from being a city, and she felt more at home here than in Phoenix or Albuquerque.

But by the third week in Sedona she was becoming restless; and she knew she would have to find something to do or she would soon be climbing the walls with boredom. She knew it would be unwise to look for a job at her usual profession, for somewhere she had read that people could be traced through the patterns of their work and recreational interests. So it would have to be something low-profile and, unfortunately, low-paying.

She found there were few job opportunities in Sedona, but at last she obtained employment in a barbecued-ribs-and-chicken place. The pay wasn't much, but the hours weren't too long, the work wasn't too arduous, and it kept her busy.

She also found a small furnished apartment to rent within walking distance of her job, and she opened a checking account in a local bank under the name of Janet Marlowe. She hesitated for a long while before finally deciding not to deposit what was left of the twenty thousand in the bank. She fully realized that it might be foolish to keep the money on her person or to hide it in the apartment; she could easily lose it, or she could be mugged. On the other hand, she might have to leave at a moment's notice, and having to wait until the bank was open to get her money would put her in far greater danger. According to all reports, Sedona had a low crime rate. She could only hope that such reports were true.

She enjoyed her work, and the people she worked with were friendly and helpful to her.

One girl, not yet twenty, was *too* nice. Kathy Dennis was solicitous when she learned that Julie was a stranger in town and had no boyfriend.

"Girl, you must be awful lonely, knocking around all by yourself," she said to Julie.

Julie shrugged. "It's not so bad. In fact, I don't mind at all being by myself."

Kathy's brown eyes were shrewd. "I'll bet you broke up with someone, right? That's why you came here, to get away from a bad scene?"

Julie looked away evasively. "You could say that, I suppose."

"Honey there are a lot of nice guys around. I could introduce you to some, if you'd like."

Julie stopped herself short of a hot retort and said merely, "Thank you, Kathy, I appreciate that, but I can find my own guy if I decide I want one."

Kathy looked at her appraisingly. "Well, you're not too bad-looking, I'll say that, although you would look a lot better if you'd do something with your hair, use a little more makeup and wear some sharp clothes."

"Anything else?" Julie asked, feeling a mixture of amusement and pique. Her disguise was evidently working, but she wasn't sure she liked being thought dowdy.

"Well, yes," Kathy said, shaking her head. "You keep acting the way you have been, you'll never get a man. If a guy even gives you the time of the day, you get skittery as a bug. Some guy must have really come down hard on you."

After that conversation, Julie tried to relax, realizing that Kathy was right. There was no earthly reason she should be afraid of some man who'd lived in Sedona all his life. It was only strange men that she had to be wary of. And, she admitted to herself, she was lonely. With every passing day it seemed that any possible threat to her became less. Either she had managed to hide herself well enough or Rosellen had given up.

Christmas came and went, and she felt even lonelier. She didn't even dare to send the Malones a Christmas card; it was just too risky.

One man who came into the restaurant for lunch almost every day was Dan Renfro, a salesman from a real estate office just up the street. He was around thirty, ruggedly good-looking, with laughing gray eyes and unruly blond hair. He was amiable, quiet-spoken, with none of the glibness associated with salesmen. He wore Western clothing, right down to the cowboy boots, but that was hardly unusual; half the population in Sedona wore Western clothing.

He always had a pleasant word for Julie and finally one afternoon, after he finished his lunch, he drew her aside. "Janet, there's a new Robert Redford movie showing in Flagstaff tonight. Would you like to go with me? We could have dinner first, if you'd like."

Julie was a little taken aback. She saw Kathy watching her and knew that the other girl had overheard. She said quickly, "Why, yes, Dan, I think I'd like that."

"It's a good forty-five-minute drive to Flagstaff. What time do you get off?"

"Five o'clock."

"Suppose I pick you up at six? That give you enough time?"

"I think so."

''Six it is, then. You'd better dress warmly. It gets cold up there on the mesa this time of year.''

Julie gave him her address, and he departed with a wave of his hand to Kathy.

''Well! You're finally taking the plunge, I see.'' Kathy's voice held a tinge of envy. ''Dan's been coming in here as long as I've been working here, and he's never made a move on me. I was beginning to think that he was gay.''

''What do you know about him?''

''Not much,'' Kathy said with a shrug. ''I understand he's been in Sedona for two years. He's a nice, quiet sort of guy, never comes on strong. And he's not a chaser. Far as I know, you're the first. I understand he went through a messy divorce out in California and came here to get away from it.''

DAN RENFRO WAS ON TIME. He was dressed casually, with a mackinaw over a sports shirt. He nodded with approval when he saw that she had on pants and boots, with a heavy sweater around her shoulders. ''I see you took my advice.''

She smiled. ''Oh, I'm from the northeast, I'm used to the cold. In fact, it might be a welcome change.''

''I'm a native Californian, one of the rare breed. So I'm accustomed to mild weather. That's one reason I chose Oak Creek Canyon. Never gets too cold, and hardly ever gets too hot.''

Outside, Dan indicated a pickup truck. ''I guess I should have warned you about my mode of transportation. Maybe you don't much fancy going on a date in a pickup.''

"I don't mind at all. In fact, it might be kind of fun. I notice that many people own pickups out here. I've never ridden in one. I've always thought they were used mostly by ranchers."

"Maybe they once were, but as you say, many people drive them now. Since the agency supplies me with a car to drive house-shoppers around, I can indulge myself. A four-wheeled vehicle like this is great for knocking around in the desert, any rough country. I have a sort of hobby, gold hunting." His laugh had a hint of embarrassment.

They were at the pickup now. He opened the door and gave her a hand up onto the high step and into the cab. It was roomy inside and quite comfortable.

"A gold hunter? Have you ever found any?" she asked as he got in behind the wheel.

"Nothing worth bragging about." He started the pickup and drove away. "But it's fun to poke around the countryside on my days off and look. There are all sorts of stories about lost gold mines in Arizona. Who knows, I might stumble onto one same day. But mostly I do it for fun, that sort of thing. I've been a city boy all my life—Los Angeles. Now it's great to be out in the open, knowing there isn't another soul for miles."

"I don't know. It's all kind of scary, all this open space." Julie shivered slightly. "I'm still not used to it. But I must say it's beautiful."

They were beginning to climb now on the steep switchback road. Oak Creek Canyon was down below them, and there were pines alongside the highway. Julie noticed that Dan was a good driver, with excellent reflexes, and that he rarely took his gaze off the winding road.

"How much of the state have you seen, Julie?" he asked.

"Not a whole lot," she admitted. "Just Phoenix and Oak Creek Canyon. Oh, I did go over to George for a day."

"Well, as the saying has it, you ain't seen nothing yet. Monument Valley, for instance. And there's the Grand Canyon. That's something else, it really is. I can never get enough of it. I've been up there a half dozen times since I've lived here."

"I do want to see it. I've heard a lot about it."

"Nothing you've heard can do it justice. Maybe we can drive up some time on your day off." He darted a sidelong glance at her. "It's not all that far from Sedona."

She tensed, then forced herself to relax. "We'll see how it goes, Dan."

IT WENT VERY WELL—the evening, at least. They had fine steaks at the Western Gold Dining Room, then enjoyed a good movie. It was the first movie Julie had seen since before she'd gone to Key West. Dan was good company, easy to be with. It was nice to spend time with someone with whom she could be herself, or as much of herself as she could be under the circumstances. She spent a relaxed evening, almost succeeding in forgetting her troubles.

When they arrived back home, Dan saw her to her door. Instead of kissing her good-night or even attempting to make a pass, he took her hand in both of his and looked deep into her eyes.

"I've had a fine evening, Janet," he said in a husky voice. "It's been a while since I've enjoyed myself like this. This is a small town, insofar as its permanent residents are concerned, so I'm sure you've been told something about why I came here."

"Yes, I understand you're divorced."

"That's right, I am. But it's been two years now, so you'd think I'd be recovered, wouldn't you? To tell you the truth, I guess I've been gun-shy. I just didn't have the inclination to ask a woman out. You're the first."

"Then I suppose I should feel flattered," she said with a soft smile.

"I don't know about that, but I certainly hope this isn't the only evening we'll have together."

"I enjoyed myself, too, Dan. And I would be delighted to go out with you again."

"Great!" He squeezed her hand gently, then smiled. "Maybe you'll go up to the canyon with me? It looks like it's going to be a short winter. Maybe I can even talk you into going muleback down into the canyon."

She stared. "On a mule?"

"They take sightseers down into the canyon on mules, all the way to the Colorado River."

"I don't know, I'm not much of a rider," she said dubiously. "And I've certainly never ridden a mule."

"They use mules instead of horses because mules are more surefooted. The trail going down into the canyon is a real switchback, with steep drop-offs. But it's safe enough." His quick smile came. "There is always a guide along, and they haven't lost a tourist yet."

Julie started to say, "We'll see," but quickly changed her mind. "That sounds like fun, Dan."

"Good! I'll watch the weather reports for a good day. In the meantime, how about dinner again soon?"

"All right."

"Then I'll say good-night."

"Good night, Dan."

He waited until she had opened the door and clicked on the inside light. Then he nodded and turned away.

Inside, Julie leaned back against the closed door, a musing smile on her lips. It was nice to feel wanted, to have the attention of a man again.

The apartment was small, with just a living room, a bathroom and a kitchenette. The couch made into a bed. Pushing away from the door, she went into the bathroom and checked the tank of the toilet. The waterproof plastic bag with the money was still there, taped to the inside of the tank. She supposed that wasn't the most original place to hide money, yet it was the best place she could think of; it would certainly be foolish to carry the money on her person, and she had to hide it someplace.

OVER THE NEXT MONTH Julie went out with Dan Renfro three times: twice for dinner, and the third for an all-day drive out into the countryside. It was an exciting day, different from anything Julie had ever experienced. They traveled over roads that were little more than tire tracks, but Dan's pickup had little difficulty.

The day was beautiful, clear but cool, and the scenery was breathtaking. Julie was really a small-town girl. During her childhood in Key West and the later years spent in Moorestown, the country was within a short drive of either place. However, the countryside there was nothing remotely like this. She felt dwarfed by the immensity surrounding her.

Dan had brought along a picnic lunch, and they stopped in the early afternoon at a spring in the shadow of the multicolored buttes towering above them. Dan had been mostly silent during the long, arduous drive, concentrating on his driving, only occasionally pointing out an animal or some particular point of interest that he wanted her to notice.

But when they were in the green oasis around the spring, the picnic lunch spread out before them, he turned his full attention to her. "Well, what do you think so far?"

She brought her attention back with an effort. She had been reminded painfully of the picnic lunch she had shared on the island with Shell Phipps.

"What can I say?" She shook her head. "All this is pretty overwhelming."

He nodded. "That's what I thought when I first came out here, but it grows on you." A shadow crossed his face. "Of course, I was running then, running from my ex-wife, and full of self-pity. When I finally realized that you can't run away from your problems, I emerged from the fog and almost decided to return to L.A. and face up to everything. Then I suddenly took a look around and realized what a damned fool I'd be for leaving all this. I've never once regretted staying here.''

As he poured two plastic glasses of wine and gave her one, Julie heard his words echo in her mind: ''...you can't run away from your problems...'' What would he think about the problem she was running away from? What a relief it would be to tell him everything!

Then he said, ''And you, Janet? What are you doing in Sedona? I know you haven't been here too long.''

She knew then that she couldn't tell him the truth. If he believed her he might want to help, and she had no right to involve him in her troubles. She remembered what she had led Kathy to believe, and she said, ''I'm out here to escape an emotional problem, too. Oh, not quite like yours, no divorce, just a shattered romance. I'm from the east coast, like I told you, and I've always wanted to see the West.''

''Are you over him?''

''What?'' she said, startled.

''I said, are you over him, this guy you were involved with?''

''Yes. At least I hope so.''

''Good. I hope so, too.'' He touched her hand. ''That leaves the way clear for me.''

Her first instinct was to snatch her hand away. The last thing she needed right now was an emotional attachment. If she had to run again at a moment's notice, she would only leave more hurt behind.

Something of what she was thinking must have been mirrored on her face, for Dan said quickly,

"Oh, don't worry, I'm not going to rush anything." He smiled wryly. "I've waited this long to get involved again, so a little longer shouldn't be any great hardship. It'll give us both time to be sure we're well again."

Julie relaxed then, smiling over at him. What harm could it do? She had to admit that Dan, by his attention, by just being there, had filled a void in her life.

IT WAS QUITE LATE when Dan dropped her off at the apartment, much later than they had planned, and Julie was pleasantly tired. The fresh air and the day's long drive had been invigorating and exciting, but now she was feeling it. For one of the few times over these past months she went to sleep almost at once.

She was never quite sure what time it was when she awoke, and she wasn't sure at first what had awakened her. She lay with her eyes open, scarcely breathing. The apartment was very dark with the drapes pulled, and she never left a night light on.

Then she heard it—an alien sound. There was someone in the apartment! She strained her ears, listening hard. It came again, and she placed it; the sound was coming from the bathroom.

The money, the money taped inside the toilet tank!

The .25 automatic was across the room in a chest of drawers, in a spare purse. She had gotten into the habit of carrying it, but she'd seen no reason to carry it in Dan's company. There had been the possibility that he might inadvertently discover that she was carrying a gun. She'd gone straight to bed tonight, without a thought of the gun.

She sat up slowly, carefully, on the side of the bed, her feet feeling for the floor. As she stood up, she heard another sound from the bathroom. She started across the room toward the chest of drawers, resisting the urge to hurry. With her third step a floorboard squeaked loudly under her feet.

She froze, listening. When she heard nothing, she started forward again. Two steps away from the chest, she heard a sound like a rush of air behind her. She lunged for the chest, hand groping blindly for the top drawer. Before she could find the handle, powerful arms wrapped around her from behind. She opened her mouth to scream, and a hand clamped over it. She struggled wildly and the arms tightened around her, then slammed her against the chest of drawers. The breath was driven from her.

As she gasped for air, the arm around her chest was removed, but the hard male body held her pinned helplessly.

Then she felt a prick of pain in the back of her neck. Immediately she grew dizzy and consciousness began to fade. She struggled once more, but weakly this time, and then she was gone, spiraling down into a long, bottomless tunnel of blackness.

SHE AWOKE SLOWLY, as if surfacing from a deep well. It took a few moments for full awareness to return. She was lying on her back on the floor before the chest of drawers, and the apartment was still dark. She listened through the buzzing in her ears and finally decided that she was alone.

She sat up and was assailed by a wave of dizziness followed by nausea. She had to lie back down for a moment. Gingerly she felt the back of her neck where she had felt the stab of pain; it was sore to the touch. In a bit she grasped the side of the chest of drawers and pulled herself up by degrees. Finally on her feet but still unsteady, she fumbled in the drawer for her purse and opened it. Her fingers touched cold metal, and she took out the gun. At least the burglar hadn't taken that.

Gripping it in her hand, she started toward the bathroom, weaving on her feet. A violent nausea seized her. She dropped the automatic onto the bed and went at a stumbling run toward the halfopen bathroom door.

She swept her hand down the inside wall, turning on the light. Even as she dropped to her knees before the bowl, retching, she had a flashing glimpse of the tank, the lid off. The plastic sack with the money was gone.

"I FIXED HER GOOD this time, Rosellen!"

"How? You didn't kill her!"

"No, no. You told me to wait for that. No, I broke into her apartment here in Sedona. I made off with all the money, what was left of it, over seventeen thousand dollars. You know where she hid it? In the toilet tank, of all places!"

"Was she at home?"

"I went in the first time while she was out, out in the desert with some guy. I snooped around and found the money, then waited until she was in bed and sound asleep. I made noises enough to wake her up. I wanted her to know that someone was invading her turf. I wanted to scare the shit out of her."

"That seems a little foolish," Rosellen said tightly. "What if she recognized you?"

"No way. I slipped up behind her, gave her a shot from a tranquilizer dart, and she went out like a light. When she woke up, I'm sure she just thought it was a random burglary. If she thinks otherwise, what difference does it make? You wanted her hassled, right? You wanted her to know that no matter where she goes or what she does, she can't escape you. Well, now she knows."

"Well, all right. Just don't get carried away before it's time." Rosellen was silent for a moment, thinking. "The old lady died in her sleep last night."

"Stella Devereaux?"

"Yes. I want you to fly back here for the funeral. It's the day after tomorrow. I think you should be here."

"But what about Suellen? What if she takes off again? I had hell's own time finding her this time!"

"She can't go very far now, without the money. The other day you told me she had a job but was making very little money."

"That's true enough. She's working for chicken feed. It'd take her forever to save up enough money to run far."

"Then I want you to fly back to Key West. Probably only for a couple of days. My plans may change now that the old bitch is dead. By the time you get here, I'll have it all worked out."

SEVENTEEN

JULIE LAY SLEEPLESS until dawn began to seep into the apartment through the drapes, trying to sort out the night's happenings.

Her first and natural impulse had been to call the police and report a robbery, but second thoughts crowded that out almost at once. How would she ever be able to explain how she, a waitress in a fast-food place, had come to possess over seventeen thousand dollars? That alone would arouse immediate suspicion. And to go further and tell them that she had hidden the money in a plastic bag taped to the inside of the toilet tank would certainly subject her to probing questions, questions that she couldn't answer, didn't dare answer.

No, she had to consider the money gone for good.

The question that nagged at her—and she kept pushing it out of her mind—was how had the burglar known she had money hidden in the toilet tank? It was a question that finally she could no longer avoid.

It seemed improbable that a random search, a search conducted while she'd slept in the next room, could have uncovered the hidden money.

Of course, Rosellen must know by this time that she had fled Key West with twenty thousand dol-

lars from the bank account. And what burglar
would carry around a needle and a knockout drug
while looting an apartment?

She remembered thinking at the time she'd done
it that a toilet tank wasn't the most original place
to hide money. It was quite possible that that was
the first place an experienced burglar would look,
so maybe an ordinary burglary wasn't so improbable after all.

She calculated swiftly. She had sixty dollars in
her checking account, and what was left of last
week's salary in her purse. Less than a hundred
dollars total. She couldn't run very far on that
amount of money.

No, she was going to take her chances and stay.
Besides, she'd had more than enough of running.
It had to end someplace, and Sedona was as good
a place as any.

At work that day her resolve was strengthened
further.

Kathy fluttered around her like a mother hen.
"Girl, what's wrong with you? You look as pale as
a ghost!"

"I didn't sleep too well last night." Julie smiled
wanly. "A touch of the flu, I guess."

"But if you don't feel well, why did you come
in? Go home, Janet."

"Oh, I couldn't do that. You can't handle the
luncheon rush all by yourself."

"I have before." Kathy shrugged. "And what
rush? The characters that come in here, they can
wait if I'm rushed. This is not a five-star restaurant, in case you haven't already noticed."

"I appreciate your concern, Kathy, really I do. But I'll be all right. I don't feel as bad as I look."

"Well, I certainly hope not. But look now, if you get to feeling lousy you just go on home."

By lunchtime Julie was feeling much better. The residual nausea brought on by whatever had been shot into her had disappeared, and the color had returned to her face. But she must have still looked a little strange, because when Dan came in at the tail end of the luncheon crowd, he frowned up at her in concern.

"You don't look too good, Janet. Do you suppose you got too much sun yesterday?"

She smiled down at him. "I don't think it was too much sun. If anything, it was too much...well, all that space, I suppose you could say."

He reached out for her hand. "Just so long as it wasn't too much Dan Renfro."

She felt a flush of pleasure as she gazed down into his eyes. Kathy's concern for her, and now Dan's obvious caring, were ample reason for her to stay around Sedona. Glancing up, she caught Kathy looking at her knowingly from across the room. Julie felt herself flushing and slowly, so as to not hurt his feelings, she disengaged her hand. "I don't think that could ever happen, Dan."

"Janet, I called a friend of mine up at the canyon yesterday. He told me that the weather has turned mild—early spring on the way, it seems. He said that next week would be a good time to take a mule trip down into the canyon."

"You're really hung up on that, aren't you, Dan?" she said in amusement.

"You'll enjoy it, Janet," he insisted. "It'll be an experience you'll never forget. When's your next day off?"

"Next Tuesday."

"Then how about it?"

"I'll give it some thought."

Just then Kathy said, "Janet, how about a hand over here?"

With a smile at Dan, Julie hurried away. She was quite busy for the next twenty minutes. When finally there was a lull, she glanced over and saw Dan still lingering over a cup of coffee. She poured herself a cup and went over to sit with him. She sighed as she sat down across from him.

Dan shook his head. "You work too hard, Janet."

"Hard work never hurt anybody," she said lightly.

"But a girl like you shouldn't be working in a place like this."

"I have to earn a living, Dan, and I've never had much work experience." She looked at him intently, wondering suddenly what he would say, how he would react, if she told him that she was potentially an heiress to a large fortune in Key West.

He leaned toward her. "But you don't have to work here."

She was momentarily startled, wondering if he had read her mind. "You mean you want to take me away from all this?" she said with forced levity.

"That's exactly what I *do* mean." His gaze was intent. "I'd like to marry you, Janet."

She sat back, suddenly out of breath. "Well, this is sure sudden!"

"Not really. To you, maybe, but I knew the minute I set eyes on you that I wanted you. It just took me a while to admit it to myself."

"Dan . . . I appreciate it. I'm flattered, I truly am." She reached over to touch his hand. "But I can't. For one thing, you hardly know anything about me. . . ."

"I know all I need to know." He took her hand in his. "Anything else I figure you'll tell me when you're ready. I know that you've been badly hurt. I know that you're also badly frightened of something."

Her eyes widened. "How do you know all that? Have I really given myself away?"

"To me you have. Maybe no one else noticed, but I have. No, wait." He held up a hand. "I'm not asking you to tell me, not until you're good and ready. All I'm asking is the chance to protect you from whatever it is that's frightening you."

THE FUNERAL of Stella Devereaux was heavily attended, the crowd numbering well over a hundred people.

Claude Henderson stood to one side of the grave site with Shell Phipps. "This crowd is a testament to the Devereaux name," Henderson said, turning to Phipps. "Stella Devereaux may have been an invalid and pretty much of a recluse during her last years, but I'd venture to say that most of the old-time residents of Key West are in attendance today."

Shell merely nodded. Henderson followed his glance to where a woman in mourning clothes, wearing a dark veil, stood between Pippen Delacroix and Helen Bronson. He noted a man standing with them and said, "Who's the young man in the dark gray suit standing on the far side of Pippen?"

"That's Ken Dawson, Julie's—or rather Suellen's—fiancé."

Henderson stared appraisingly at his associate. "I must say, Sheldon, that I'm rather surprised that you came today. You've kept pretty much to yourself these past few months."

"I tried to explain all that, sir," Shell responded. "I've been trying to find Suellen."

"I heard your explanation, yes, but I fail to understand it."

"I felt somehow responsible for her."

"I thought I made it abundantly clear that when she disappeared this second time, the firm's responsibility had been discharged."

"Maybe the firm's responsibility, but not mine."

"You also have a responsibility to the firm, Sheldon. You are a junior partner. Your name is on the masthead. I had Miss Harris run a check. In the past four months you have been in the office a total of ten days. That is scarcely the action of a responsible member of the firm!"

"I'm sorry about that, sir, but I have to do what I think best."

"I must tell you that I would have demanded your resignation long before this but for the fact that I have grown fond of you, and because I took into consideration your contributions to the firm in the past. Tell me, Sheldon, *are* you enamored of Suellen?''

"Enamored?" Shell gave him an amused look. "That's rather an old-fashioned word, but I suppose it's accurate enough. I love her, sir."

Henderson grunted. "And how does she feel about you?"

"That's rather hard to say," Shell said with a shrug. "It's been months since I've seen her. The last time I did, in Moorestown, she ran from me."

"*Ran* from you. Good heavens, man, that's rather odd, wouldn't you say?"

"She still thought someone was trying to kill her."

"Well, she doesn't seem to be frightened now." His glance went to the graveside. "And it would seem that your efforts to find her were a waste of time and effort. She came back on her own."

"It would seem so, wouldn't it?"

"Do you know where she's been? Why she ran from you like that? Have you spoken to her?"

"No, sir. I was as surprised as anyone when she showed up for the church services this morning."

"Well, at least you won't have to look for her anymore. Hopefully we'll be graced with your presence at the office again. And that reminds me . . ." Henderson placed a hand on Shell's arm. "I am going to call a meeting of all the legatees at Devereaux House for ten in the morning. Naturally, you will be there."

They fell silent as the minister spoke the final words of the service in rich, resonant tones.

Henderson watched impassively. He had never cared much for funerals, believing them to be a barbaric ritual; yet he knew it was proper form to attend the funerals of deceased clients. It seemed to him that most of the funeral services he'd attended recently were those of his contemporaries, and it tended to make a man all too uneasy about his own mortality. At least Stella Devereaux had been a few years his senior.

He saw now that the mourners were all turning away and Suellen was heading toward them, with Pippen, Helen and Ken Dawson trailing in her wake.

Suellen stopped before him, throwing back her veil. "Mr. Henderson, how nice of you to come," she said in a throaty voice.

Henderson inclined his head slightly and said formally, "Stella was an old friend, as well as a valued client."

"Yes, I understand. Poor Grandmother." She glanced at Shell. "And it was thoughtful of you to come, also, Shell."

"Julie, where have you been?" he said in a low voice. "I've looked everywhere for you."

"I know, I'm sorry. But this isn't the time to talk about that, Shell." She turned as the others ranged alongside her. She took the young man's arm and drew him forward. "Mr. Henderson, I don't believe you've met Ken Dawson. This is Mr. Henderson, Ken, Grandmother's attorney. Ken is my fiancé, Mr. Henderson."

"How do you do, sir? I'm sorry we couldn't have met under happier circumstances."

"And I also, Mr. Henderson. Julie...uh, Suellen has told me how nice you've been to her."

Ken held out his hand, and Henderson took it.

"Since most of the principals are here, I will take this opportunity to apprise you of...uh..." Henderson cleared his throat. "I realize this may be a little premature, but I wish to expedite the reading of the will in the morning at ten in Devereaux House. I trust you will all be present. Suellen? Pippen? Helen?"

Suellen regarded him gravely. "Whatever you think best, Mr. Henderson."

"Well, I happen to think it is a little callous," said Helen Bronson dourly. "With poor Stella hardly in her grave."

"Oh, don't be a ninny, Helen!" Pippen snapped. "Stella was a better businesswoman than any of us, she would have wanted all business matters settled as soon as possible."

Helen sniffed. "I would expect you to say that."

Henderson interjected smoothly, "I thought it best to do this while Suellen is with us."

"I won't disappear between now and then, Mr. Henderson. I give you my solemn promise on that."

As THEY DROVE up to Devereaux House shortly before ten the next morning, Henderson asked, "Did you ever get the full story from Suellen, Sheldon?"

Shell shook his head. "Not yet. I haven't been able to see her alone yet. I tried last night but couldn't even get her on the phone."

"Perhaps after today matters will settle down and everything will return to normal."

Henderson depressed the doorhandle and got out. Briefcase under his arm, he waited for Shell to come around the car and join him.

Instead of Pauline, Helen Bronson answered the door. "The others are all waiting for you in the living room," she said with a jerk of her head.

"Helen, why didn't Pauline answer the door?" Shell asked. "Is she sick or something? I didn't notice her at the funeral yesterday, either."

"Oh, didn't you know? She and Suellen had a big fight the day Suellen came back, and Pauline packed up and left in a hurry. I think she just plain quit."

Helen started down the hall toward the living room. Shell detained Henderson with a hand on his arm. "Sir, I'm sorry to have to tell you this, but I may have to leave again at a moment's notice."

Henderson turned on him, his voice cold. "I thought that was all over. Suellen is back, I should hope to stay this time. Or do you expect her to vanish again?"

"I'm sorry, Mr. Henderson," Shell said without looking at him. "It's personal. I can't explain now."

Henderson's temper slipped. "I will not stand for any more of this kind of irresponsibility, young man! You are an associate in the firm. If you find it too onerous to fulfill your duties, perhaps we should think of terminating your services!"

"You do whatever you have to do," Shell said quietly. "I really can't blame you for feeling that way."

Henderson kept his temper tightly reined, but it was obvious that he was raging inside. Without another word he marched into the living room. Suellen and her young man sat side by side on the couch. Pippen was in an easy chair, a cup of coffee in one hand, a smoldering cigarette in the other, and Helen Bronson was just seating herself.

"I see that everyone is present, except for Pauline," Henderson said, his anger making his voice harsh."

"She was fired," Pippen said unpleasantly. "Fired for insolence. Stella has been letting that woman get away with murder for years. Besides, why does she have to be here?"

"She does receive a bequest in the will. However, I can contact her later." He sat down on the end of the couch, opened his briefcase and took out a thin, blue-backed document. He also took out a pair of glasses, polished them meticulously, then placed them on his nose. He frowned over them at Ken Dawson. "May I inquire as to why your young man is here, Suellen? He is not concerned in these proceedings."

"Oh, but he is." Suellen hugged Ken's arm against her. "Whatever concerns me concerns Ken." She glanced over at Shell, her expression unreadable.

Henderson followed her gaze. Sheldon was standing just inside the door, his face tight with displeasure as he returned Suellen's stare.

"Do sit down somewhere, Sheldon," Henderson said irritably.

Shell nodded curtly and found a seat to one side, his gaze still on Suellen.

"Now." Henderson cleared his throat and opened the blue-backed document. "I am sure that most of you are already familiar with the terms of Stella Devereaux's will, but I will summarize briefly, then read it word for word in compliance with the law. Stella's personal fortune was not great, yet it was substantial. Aside from the bequest to Pauline, her entire estate is equally divided between Pippen Delacroix, Helen Bronson, Rosellen and Suellen. And since you, Suellen, are the only survivor of the two girls, your sister's share will pass to you." He glanced up at her. "The trust your father established for you and your sister will end within sixty days. And again, since your sister is deceased, the entire trust will revert to you. A considerable sum, if you are not already aware, in excess of five million . . ."

ON BOARD the *Adventuress*, the telephone rang. Rosellen picked up the receiver. "Hello?"

"Why did you just take off like that, Rosellen? I haven't been with you in God knows how long!"

A smug smile curved her mouth. "I know, big guy, I know. You think I don't want you, too? But it's too risky right now for us to be together. You heard what that old poop of a lawyer said. In sixty days the money, all the money, will be mine! Five million! I knew it was big bucks, but I had no idea it would be that much."

"Why is it so risky? I can wait until late tonight, then sneak on board your boat."

"No! I'm going to get rid of the boat. I'm taking her out tonight and sinking her."

"But why? That boat's worth a lot of money."

"Not compared to five million dollars. I want nothing left of the life I've led for the past eight years. True, she's been renamed and painted and pretty well disguised, but there's always a slight chance someone might recognize her if I sold her. And if I kept her, took her to Key West as mine, the risk would be even greater. No." Her voice was decisive. "Tonight the *Adventuress* dies, as does Rosellen Devereaux, for all time."

"If you sink her out at sea, how'll you get back to land?"

"There's a dinghy on board with an outboard motor. When I reach land again, at a desolate spot I know, the dinghy goes to the bottom, as well."

"I could come up and give you a hand," the voice on the phone said hopefully. "That's a big job for a lone woman to have to handle."

"I've handled bigger!" she retorted. Then she softened her voice slightly. "I have another chore for you to do, big guy. I want you to go back to Arizona immediately. It's time to end it now. I enjoyed the little game of cat and mouse with dear sister, but now that Grandmother's dead it's time for me to assume my place as Suellen. I was always a little afraid that the old witch could tell us apart. I always thought that she was the only one who could. Well, now she's gone."

"You mean you want me to finish it now?"

"That's exactly what I'm saying, yes. I want my sister dead now, as quickly as possible."

"There's the possibility, you know, that she might be identified by the police even after she's dead. That has occurred to me before, but I haven't mentioned it."

"How? Neither one of us has ever been finger-printed. And you said she now has identification papers showing her to be Janet Marlowe."

"Yes, that's all true enough."

"Then how can she be identified?" Her short laugh was savage. "In essence, my dear sister is already dead. All that remains is to bury her. Do it!"

EIGHTEEN

THEY WERE ON THEIR WAY to the Grand Canyon. Although it was still March, the weather was comparatively mild. As they drove northwest out of Flagstaff, Julie could see only a few patches of snow in the deep shadows of the pines.

She glanced over at Dan at the wheel of the pickup. He was singing tunelessly under his breath. He was a good, kind man, she thought with a sudden rush of affection. Yet she doubted that she would ever really love him. There hadn't been the electricity that had sparked with Shell. . . .

She almost forcibly thrust all thought of both men out of her mind.

As though sensing her gaze on him, Dan abruptly turned his head. He grinned lazily. "My humming bother you? I know I can't carry a tune in a bucket, but I sometimes do a little humming when I'm on a long drive like this."

"Oh, your humming doesn't bother me," she said hastily. "On the contrary, I was thinking that you sounded happy."

"I am, I am," he said cheerfully. "Why shouldn't I be? I'm with a pretty girl, a girl I really like, and I'm looking forward to a nice, carefree couple of days." He reached over, caught her hand and squeezed. "I have two cabins for us at the Bright Angel Lodge. It's quite old, but comfortable enough, and it's perched right on the south rim of the canyon.''

Julie made an involuntary sound of surprise. And then she felt herself blushing. She sneaked a glance at Dan and saw that he had turned his attention back to the highway but was smiling slightly.

"I don't mean to rush things, Janet," he said softly. "When it's time, we'll know it."

He baffled her sometimes. In this time of "My pad or yours?" at first meetings, he was an anachronism. He had kissed her a couple of times, and she had felt the sexual response in both of them, yet he had never pushed it; he had never made what could be truly called a pass. She didn't know whether to be grateful or piqued. But then, perhaps he was right—when the time came, they would know it.

It was shortly after noon when they approached the cluster of buildings on the rim. They passed the old railroad station first and then pulled into the half-empty parking lot in front of the lodge proper. It was midweek, and the crowd wasn't too large.

But Dan drove on through the parking lot and toward one of the lookout points. "You have to have at least a look at the canyon first before we check in."

He nudged the pickup against a log barrier, and they got out of the vehicle and approached the stone wall that edged the canyon at that point. As Julie leaned over the wall, the canyon opened up before her, taking her breath away, like an explosion of the senses.

The wide, deep cut into the earth plunged breathtakingly down until far below she could see the brown ribbon of the Colorado. The colors were stunning—brown and red and tan hues, with patches of green where shrubs clung to the steep slopes. Across the giant chasm and on what she knew must be the north rim, Julie could see snow.

And to the west, hovering right along the rim of the canyon, blue-black clouds boiled, a curtain of rain joining them to the earth. As she watched, forked lightning flashed brilliantly, causing her to jump.

"It's magnificent, Dan!"

"Yes, isn't it?" he said blissfully. "When I come up here and look at all that, whatever troubles I have suddenly seem almighty puny."

"But you expect me to ride a mule down into that?" She gestured down below.

"Don't knock it until you've tried it. Let's see—" he leaned across her, peering down "—it's time for the mule train to be returning. Yes, there it is!"

Julie followed his pointing finger. She squinted and finally made out a narrow trail snaking down the face of the cliff, and far below she could see a mule train. The perspective from where she stood made the animals and their riders appear very small and fragile in the vast vertical landscape.

Dan started the pickup, backed it up and drove back to the parking lot in front of the lodge. As Julie started to push down the doorhandle, Dan said, "Wait a minute." Fishing in his pocket, he dug out a set of keys and dangled them before her. "I always carry an extra set of keys for the pickup. You hang on to these while we're here.''

''But why should I have a set of your keys?''

''Because I'm absentminded and have a bad habit of locking myself out of the truck,'' he said with some embarrassment. ''Besides, you might want to drive the pickup somewhere yourself.''

''I doubt that very much,'' she said, taking the keys. ''Anyway, I don't think I could drive this monster. You know, I've only driven a stick shift one time in my life.''

''It's not all that difficult. You'd soon get the hang of it.''

He got out, then came around to open the door on her side. He got their two bags out of the pickup, and they went into the lodge. After they had registered and gotten their room keys, they went down the side hall and outside again.

On the way up, Dan had explained to her that he had been lucky to get cabins for them. ''They only have fourteen cabins, and they're usually reserved well in advance, but they had some last-minute cancellations. Yours not only has a view of the canyon, but a fireplace, as well.''

At the door to her cabin, Dan said, ''Mine is down the way a bit. Why don't you rest for a bit, then I'll come by for you. We'll explore for a while, then have drinks and dinner. I thought we'd attend a lecture this evening given by a park ranger at the Shrine of the Ages building, if that's all right with you.''

''That sounds fine, Dan,'' Julie said with a nod.

FOUR HOURS LATER they paused again before the door to Julie's cabin. They had enjoyed a good dinner and an interesting lecture and slide show on the canyon and its history and had walked along the rim for a bit after the lecture, until the chill of the evening had begun to penetrate their clothing.

"I have a bottle of brandy in my bag. We could build a fire," Dan said.

She looked at him without speaking.

He cupped her chin in his hand, running a thumb along the line of her jaw. "I said I thought we'd know when it was time," he said softly. "Well, I think the time is now. Do you agree? If not, I won't push it."

"I agree," she said in a voice that was little more than a whisper.

He nodded. "I'll be back in ten minutes."

Inside the cabin, Julie had a few second thoughts. Should she be doing this? It wasn't that she didn't want him. Dan was not only kind and gentle but personable, and she knew instinctively that he would be a good lover. But if she took this step she would be making a commitment, and she would be involving him in her life and consequently her problems. Did she have the right to do that to him?

Still musing, she walked over to the fireplace. It was chilly in the room. Logs and kindling had already been laid for a fire. Julie used one of the long wooden matches provided to start the fire. Removing her shoes, she sat down on the floor and leaned back against the chair. The logs were burning merrily by the time a knock sounded on the door.

"It's unlocked, come on in," she called out.

Dan came in carrying a bottle of brandy. He stood scowling down at her. "That's not very smart, Janet, leaving the door unlocked like that. Even up here you never know what weirdo might happen along."

"You're right, I shouldn't have," she said meekly. And he was indeed right, she thought. Considering that there was someone out there searching for her, it was stupid to leave a door unlocked. But it seemed so isolated here, so far away from any threat, that she hadn't given a thought to Rosellen or anyone else all evening.

Dan came back from the bathroom with two glasses. He splashed brandy into them, gave Julie one, then sat down on the floor beside her. He warmed his hands before the fire. "That feels nice. There's still a nip in the air up here."

"Maybe they'll have to cancel the mule train tomorrow," she said hopefully.

"No way," he said, laughing. "No way you're going to get out of that. As a matter of fact, I had a chat with my guide friend after the mule train came back this afternoon, and he assured me that it's on for tomorrow."

Julie took a warming sip of brandy, looking at Dan's profile as he stared into the leaping flames. The firelight gave a bronze glow to her features, and he had the look of a member of some ancient Indian race.

"Tell me about your marriage, Dan," she said abruptly.

He threw a sharp glance to her, seemed about to demur, then shrugged. "If you like. But there's really nothing to tell. We were both too young when we got married, right out of high school. We weren't really prepared for life *or* marriage. We both worked. Annette was a secretary with an insurance company, and I worked at several jobs, none worth bragging about. I was managing the sales force for a used car agency when we got divorced, and the job was a dead end.''

''What happened? The divorce, I mean?''

He took a drink of brandy. ''Nothing earth-shaking. Like I said, we were too young when we got married. We drifted apart. Or maybe grew apart would better describe it.''

''That isn't what I heard. I was told that it was a bitter divorce.''

He gave her another sharp look. ''You heard that, did you?''

''I'm sorry, Dan.'' She touched his hand. ''I shouldn't listen to gossip, and it's none of my business, anyway.''

''No, it is your business, in a way, and it *was* bitter, at least on my part. Or so I thought at the time. I caught Annette in bed with another man. I felt betrayed, stripped of my manhood, all the old clichés. But Annette is not a bad person, and I never stopped to think that I should share some of the blame. She had to be looking for something I couldn't, or wouldn't, give her. I came to see that after I was out here for a while, when I could think rationally again.''

''You're a perceptive man, Dan. Not many men would look at it like that.''

"Not so perceptive." He gave a snort of laughter. "I just grew up a little. A little late, I guess, but that's better than never."

And now it comes, Julie thought, the questions for her. Yet she had no right to complain. She had opened the door.

He surprised her. He set his glass down and turned to her, taking her into his arms, all in one supple movement. His mouth came down hard on hers. Caught by the suddenness of it, she stiffened and started to draw away. Then she felt a leaping response to his kiss and she went lax in his arms.

Although he was gentle about it, there was a demanding maleness about him now, and she responded fully to it as he rained kisses on her cheeks, neck and ears, his hands roaming over her body, molding her breasts and thighs. Although warm now from the heat of the fire, she grew warmer still under the pressure of his lips and the stroking of his hands. Desire surged in her and she longed for the torment and oblivion of passion, however brief. She recognized that her feeling was purely physical, with perhaps a leavening of affection, and this brought a touch of sadness, a sadness that was gone as Dan stood, drawing her up with him.

"I've wanted you for months now," he said huskily. "I don't want to wait any longer."

"I know, Dan," she whispered against his lips. "And you don't have to wait any longer. It's time."

They undressed one another by the light of the dying fire, stopping now and then to kiss and embrace. Although both were breathing heavily now, and Julie was on fire with need, there was nothing frantic or hurried about it. A part of Julie's mind wondered about this. She knew that Dan had not made love to a woman since his divorce, and this had to mean that he was showing remarkable restraint.

It wasn't until they were naked together on the bed that his desire became overriding.

"Janet . . . ?" he asked, his voice raw with passion.

"Yes, Dan. Now."

Her heart was racing, the blood rushing through her veins like fire. She gasped and arched up to meet him as he joined them together.

In passion's heat she forgot everything but the man in her arms. The world, the room—it all receded, and the bed became the center of her universe, the core of her consciousness. It seemed to her that this was the first time she had truly functioned as a woman in an endless time, and such was the rich fullness of her emotions that she felt unshed tears gather at the corners of her eyes.

When the storm had passed and they lay together in each other's arms, Dan said, "I want to hold you like this for the rest of my life, Janet. Marry me."

"Hush, Dan." She placed her fingers lightly across his lips. "Not now."

He touched her bare breast and laughed softly. "I can't think of a better time."

She closed her hand over his, pressing it against her breast with a shiver. "You don't understand, Dan. There are many things you don't know about me. Even if I wanted to get married, and I'm far from sure that I do, I couldn't at present."

Again she expected a flood of questions. Instead, he shrugged. ''Promise me you'll tell me when you're ready. I'll still be around.''

THE MORNING WAS CHILLY before the sun inched up and began to warm the air. By that time they were crawling down the narrow, serpentine trail. Julie was bundled up in a jacket and Dan was wearing his mackinaw. She had only ridden a couple of times in her life, and then it had been on a horse, with a relatively smooth gait. Riding a mule, she soon found, was something like riding a mechanical horse that went only one way—straight up and down. Already, only an hour from the corrals up above, she was stiff and sore.

Their guide, a tall, raw-boned man with a laconic sense of humor, told them to call him Buck Horn. ''That's not my real name, of course,'' he had told Julie as they prepared to leave the corrals. ''But who would want to be led down into the big ditch by a guy named Sylvester Buckingham?'' He turned to the others and raised his voice. ''Now there's nothing to be frightened of, folks. Don't try to guide these critters. Just let them have their heads. They could go up and down the trail blindfolded. And no matter how dangerous the trail may look at first, these mules are perfectly safe. It wouldn't do you any good to try and use the reins on them, anyway. They're ornery and they're going where they want to, irregardless.''

Despite the guide's reassurances, Julie had clung to the saddle horn in fright for that first hour. The trail was very narrow in places; on her right the cliff face was so close she could brush it with her elbow, and on her left the ground plunged steeply away inches from the hooves of the mules. A single misstep could send animal and rider plunging down forever, it seemed. Yet after a while her confidence grew in her mount and she began to relax and observe everything around her.

Dan, riding in front of her, would turn now and then for a few reassuring words and a smile. At the start he had told her that he would ride in front of her on the way down and behind her on the way back up. "So if you fall I'll be there to catch you," he had said with a grin.

"Don't say that!"

"I'm sorry, Janet. You heard what Buck said. There is absolutely nothing to worry about. Except you'll be sore as the devil for a few days after. You'll probably want to kill me."

As they rode farther down, an occasional glimpse of the Colorado could be seen far below, and sometimes the trail would take an unexpected twist and Julie could see back up to the rim, where people were waving at them.

And then finally, just short of noon, the trail leveled out, going relatively straight.

Dan twisted around to look back at her. "We're just about to the plateau where we'll be stopping for lunch. You can walk out to the end and look down at the river. We won't go all the way down to the river itself."

"It seems to take a long time."

He grinned. "Next time we'll go across the river and spend the night in the lodge there. I thought this one-day trip would be enough for you the first time."

When they finally stopped in a grove of trees by a stream trickling down toward the river, Dan dismounted quickly. "Wait, don't try to get down until I can give you a hand."

He came back and held a hand up. Julie slid off awkwardly. When her feet hit the ground, her knees buckled and she would have fallen if he hadn't supported her. Dan was keeping a straight face only with an effort.

"I warned you," he said.

At a cry from across the way, Julie turned in time to see a heavyset woman crumple to the ground. Buck Horn hurried forward and helped the woman up.

"I see what you mean," Julie said ruefully, rubbing her numb buttocks.

Dan gave her his arm over to a boulder and eased her down. Buck Horn was unloading lunch boxes from one of the pack mules. Dan went over to help and soon returned with two boxes. Opening hers, Julie discovered two hard-boiled eggs, two sandwiches—ham and tuna salad—and a wedge of chocolate cake. She realized that the air and the unaccustomed exercise had given her an enormous appetite, despite the large breakfast she had eaten.

After all the lunch boxes had been distributed, Buck came over to sit beside them with his own lunch.

"Have you been doing this long, Buck?" Julie asked.

"A spell," he said with a shrug. "Couple of years."

"Do you like it?"

"It has its good points and its bad points. The work ain't hard, but some of the people you have to deal with are a pain in the rear end. But at that they ain't as bad as some of the characters that patronized that dude ranch down to Wickenburg where I worked before I came up here."

Finished eating, Julie sat with her knees drawn up, her arms wrapped around them, watching him with interest. "And what did you do before that?"

"Oh, a little cowpunching, a little rodeoing." He leaned back against a tree trunk, took out a sack of tobacco and papers and deftly rolled a cigarette.

Julie watched him, fascinated. When he had it in his mouth and lighted, she clapped her hands. "You *must* be a real cowpuncher. I've never seen anyone do that but movie cowboys."

"Aw, shucks, ma'am," he drawled. "Tain't nothing. All us cowpokes learn to roll our own. You out there in the breaks long enough looking for stray dogies, you run out of tailor-mades."

Julie threw back her head and laughed wholeheartedly.

"Don't let that aw-shucks act fool you, Janet," Dan said. "Buck was damned good at rodeoing. He won the belt for bronc busting a few years back. Pendleton, wasn't it, Buck?"

"Yep. But the trouble with bronc busting is they got it the wrong way around. It's not the broncs get busted so much as the rider. That last season I had on the rodeo circuit busted me up pretty good. I broke a leg and some ribs, and the doc told me that if I didn't quit I'd be in a hospital for the rest of my life." He took a last draw from the cigarette and carefully ground it out in the dirt, then nodded his head at Dan. "And speaking of damned fool things, Janet, you know what this guy wants to do? He's put in an application to join the park rangers."

Julie glanced at Dan with raised eyebrows. "Is that true, Dan?"

Dan colored slightly. "Yes, it's true. I don't know whether I'll make it or not, but I've applied."

"Hell," Buck said, "he probably makes three times as much money in the real estate business as he would in the park service."

"Money isn't everything," Dan said defensively.

"Now where have I heard that before?" Buck said with a soft snort of derision. He uncoiled his long length and got to his feet. "Well, if you guys are going to walk out to the point you'd better get a move on. We'll be starting back up to the rim in about an hour."

Looking around, Julie saw that most of the people had finished their lunch and were walking along the wedge of land leading toward the river. Dan got to his feet and gave her a hand up.

As they strolled toward the point, he said, "I suppose you think I'm foolish for trying to get into the park service?"

She squeezed his arm. "Not if that's what you really want to do."

"Well, I'm tired of selling things. First cars, now real estate. I don't mean to sound altruistic, but I want to do something that serves some purpose. And since I love the canyon, I figure this is the best place to do it.''

"Then I say good for you!"

"Do you think you'd like to live up here?"

"Dan," she said with a hint of warning in her voice as she unhooked her arm from his.

"No, no, I didn't mean that. I promised, and I'll keep to my word. But I mean a job up here. They always need people to work in the dining room, and it certainly pays more than the place where you work now."

"Money isn't everything."

He looked briefly disconcerted, then laughed. "Touché!"

They reached the edge of the plateau and stopped. The Colorado was still some distance below, but it could be seen clearly now. What from above had looked like a brown ribbon was actually a racing current of water, boiling white in places. Julie groped for Dan's hand, gripping it tightly as they walked along the edge of the plateau.

In a moment Dan pointed across the river, to a smaller canyon running north from the river, and a spot of green.

"That's the lodge where people stay overnight," Dan said.

"That might be fun . . . some other time," Julie said. "But I'm just as happy we settled for the one-day trip." She glanced back over her shoulder. "Shouldn't we be getting back? People seem to be returning."

"Okay."

They turned back toward the spot where the mules were corralled.

A short while later they were all mounted and on the trail up. Julie rode in front of Dan this time. She hadn't realized just how sore her thigh muscles were until she was in the saddle again; the insides of her thighs were also becoming chafed. After a bit her stiffened muscles loosened, and it wasn't quite so bad, but she hated to think how sore she'd be in the morning.

They wound around the switchbacks, the mules moving slowly, methodically. The clip-clopping of their hooves rang musically against the side of the canyon.

About a half hour from the rim, Buck Horn began to sing. His voice wasn't the best, but it was loud and clear. The song was "Tumbling Tumbleweeds." One by one the others all joined in, their voices rising loudly.

Julie called back over her shoulder, "Dan? I don't hear you singing."

"I can't sing, for Christ's sake."

"But you can hum, I've heard you." She twisted around, ducking her head to laugh back at him.

"Humming is different—"

In midsentence his face flowered red and he tumbled off the mule. As Julie stared in shock, he hit the ground and began to roll down the cliffside, and a cracking sound echoed off the walls like thin, distant thunder.

TWO HUNDRED YARDS AWAY just below the rim of the canyon, the rifleman cursed. He had had Suellen right in the cross hairs of the scope, but she had ducked her head just as he'd squeezed the trigger.

He had missed, hitting the man behind her—the guy she had come up with in the pickup.

Now the group down there was milling around, and he didn't dare wait around for another shot at Suellen. He was exposed enough as it was, and soon people would be scrambling around the rim looking for the source of the shot. He dropped the rifle to the ground and stood up cautiously, looking around. He had been lying prone in a little depression between two boulders, a few yards below the rim of the canyon. He swept the area with his glance but saw no one close by.

He clambered up to the rim, still unobserved so far as he could tell, and began walking unhurriedly toward his car parked about fifty yards away. As he walked he stripped off the surgeon's gloves he wore and crammed them into his pocket.

As he drove away, his thoughts were on Rosellen. She was going to be absolutely furious when he told her that he had failed. For a moment he toyed with the idea of not calling just yet, not until he had made another, successful attempt. But the alarm would be out now, and it would be too risky to try again too soon. He would have to wait a few days, at least.

He sighed. He had no choice but to call Rosellen. If he didn't and she learned about the abortive attempt, she would be even more furious. He couldn't take a chance of losing her, and the money. Rosellen and the Devereaux millions were of equal importance to him. And he had gone too far, done too much, to lose out now.

IT TOOK A GREAT DEAL OF EFFORT but Rosellen managed to keep a hold on her temper. "All right, I agree," she said into the phone. "We'd better let things cool down for a few days. Just keep a close watch on her, don't let her get away again."

"Okay, baby. I'll watch her, don't worry. And I'll call you again around this time tomorrow."

In that instant Rosellen made up her mind. "No, that's not necessary. I'll be away for a bit, three or four days. I have to go up to Miami."

"Why do you have to do that?"

"Personal business," she said curtly, and hung up.

She paced the bedroom, thinking hard. She was back in her old room in Devereaux House. Or rather, Suellen's old room. But then, she was Suellen now, wasn't she?

She knew what she was going to do now. She was flying to Arizona on the first flight she could get out of Miami. There would be no foul-up this time; she was going to take care of Suellen personally. In a way she was glad that this attempt had failed. She was going to take great pleasure in killing her sister herself. Besides, if you wanted a job done well, do it yourself, don't depend on someone else.

The phone started to ring again. Rosellen let it ring as she paced the room. It rang for a long time, then finally stopped.

The moment it stopped, she picked up the receiver and dialed the reservations desk at the Miami airport to inquire about the first available flight to Arizona.

NINETEEN

FROZEN WITH SHOCK, Julie sat where she was without moving, staring at the riderless mule behind her. The cold recesses of her mind held but two thoughts: Dan was dead, and she knew that the shot had been meant for her!

Dan was dead!

Her skin shrank at the thought of it, and it was all she could do to keep from moving back under the overhang, making herself as small as possible.

She glanced down at the trail below and saw Buck Horn and the other guide bending over Dan's body. Now Buck looked up at her and shook his head dolefully.

The other riders, strung out along the trail for a hundred yards or so, were sitting white faced, clutching their saddle horns. One woman, on the mule behind the one on which Dan had been riding, was sobbing loudly. Julie herself was too stunned to cry. The entire occurrence seemed nightmarish and unreal, and yet a part of her knew that it had happened.

Pursuit had caught up to her again, and this time someone was dead, an innocent who had had no part in all this; but for her, Dan Renfro would still be alive. By simply being with him she had dragged him into the dangerous orbit of her past.

In a moment Buck came back up the trail. "All right, folks," he said loudly. "Let's head for the rim." He came to Julie and touched her arm briefly. "You, too, Janet. There's nothing you can do here." He called down below, "Jack! I'm taking us on up. You stay here with Dan until the medics and the rangers get here."

In a few minutes the mule train was moving again, the riders silent and pale.

Julie felt terribly exposed. Was the rifleman still up there? Would he try again? Such was her despair that she thought it might be best all around if she *was* killed.

Then her despair changed to anger. Rosellen had gone too far! To kill an innocent person, even if inadvertently, was too much. Her sister was responsible for Dan's death, and she had to pay for it.

They made the rim and the mule corrals without further incident. As Julie dismounted and stood swaying on numb, uncertain legs, she saw Buck making his way over to her accompanied by a man in a park ranger's uniform. The ranger carried a walkie-talkie and was speaking softly into it.

"Janet, this is Harlan Carter," Buck said. "He's the man temporarily in charge of the investigation. Harlan, this is Janet Marlowe, a friend of the...a friend of Dan's. You're from Sedona, right, Janet?"

It took an effort for Julie to speak. "Yes, that's right."

Carter had removed his hat and stood twisting it in his big hands. "I'm sorry we had to meet under such circumstances, Miss Marlowe. Were you a good friend of Renfro's? Engaged or anything?''

Julie hesitated briefly. ''No, we weren't engaged, just good friends.''

''Had you known him long?''

''Not long. I've only been living in Sedona for a few months.''

''There are some questions I must ask. But they can wait until you've freshened up and had some time to yourself. I will have to question everyone who was on the mule train, just in case they saw anything. Some of them aren't staying at the canyon, so I must catch them before they leave. You are staying at the lodge, I understand?''

Julie told him that she was and gave him the number of her cabin.

''The lodge is providing us with a room for the interrogations. If you will come to the lobby in about an hour you will be told which room to go to. By that time there'll be someone from the Coconino sheriff's department here to take charge of the investigation.''

Julie nodded and was permitted to leave. It was painful walking to her cabin, but she was so occupied with thinking about what had happened that she scarcely noticed the discomfort.

Once inside her cabin, where she and Dan had made love only last night, it all crashed in on her. She crumpled onto the rug in front of the cold fireplace and wept bitterly. She hadn't loved Dan Renfro, but he had been a fine man, and the sense of loss was overwhelming. It wasn't fair that he should die like this, from a bullet meant for her!

She had, even if indirectly, been responsible for the death of an innocent man.

Her anger at her sister returned, stronger than ever, and her tears stopped.

She had dimly realized all along that somewhere along the way she would have to stop running, that she would have to turn and fight back if the pursuit continued; but over the past months in Sedona she had begun to relax, thinking that Rosellen had either given up or had failed to find her.

Now it was abundantly clear that neither was the case. Rosellen would never give up and she, Julie, could never escape.

She thought of the burglary again. It hadn't been a random burglary; she had been the intended victim all along. But why hadn't the man in her apartment killed her then instead of just putting her out with some kind of drug and stealing the money? There had been no doubt that the intent today had been to kill, and almost certainly it was the same man. What had changed between the time of the burglary and today?

She remembered then—it was only a few weeks until her twenty-fifth birthday, hers and Rosellen's, and on that day the trust was due to terminate.

Rosellen was no longer just pursuing and tormenting her, she wanted her dead so there would be nothing in the **way** of her becoming Suellen and inheriting all the money from the trust. Or maybe she was already posing as Suellen! Who would know the difference?

This thought brought Julie to her feet, and she almost bolted from the cabin. Then she restrained herself. She couldn't leave the lodge right away, not until after she was questioned. If she did it would look suspicious, probably suspicious enough to bring the police after her.

She went into the bathroom, removed the dirty clothes she had worn down into the canyon and took a quick shower. It wasn't until she was dressed in fresh clothing that she remembered something else. Dan had given her an extra set of keys to the pickup. She dug into her purse, and there they were. Clutching them in her hand, she was tempted once again to leave immediately. No, she had to wait. After all this time, another few hours would hardly matter.

She left the cabin and walked to the lodge. At the desk she was directed down the hall to the meeting room that had been turned over to the park rangers for the interrogation of those people on the mule train.

Buck Horn saw her enter the room and came over to meet her. "Are you okay, Janet?"

She nodded mutely.

"As you can see, they're about finished with the others. You'll be the last one, since you're the only person aside from myself who knew Dan at all, and I was little more than a casual acquaintance."

"Have they learned anything?"

"Naw. Nobody saw anything out of the ordinary, nobody contributed a damned thing. Harlan says they have men scouting around the rim where the bullet came from in the hope of finding someone who saw the shooter, in the hope of finding *anything*."

"I'm afraid I won't be of much help, either."

"Probably not. It's all just routine, Janet."

At that moment Harlan Carter beckoned them from across the room, and Buck escorted her over.

"Miss Marlowe," Carter said, motioning to a heavyset man sitting at his side, "this is Charlie Wellman from the sheriff's department. They're officially in charge now, but since I started the interrogations, I will continue. Charlie, this is Janet Marlowe."

Wellman nodded soberly. "If I think of anything that Harlan doesn't cover, Miss Marlowe, I'll interrupt."

"We'll try not to keep you too long," Carter said. "I hope you can help us. At least you *knew* Renfro."

Julie sat across the table from the ranger. "I doubt I can be of much help. As I've already said, I've only been in Sedona a few months. As for knowing Dan, I've been out with him a few times, that's all."

"But you can at least tell us what kind of a man he was, who his friends were and if you know of anyone who might wish him dead."

Now was the time to spill the whole story, she thought fleetingly. Then the moment was past, and she heard herself saying, "Dan Renfro was one of the nicest men I've ever known. I can't think of anyone who would want to kill him."

Carter's long, weathered face took on a slight smile. "I've learned, Miss Marlowe, that there are few of us who don't have one or two people who'd like to see us dead. But no matter. Please tell us what you know about Dan Renfro."

Julie told him everything she knew. At the finish she said, "I suppose if anyone held a grudge against Dan it would have to be his ex-wife, but she's out in Los Angeles, as far as I know. And I hardly think she would choose this way to..."

Carter was nodding. "Yes, it hardly seems the method a woman would use to kill. What do you think, Charlie?"

The sheriff's man said, "I'll get off a wire to the Los Angeles Police Department and have her checked for an alibi. But I agree, it's probably a dead end." He glanced at Julie. "Miss Marlowe, do you know any of the deceased's business associates at the real estate agency in Sedona?"

Julie shook her head. "Not by name. Dan came into the restaurant where I work a few times with people I assume worked with him."

"They'll be checked out, as well." Wellman looked down at the pad on which he had been taking notes. "Is that all you can tell us?"

Julie took a deep breath. "I'm afraid so."

Carter said, "You'll be going back to Sedona?"

"Yes. Shortly, if you're through with me."

"I think you've given us all you know. What do you think, Charlie?"

Wellman said, "Yes, Miss Marlowe, you may go back to Sedona, but keep yourself available in case we need to get in touch. May I have your address and telephone number?"

Julie gave him the requested information.

As she got to her feet to leave, a man came hurrying in. "Charlie, we found a rifle and an ejected shell!" he said excitedly.

Wellman said sharply, "Any sign of the shooter?"

"Nope."

"No one saw him?"

"Nobody we can find would admit to it."

"The rifle, where is it?"

"Right where we found it. I thought you'd want a look before we moved it."

"Good thinking, Sam." Wellman got up with a sigh. "I suppose if we're lucky, *real* lucky, we'll find prints on the weapon, but I'm not holding my breath." He nodded to Julie. "Goodbye, Miss Marlowe. If we need you, I'll be in touch."

As the others hurried out, Buck Horn said, "You need help with anything, Janet?"

"No, I can manage, thank you. Oh, about Dan's things in the cabin...I don't feel up to packing them."

"I'll handle it. They're impounded for the time being, anyway. So long, Janet." He touched her elbow. "I'm damned sorry this had to happen."

"Thank you, Buck. Goodbye."

As she walked out of the interrogation room, Julie breathed a sigh of relief. She had been expecting someone to mention Dan's pickup, but apparently it had escaped everyone's mind. She checked out at the desk. Fortunately, Dan had paid for the cabins in advance, so she didn't owe any money.

In the cabin it took only a few minutes to throw her things into the small bag. Outside in the parking lot, as she keyed open the door to the pickup, she caught herself glancing furtively around, as though expecting to be challenged any second by someone shouting, "Stop, thief!"

There was no challenge, and she finally got behind the wheel of the pickup. She looked dubiously at the manual gearshift on the floor and at the clutch pedal. Her only experience with a shift dated back to her high school days.

She adjusted the seat and then gingerly fiddled with the gearshift until it was in what she thought was neutral. To be on the safe side she also pushed the clutch pedal to the floor before turning the key. She breathed a relieved sigh when the motor started without incident. It took her three tries before she found reverse and managed to back the pickup out of the parking slot.

Driving very slowly, she started ahead, the pickup advancing in a series of jerks. But by the time she had maneuvered it out of the parking lot and onto the access road she was a little more confident.

On the highway leading south out of the park she had the pickup pretty well mastered, but she kept under the speed limit, sitting tense and rigid behind the wheel. It was completely dark by the time she passed through the park entrance. Travel was light, yet there were some vehicles going both ways. Julie glanced up into the rearview mirror from time to time, wondering if she was being followed.

It was impossible to tell for sure. Since she continued to drive well under the speed limit, cars were backed up behind her; occasionally one would pass her with an angry blare of its horn. After about ten miles from the park there was only one set of headlights behind her. The lights hung there mile after mile, speeding up when she did, slowing down when she did.

At the junction where Highway 180 branched off 64, Julie pulled the pickup into the parking lot in front of a restaurant. She switched off the motor and the headlights, then twisted around to stare at the car that had been trailing her. It seemed to hesitate briefly, then accelerated. She watched it until the taillights were out of sight. It was only then that she realized her hands were slippery with perspiration from gripping the wheel for so long and so tightly, and the muscles of her neck and shoulders throbbed like an infected tooth.

Locking the pickup, she went into the restaurant, ordered a sandwich and coffee and asked for a couple of aspirins. She was directed to the washroom, where she washed her face and hands and swallowed the tablets.

As she looked at herself in the mirror—eyes huge, with blue circles like bruises under them— she was threatened by another onslaught of tears. Angrily she tore off the mousy wig and threw it into the trash receptacle. There was no longer any need for a disguise. Whoever was hunting her certainly knew who she was. From this moment on she was Julie Malone. No, Suellen Devereaux! She was going to go back to Key West—if she could successfully elude pursuit and death—and fight for her inheritance. And fight Rosellen!

Feeling somewhat better, she marched back into the café and ate the sandwich and drank two cups of coffee.

IT WAS CLOSE TO MIDNIGHT when she drove through Flagstaff. As she approached the turnoff to Sedona, she was strongly tempted to keep right on driving east on Highway 40 and head for Florida. But she realized that would be foolish. She had about thirty dollars in her purse, hardly enough to buy gas to get her into Texas. She needed what little money she had in the bank in Sedona, and even with that she would be hard-pressed to make it. She would have to sleep in the pickup and eat lightly. There certainly wasn't enough to purchase a plane ticket. And there was the .25 automatic back in her apartment.

She refused to think about the fact that a police bulletin might soon be broadcast, for she was in effect stealing Dan's pickup. If she moved quickly enough, she might be able to stay ahead of the police. And she was certain that Dan would have wanted her to use the truck.

She swung south on the highway to Sedona, dreading the drive down the mountain into the canyon. She was more comfortable with the pickup now, yet she remembered those switchback curves with a shudder of fear. Fortunately, there was almost no traffic on the road this late.

When she eventually reached the comparatively level floor of the canyon, Julie hit the steering wheel with the heel of her hand and shouted, "I made it!"

Grinning, she felt that she could handle anything now, overcome any obstacle. Sedona was dark and quiet as she drove to her apartment. As she let herself in and switched on a light, she found herself holding her breath and realized that subconsciously she had been expecting someone to be waiting there for her.

But the apartment was empty, and the .25 automatic was in the drawer where she had left it. She chained the door, checked to make sure that all the windows were locked and quickly undressed.

She glanced at her watch as she got into bed— almost five o'clock. She went to sleep with the automatic under her pillow.

For the first time in months the nightmare returned. Trapped in a maze of mirrors, she wandered helplessly, seeing her reflection mirrored a thousandfold. And then Rosellen was there, grinning like a death's-head, taunting her, beckoning her toward destruction and death.

Julie awoke with a scream, mouth dry, head pounding. It was already sunup, but she still felt tired and lethargic. She went into the bathroom for a glass of water, then crawled back into bed. Just another hour, then I'll get up, she thought.

When she awoke the second time, she saw with dismay that it was almost noon. She had slept half the day away!

She took a quick shower, had a skimpy breakfast and packed the few things she intended to take with her. At least, since she was supposed to be off work today, no one at the restaurant would wonder about her. Her rent was paid until the end of the month, and as far as she could remember, there were no other loose ends dangling.

But by the time she had closed out her bank account and headed the pickup north, it was the middle of the afternoon. She was not going to get very far before dark, since she knew that it would take her some time to negotiate the mountain road up onto the mesa and Highway 40.

There was considerable traffic on the road, and although she couldn't be certain, she assumed she was being tailed. Well, let whoever was tailing her follow her all the way to Florida! It didn't seem too likely that they would dare do anything on such a busy highway. She could well imagine her pursuer's confusion at the direction she was heading. On the other hand, Rosellen might be pleased to know that she was returning to Key West for a final confrontation.

It was dusk by the time she saw a highway sign stating that Holbrook was six miles ahead. Traffic was light, yet Julie kept to the right-hand lane, keeping her speed just below the posted limit.

An uncomfortable feeling began to gnaw at her. She glanced into the rearview mirror and saw several cars strung out behind her in both lanes. Then she spotted a green Ford two-door in the left-hand lane next to her and realized it had been there for some time, keeping pace with her. Since the pickup cab was higher, she couldn't see into the car except to note that the passenger seat was empty.

She slowed the pickup abruptly, hoping to glimpse the driver through the back window of the Ford. But the other driver, as though anticipating her maneuver, also slowed, keeping pace with the pickup.

That removed any doubt in her mind—the driver of the Ford was definitely following her. So much for her belief that she wouldn't be harmed on a busy highway! She reached into the open purse on the seat beside her for the automatic. But as soon

as her fingers touched the cold metal, she with-
drew her hand. What was she going to do with it?
Shoot at the other car while they were both traveling at forty miles an hour?

Now horns were blaring behind them. Looking
into the rearview mirror, Julie saw that both lanes
were still blocked, with a string of cars behind the
Ford and the pickup.

She tromped on the accelerator, shooting ahead.
This time, instead of keeping abreast of her, the
green Ford remained back, changing lanes to fall
in behind her. The cars that had been held back
began to pass the pickup. Julie tried to see the
driver of the Ford in her mirror, but it was too
dark, and the headlights of the passing cars blinded
her.

Soon the cars had all caught up and passed her
except for the Ford and one other set of headlights
about a half mile back. Then Julie noticed the Ford
pull out and move up alongside her, again traveling in tandem. After about a mile the Ford began
to inch ahead, and she wondered if she had been
mistaken. Maybe the Ford wasn't following her
after all but was being driven by some highway
cowboy who only wanted to hassle her a little.

And then she suddenly went tense. Instead of
pulling on ahead, the Ford hung even with her
front bumper and began to edge over into her lane,
only inches from the pickup. The driver was trying
to force her off the road!

Heartbeat quickening, Julie let up on the accelerator, dropping back just in time as the Ford
swerved and would have struck the pickup. The
Ford went on for a quarter mile, then began to

drop back again. When it was once again almost even with her, the Ford swerved once more and Julie was forced to slow even more.

The other driver must be mad, she thought frantically. If they collided, they might both be killed!

This time when the Ford shot ahead, it changed over into her lane. In the glare of the pickup's headlights she could see the silhouette of the driver, but she could see only enough to make out that the driver was a man.

The Ford started to slow, dropping back until they were almost bumper-to-bumper. Then Julie realized the driver's intent. He was trying to force her to stop. And if that happened, there was no doubt in her mind that he would kill her.

She slowed even more, and so did the other vehicle. She glanced up into her mirror and saw the car behind her coming up fast. And then the trailing car changed into the left-hand lane and sped past her.

Still, the Ford was slowing. Gritting her teeth in a surge of fury, Julie stepped on the accelerator. Motor roaring, the pickup leaped forward. She hit the Ford's bumper at about forty miles an hour. The impact jarred Julie. The Ford was sent careening ahead, weaving as the driver fought for control. Once again, Julie floored the accelerator and darted ahead.

The second collision was much harder than the first, and there was the sound of metal crunching and glass breaking. The front end of the Ford whipped left, then right, and swerved off the road. There was a shallow ditch running alongside the highway, and the Ford nosed down into it, coming to a jolting stop.

Julie kept going, risking a quick glance back. At least the Ford was out of commission temporarily, if not permanently. Trembling and shaken, she drove on toward the lights of Holbrook.

TWENTY

As Julie drove into the outskirts of Holbrook, she began looking for a motel, one where she could park out of sight of the highway.

Despite her earlier resolution not to make any regular overnight stops along the way to Florida, she realized that she was too strung out by her encounter with the Ford to drive any farther tonight. She knew that she wouldn't get any real rest in the cramped cab of the pickup.

At any rate, she seemed to have lost her pursuer for the time being; and she hoped that if she could park out of sight of the highway he would conclude that she had driven straight on through Holbrook.

Coming off the highway exit onto a city street, she passed a small carnival ablaze with lights; then, a block farther on, she found the motel she was looking for.

She signed the register, writing Julie Malone for the first time in months. It might be a mistake, but she really didn't care. She had hidden long enough.

Once in her room, after a quick shower, she found that she was too keyed up to sleep. Perhaps a walk would calm her down, she thought. She had been sitting for hours. Putting on her jacket, she picked up her purse and left the motel. The hard bulk of the .25 automatic in her purse was reassuring.

It was a pleasant evening. The sky was clear, the stars bright, and the air had a pleasant nip to it. Julie inhaled deeply. It felt good to be outside in the open.

Looking around, she tried to decide which direction to take. The streets were well lighted, and there were other pedestrians on the sidewalks, most of them moving in one direction. In the distance she could hear the sound of a calliope—what she had always thought of as merry-go-round music.

The carnival, of course. That was where the other pedestrians were headed. She smiled to herself. Why not? She hadn't been to a carnival in years. She might as well look it over. She really should eat something, and she could probably get a hamburger or a hot dog there. And Julie knew she would feel safer in a crowd.

Feeling some of the tenseness leave her, she followed the sound of the music, and the other pedestrians. Inside the carnival grounds Julie soon realized that there were really not that many people on the midway. The carnival was a scruffy affair and looked to be made up of leftovers from other, failed, shows.

Although the calliope music boomed loudly, the merry-go-round itself was very small, evidently only for children, and the tiny carved horses looked forlorn and weary. A few children sat astride the horses' worn back, solemnly whirling to the raucous music.

Gazing around, she saw that the other rides were as badly in need of repair as the merry-go-round.

Creaking and groaning, their paint peeling, they looked unattractive and dangerous. Thrill rides had never appealed to her much, anyway.

The half-dozen canvas tents had a similarly bad appearance. Patched and dirty, they looked as if a good stiff breeze would blow them down.

Clutching her purse tightly under her left arm, Julie looked around for a food vendor and spied a dirty white booth with the words Hamburgers, Hot dogs, Soft Drinks in red letters on its not-quite-square sides.

Several people were crowded around the booth, and Julie lined up behind a fat man wearing brand-new blue jeans and a bright red jacket. Standing there behind him, she suddenly realized just how alone she was. In distance, of course, she was close to these strangers—no more than a few inches—but in reality she was totally alone, as alone as she had ever been in her life.

Resolutely pushing this gloomy thought out of her mind, she approached the greasy counter and asked the woman behind the window for a hamburger and a diet soda. The unattractive woman nodded sullenly but looked right through Julie, as if she did not exist.

Julie shivered. Now that she came to think of it, all the carnival employees she had seen so far seemed to have a vulpine look about them. Or was it just her overactive imagination? In her present keyed-up mood she knew that she was vulnerable and oversensitive.

The hamburger was greasy and overcooked and the soft drink was flat, but Julie, conscious of her hunger now, forced herself to finish them.

Then, feeling the need for something to remove the taste of the hamburger, she bought a candy apple. She was unable to resist the hope that this, at least, would be as she remembered from her visits to carnivals in the past.

Surprisingly, the candy apple was quite good—the apple crisp and fresh and the sticky cinnamon candy coating hot against the cool meat of the fruit.

A bit cheered, Julie strolled along the midway, examining the games and enduring the shouts of the barkers: "Hey, lady, try the ring toss! Win a prize! It's easy, lady. You just gotta knock down the bottles. Come on, lady, be a sport! Just twenty-five cents a throw, a quarter of a dollar."

Feeling harassed by their urgings, she turned toward a rather large side tent from which came the sound of loud mechanical laughter.

In front of the tent was the figure of a large woman in a bright housedress. Larger than life, she moved jerkily forward and back, holding her ample mechanical waist. The laughter roared from her open throat.

Like everything else at the carnival, the mechanical figure was in disrepair, and this made it seem somehow frightening to Julie. The sign above the laughing figure said: Fun House—House of Mirrors.

A fun house. Well, she could certainly use a few laughs. Tossing aside the stick from the candy apple, Julie bought a ticket and entered through the tattered flap.

As fun houses go, this one wasn't much, Julie thought. There was the usual large turning barrel and jiggling walkway, and the distorting mirrors that made you appear very tall and thin or very squat and misshapen. Julie was beginning to wonder whatever had possessed her to buy a ticket when she came face-to-face with her own reflection. She stopped short with a muted cry as the memory of all her mirror dreams came back to her in vivid, frightening detail.

Breathing shallowly, she clutched her purse and stepped quickly around the mirror. She was confronted by a half-dozen reflections of herself.

Filled with sudden panic, she almost turned and bolted from the tent, but then she realized that she had entered the House of Mirrors. There was really nothing to be afraid of except her own fears.

Drawing a deep breath, she deliberately slowed her breathing, standing still, until she felt a measure of calmness return. She had vowed that she would run no more, so why should she flee from her own reflections? She would very calmly make her way through the mirror maze, and then she would return to the motel and get a good night's sleep.

Straightening her back in determination, she stepped forward into a hard mirrored surface.

Again she experienced a surge of panic, and again she controlled it. The confusion was supposed to be part of the fun of the House of Mirrors; and although at the moment it didn't seem to Julie to be particularly enjoyable, there was really nothing to get alarmed about. She simply must keep her head and find her way out.

Moving ahead more slowly now, holding her right hand out in front of her face to avoid any further mishaps, she walked forward. Dozens of other Julies moved with her.

She shivered slightly, wishing that she would see the image of someone else. In the other rooms of the Fun House she had seen several other people, but now she seemed to be quite alone except for her white-faced reflections, which moved in eerie unison with her.

She turned yet another corner and again faced a bank of confusing replications of her own face and figure. Stopping short, she reached out a hand tentatively and slid it along the glass, feeling for the next turning.

As she did so, she frowned. Something was wrong.

Staring at her reflection, she felt as if a cold hand were squeezing her spine, for the reflections had changed. The faces staring back at her were hers, but they were smiling coldly, and the clothes were not the same. There was no jacket!

Julie fell back against the cold glass, her breath exploding in a muffled cry.

The reflections were delighted. Their heads nodded, and their smiles widened as Rosellen's voice echoed throughout the chamber: "Well, we meet again at last, dear sister, and believe me, it *will* be the last occasion!"

The sudden appearance of her sister was a shock, yet Julie was not really surprised that Rosellen should be here, in a house of mirrors in a small town in Arizona. It seemed inevitable. And she had promised herself that she would no longer run, that she would face Rosellen, whatever the outcome. Now that confrontation was at hand, she had to act with courage and dignity.

Her hands trembling, Julie opened her purse and put her hand inside it, grasping the cold handle of the automatic. Its steely touch reinforced her determination. She would use it if she had to. She would not let her sister kill her easily.

Rosellen's voice was now amused. "Are you surprised, Suellen? Did you really think that I couldn't find you? I could have had you killed several times during these last few months, but as I told you, I wanted you to be afraid. I wanted to see you run!"

Julie had to struggle to keep her voice steady. "I've stopped being surprised by anything that you do." She looked closely at the mirrors, trying to distinguish the real Rosellen from among the reflections, trying to ascertain from which direction her voice came.

"But why did you send someone after me at first, instead of coming yourself?" she continued.

The dozens of Rosellens smiled, but their eyes were cold. "That was just to worry you, dear, to keep you afraid and running. Now that it's down to the final wire, so to speak, I decided to have the pleasure of doing the job myself. And it *will* be a pleasure, have no doubts about that."

Julie's gaze continued to search desperately. Where *was* the real Rosellen? "And I suppose you derived pleasure from having an innocent man killed, a perfect stranger to you?"

The reflections shrugged in perfect unison. "I suppose you're talking about your friend at the Grand Canyon? Why should I regret that? After all, it must have caused *you* some pain, and casualties can be expected in any war.''

Julie did not try to keep her disgust and anger from showing in her voice. ''War? This hadn't been a war, Rosellen, it's been simple murder all along. But you seem to have a taste for murder, don't you? First... what was his name? Huey? Then Mother, then Dan! I suppose you might say that your talent for murder is the main symptom of your madness!''

Rosellen's many faces twisted, and her voice rose to a shout. ''Don't say that! Don't ever say that! You stupid little bitch! If there was something wrong with my mind there would be something wrong with yours. We're identical, remember?''

Julie shook her head. ''Only in appearance, Rosellen. In every other way we're miles apart. It was *you* who did the killings, not me. It was you who seduced our father and drove him to his death!''

Rosellen's face twisted again and then smoothed out as if by magic. She chuckled, the sound echoing eerily.

''You're trying to get me going, little sister. And I almost let you! But I've always been too clever for you, haven't I? You're right, we're not alike, except on the outside, because *I* am far superior!''

''Well, if you are so superior, and if you are going to kill me anyway, why not tell me how you did it? I know you had someone helping you. Was it Shell? Or was it Ken? And where is he now?''

Rosellen's laugh was almost musical. ''My helpful friend? He informed me where you were staying in Sedona, and I arrived there just in time to follow you both when you left today. As for where he is now, I suppose he's on the highway, where you left him. That was really very clever of you. I didn't think you had it in you. As to who he is, well, I think I'll just let you guess."

Slowly Julie began to move forward, hoping that the movement would separate Rosellen from her mirrored doppelgängers; but Rosellen's reflections moved, too, and now there were two sets of images, Julie's and her twin's.

Rosellen's voice became mocking. "Anxious to end it all, sister dear? Well, all right then, I'll accommodate you. I suppose I've had as much sport out of you as there is to be had."

There was a note of finality in her sister's voice, and Julie quickly pulled the automatic out of her purse. And then she saw that Rosellen held a similar weapon.

Rosellen laughed tauntingly. "You see, it will be a fair fight, except that I have experience with a gun and you haven't! Oh, I'm really enjoying this, and when it's over I'll enjoy all our money. Goodbye forever, sister dear!"

Rosellen's last words were interrupted by the sound of metal against glass, and in the mirrors that reflected the image of her sister, Julie now saw another figure—Ken Dawson. The gun in his hand loomed large and menacing.

She heard Rosellen gasp as Ken's voice, thick with elation, called softly, "Suellen!"

Julie saw Rosellen, her face going pale with shock and astonishment, turn toward Ken, her gun in one hand, the other raised as if to push him away.

"No, Ken, no!" she cried frantically. "I'm not—"

Her words were drowned out by the booming of Ken's gun, and glass shattered as the bullet missed Rosellen and struck one of the mirrors.

As Julie watched in frozen horror, she saw Rosellen swing around, bringing her own gun up to bear on Ken; but he fired again, and this time his aim was true. Rosellen was hurled back, shattering one mirror and then another until it seemed that the whole tent was filled with the brittle sound of breaking glass.

Julie instinctively pulled her jacket over her head as the mirrors around her fell one by one. When she heard the last crash, she uncovered her head and gave a gasping sigh. The air was full of dust and smelled of gunpowder. The illusion of vast mirrored distances was no more.

She stood now in a space that had the dimensions of a medium-sized room. Only two of the mirrored panels that had made up the maze were still standing; the shards of the rest covered the floor like the remains of an ice palace, cold and glittering.

Across from her, standing against the dirty canvas wall, was Ken, his eyes wide and his mouth lax with shock. Between them lay the body of Rosellen, a giant bloom of blood spreading across her chest.

"Rosellen?" Ken said in a guttural voice. "Rosellen?"

Trembling, Julie brought the automatic up and gripped it with both hands, pointing it at his chest.

The expression in his eyes began to change to one of horrified realization. "No!" he said loudly. "No!"

Julie swallowed but held the gun steady. "Yes, Ken. You've killed Rosellen, not me."

He shook his head violently. "No! You're trying to trick me. Don't forget I know you, Rosellen. I know your little games. You just want to make me sweat a little."

Julie said sadly, "No, Ken. This isn't a game. It never was."

She could hear shouts now and the babble of voices from outside, punctuated by the sound of a police siren.

Ken, who was now crouched over Rosellen's body, looked up, panic making his eyes wild, as two uniformed policemen came running into the tent.

Julie felt herself sag with relief as the two officers disarmed them. There would be lengthy explanations, and no doubt an investigation, but it was over now. Over at last, and she was alive.

A HALF HOUR LATER she stood by a police car, one officer standing nearby with a watchful eye on her. She felt numb now, devoid of all feeling.

"Julie?" a man's voice said tentatively, breaking through her reverie.

She whirled to see the tall figure of Shell Phipps standing beside her, and feeling returned like the sharp pain of a sudden wound. She fell against him, fell against his warmth and strength. "Oh, Shell! Dear God, I don't think I've ever been so glad to see anyone in my life!" she cried.

The officer stepped forward in alarm. "This woman is in custody."

"It's all right, officer." Shell took a card from his pocket and gave it to the policeman. "Sheldon Phipps. I'm Miss Malone's attorney."

Julie pulled back out of Shell's arms just in time to see two men carrying a stretcher out of the remains of the House of Mirrors toward an ambulance parked before the police car.

Shell said, "Is that Rosellen?"

She nodded, swallowing. "Ken killed her. He thought she was me." She turned a stricken face up to his.

He nodded soberly. "I suspected that Ken was in cahoots with her."

She frowned at him. "But you, Shell. How on earth did you get here?"

"Well, I was hardly in the nick of time, was I?" he said with a rueful smile. "I make a lousy detective. I've been following Rosellen, but I lost her back on the highway outside of Holbrook. I just found her car down the street, and when I saw the police cars here as I drove past, I had a hunch that it all had something to do with the both of you."

"You still haven't answered my question. How did you come to be here in the first place? You were following Rosellen? Why?"

"Well, when Stella Devereaux died Rosellen showed up for the funeral and the reading of the will, claiming to be you, of course. She didn't quite bring it off, not with me, anyway. She fired Pauline, for one thing, and I knew you would never do that. And other things didn't quite ring true. So I started following her." He gazed down into her eyes. "Where was she all these years? Do you know?"

"Yes, Shell, but it's too long and complicated to go into right now."

"How much do the police know?"

"Very little at the moment. I told them that Ken shot Rosellen and was about to kill me when they burst in. I'm not sure how much of that they believe."

"Don't worry about it, honey. We'll convince them." He tightened his hand on her elbow and smiled down into her face. "I'll be right beside you until you're cleared and can return to Key West as Suellen Devereaux." His smile turned tender. "Although I doubt I'll ever think of you as anything but Julie Malone."

"Shell, can you ever forgive me for not trusting you?"

"I'm the one who should ask for forgiveness, for not believing you all along. I should have been able to convince you in Moorestown that I finally did believe you. I've been looking everywhere for you since that day."

"Oh, Shell! I'm sorry I've caused you so much trouble."

"I'm not. After you left Key West I discovered that you're the most important thing in my life. I love you, Julie, more than I ever thought possible."

"I love you, too, darling," she said with shining eyes. Past his shoulder she saw an officer, the one she had learned was in charge of the investigation, approaching.

The officer tipped his hat. "It's time to go down to the station and see if we can get this mess straightened out."

"Is it okay if I ride in with her, Officer?" Shell asked. "I'm Miss Malone's attorney."

The officer's heavy eyebrows rose. "Well, counselor! I've heard of fast ambulance chasers, but you're the fastest yet. The lady hasn't even made a phone call that I know about."

Shell looked at Julie with laughing eyes. "Oh, I've been chasing her across half the continent. It just took me a while to catch up with her."

Shell helped Julie into the back of the police car and got in with her. As the cruiser drove away, he said, "You know, my boat, the *Dancer II*, was finally found."

"Is she all right?"

"Not too bad of shape. I thought..." He cleared his throat. "I thought that after all this is over, maybe we could cruise down to the Caribbean. Maybe for a month, even longer if you like."

"Oh, I like! I'd like that very much, Shell."

She stretched up to kiss him softly. They clung together for a moment, and then she settled contentedly against him, her head on his shoulder.

Dear Friends and Readers:

In the California desert I have created a town called Oasis. Oasis is a small town, peaceful and quiet, where the citizens enjoy the view and the sunsets, away from the bustle, criminal activity and smog of the cities.

This quiet community is chosen to be the site for a large, expensive clinic, the Heinman Center, the presence of which splits the citizens of the town into opposing camps. Who are these people and how does this affect Oasis and its residents?

Zoe Tremaine, the striking, elderly woman with a secret in her past, is one of the founders of the town. She moved to the desert for the privacy and peace it afforded, the very qualities that she believes the presence of Heinman Center will destroy.

Dr. Noah Breckinridge, the young, charismatic doctor who has become the focus of much of the attention paid to the center, has mixed feelings about the job he is being asked to do.

Susan Channing, Zoe's young friend and fellow activist, is against the center, partially because her hated father, Otto Channing, the town's leading developer, is for it.

Dick Stanton, failed writer and reluctant homosexual, opposes the center because he is frightened by the specter of his own alcoholism.

And then there are the rich and famous who come to the clinic for help.

The beautiful Lacey Houston is one of the most desired women in the world, and one of the most unhappy. Millions see and admire her on the screen, but she cannot control her own life.

Todd Remington, Rem, an over-the-hill Western actor, hopes that a stay at the clinic will bring him to the attention of casting directors.

Jeffrey Lawrence, jewel thief *extraordinaire*, enters the clinic under false pretenses and with nefarious intent.

Governor William Stoddard, is counting on the clinic to control his alcoholism before the coming election.

Billie Reaper, known as The Reaper, rock star and teen idol, is an unwilling patient at the clinic, balanced on a precipice of drugs, and about to fall.

And finally, Cindy Hodges, a trendy, successful writer, sees the clinic as a source of items for her column, "Cindy's Scoops," and does not care who is hurt by what she prints.

These and others are the characters I have been living with for the past year while writing *Oasis*. I have come to care about all of them and about Oasis, and I hope you will, too.

I would love to have you join us and find out how the story unfolds, when *Oasis* comes out in November, from Worldwide Library.

Patricia Matthews